**DO NOT MISS ALAN DALE DICKINSON'S**
**PREVIOUSLY PUBLISHED CRIME-FICTION MYSTERIES:**

Charlie O'Brien, Private Investigator
Kidnap Country

The City of Brotherly Love

For the Love of Money

Charlie's Private Eye Angels

Orange County (California) Confidential

Baghdad Confidential

A Mystery in Laguna Woods

A Theft in Laguna Woods

A Kidnapping in Laguna Woods

A Shooting in Laguna Woods

In addition, a published short primer on:
How to Write (and publish) a Novel

# The Money Changer

## A CHARLIE O'BRIEN PRIVATE INVESTIGATOR MYSTERY

# The Money Changer

## A CHARLIE O'BRIEN PRIVATE INVESTIGATOR MYSTERY

BY PROFESSOR
ALAN DALE DICKINSON

COPYRIGHT © 2017 by Professor ALAN DALE DICKINSON

This novel is a work of pure fiction. The names, characters, places as well as incidents in this said novella, are either the product of this said author's very creative imagination or are used fictitiously. Any resemblance, at all, to actual persons, living or deceased, events or locales is completely *coincidental.*

Without limiting the rights under the copyrights of the United States, no part of this publication may be reproduced, stored in or introduced into a retrieval system, or transmitted, in any form whatsoever, without the prior written permission of both the copyright owner and the author of this subject book.

The scanning, uploading, and or distribution of this book via the internet or via any other means without the permission of the author and copyright owner, is illegal and is also punishable by law. Please purchase only authorized electronic (eBooks, et cetera) editions, and do not participate in or encourage electronic piracy of legally owned copyrighted materials. Your crucial support and recognition of the author's, and publisher's, legal rights are greatly appreciated.

*All rights reserved, including the right of reproduction in whole, and or in part, and in any such form whatsoever.*

ISBN: 978-1-7326283-8-0

DICKINSON PUBLISHING COMPANY
PROFESSOR ALAN DALEDICKINSON
Chairman and Chief Executive Officer

Bank of America
Vice President and Business Banking Manager (Retired)
World Corporate Lending Group
P.O. Box 3962
Laguna Hills, CA 9265

# DEDICATION

*The Money Changer*, a Charlie O'Brien, Private Investigator mystery novel, is dedicated to my beloved grandson Scott Alan and to my precious granddaughter Morgan Marie. They are the best grand kids in the whole wide world. I hope that the rest of your grandparents out there will understand my admitted favoritism.

Also, to my eldest son, David Alan, who has a heart made out of silver, and his very thoughtful, considerate and *absolutely wonderful* wife, Desiree. And, to my younger son, Mark Alan, who has a heart made out of gold, and his very talented and sweet wife Ramona.

# ACKNOWLEDGEMENTS

*The Money Changer*, a Charlie O'Brien Mystery Novel, might never have come to fruition and completion had it not been for the friendship and encouragement of a few very kind hearted people. At the top of my list, a special thank you to a longtime friend, Curt. Also, to Phyllis, my most loyal friend and supporter for forty years. And Betty, my wonderful adopted mother. To Jim Bowen, the best assistant that I ever had at the Bank. And, Chuck, my life coach, and his wonderful wife Pam. Also, Doug, a good friend and Maureen his terrific wife and former LA Rams cheerleader.

And, lest I forget, you know me, how bad Charlie's memory is getting these days, Leann, John, Lindsay, and Zach, *Dr. Anne Ford*, and Jeff Katz. Also, to Karen Fulton, Betty, Johnny and their family, Phyllis and her family, Jim and Roz, Alex and Sarah, I know I am still missing someone important to me, however, sorry, I will include your name in the front of my next novel. Thank you for your understanding.

In addition, to Howard Crawford, my very capable research analyst, computer transcriber and closest writing assistant. He spent countless hours interpreting my illegible hand written notes, and or my somewhat confusing typed story line comments. He is a very articulate and intelligent man. And he possesses a good keen eye for paragraph flow, repetition and spelling errors. Also, he has an excellent and very diverse background in several different fields of business. Thanks a million.

Last, but certainly not least, my humble 'Thank You' to all of you out there in internet eBook, or bookstore land, and finally my sincerest apologies to anyone who I may not have acknowledged.

# PREFACE

You probably have heard the term ‘dancers', all different types of professional dancers, use it all the time. It goes like this just in case you have never heard it: "I am going to bring it (everything I've got) and I am darn well going to leave it all out on the dance floor, no matter what it takes!" Think ‘American Idol' and ‘Can You Dance', et cetera—TV shows from Hollywood. Those contestants cry, argue, and schmooze with the judges and dance and sing their little hearts out and behinds off. And then they all "*Leave It On the Dance Floor*!"

Private Investigators (PI's) and Detectives, both police detectives as well as private detectives and investigators who are self employed, do pretty much the same thing. The only difference between what Old Charlie sees is that, *sometimes*, just every once-in-awhile, these types of individuals have to leave some of their ‘blood and/or some of their body parts and/or their lives, on the floor (i.e. leave it on the job!)

This applicable quote of unknown origin is sort of like the Private Investigator's own personal mini version of their vocationally *perceived* mission statement.

# CHAPTER ONE

**MY NAME IS CHARLES WARNER** Kennedy O'Brien. My best friends and fellow private investigators and police detectives just call me "*Charlie*", so why don't you? I have been described by various people and associates and clients, over the years as a quick wit, having a keen visual sense and a refusal to give in or give up, ever, a man who never panics when trouble comes *knocking on his door*.

Someone who would never, ever betray you, a man who absolutely hates terrorists, and people who try to ruin or stop democracy around the world, sociopaths (and psychopaths), rapists, and men who harm defenseless women or children.

Also, I'm described as a person in good shape (for my age anyway), with an iron fist hidden in a kid glove, someone who is much more dangerous than he seems at first glance, a man with a tough exterior but a heart made out of gold. I will not bore you with the opinions of my arch-enemies, detractors, nor my ex-spouse. You can read those for yourself on the internet under "Charlie O'Brien scoundrel".

I was enjoying one of my favorite indoor sports, no not arena football, women's indoor figure skating at the famous 'Staples

Center' in downtown LA (Los Angeles, California). The world famous LA Lakers (Pau Gusol, Kobe Bryant, Luke Walton, Lamar Odom, Derek Fisher, Ron Artest, Andrew Bynum, and Sasha Vujacic) play their home NBA basketball (National Basketball Association) games here.

The center also has several other very interesting events throughout the rest of the year when the Lakers are not using the beautiful facility. Events such as LA Clippers NBA basketball, LA Kings NHL ice hockey team, and Icescapes' shows.

Just when some of the lovely women ice skaters were making some of their terrific turns, incredible jumps, and figure eights, I received an urgent call on my encrypted cell phone from my good friend, Howard Crawford Wallace, the *Deputy Director* of the CIA (Central Intelligence Agency).

He informed me that he had just received a frantic, desperate and confidential secure satellite phone call from 'Giacippi Francis Bouchilli'. He is the Chairman of the Board of "*The Bank of Italy, LLC*", which is located in Rome (Roma), Italy. Their headquarters building, and principle office, was originally built in 1621. What a gorgeous and stately building it is said to be. It is located in one of the oldest and most prestigious parts of the very lovely and extremely historic city.

The bank has 2,000 branches located all over Italy, as well as over one hundred Corporate Banking Offices spread all around the world. Some of these are: London, Great Britain, Paris, France, Berlin, Germany, Tokyo, Japan, Beijing, China, Sydney, Australia, Montreal, Canada, Geneva, Switzerland, Moscow, Russia (former Soviet Union), Kiev, Ukraine, Mumbai, India, Dubai, UAE (United Arab Emirates), Abuja, Nigeria, Athens, Greece, Tel Aviv, Israel, Rio de Janeiro, Brazil, Caracas, Venezuela, Lima, Peru, and New York City, New York, *Los Angeles*, California, Miami, Florida, and Houston, Texas (oil money) in the United States. Just to name a few (22) of their world wide offices.

The renowned, and extremely prestigious, bank was almost three hundred (300) years old! It was originally founded in 1725 by one of the oldest royal families in Italy.

The Chairman, Mr. Bouchilli stated to Howard, that his secret internal bank auditors, had just discovered several million dollars, to be exact almost one hundred million dollars (USD) in counterfeit $100.00 US bills.

They were found in their *Central Cash Vault*, located four stories below their main branch in Roma. No one knew yet from which customer they had come, nor from which office they had been deposited. The bank's senior internal auditors, as well as the chief of the bank's internal security and threat department (Mr. Luca Perugino), were frantically trying to track down that very crucial information at this very moment.

If it got out to the public, or especially to the press media, that the *Bank of Italy* was circulating, or even in possession of, millions in counterfeit $100.00 US bills, it would be the bank's worst 'nightmare'.

The whole bank could be put right out of business with a 'run' on the bank by their depositors, or even worse, shut down by the 'Depositor Protection Agency' (Department of the Italian government) — the equivalent to the United States FDIC (Federal Deposit Insurance Corporation).

The auditors had just determined that the 'fake' $100.00 bills were printed in either Hong Kong, China; Pyongyang, North Korea; or Abuja, Nigeria. The '*funny money*' was of seemingly very good quality, however, not as good as the ones counterfeited in Moscow, Russia in the 1980's before the end of the cold war. Those were 'primo' bills and you could not tell them from the real ones except with special x-ray equipment.

Luckily for America, the cold war ended before the commies had circulated very many of them. They sent most of that 'fake' money to London, England where 'Scotland Yard and MI-5' were very quick to detect them floating around the London bank's central cash system.

I just love old sayings...you might think that is due to the fact that 'old Charlie', as they call me, is actually 'old', however, I do not think that's so. I more correctly believe that it is because I am an avid student of history, as well as a student of human nature.

Recently, for example, I read the following very intriguing quote: "Sin has many tools, but a lie is the handle which fits them all." (Oliver Wendell Holmes).

Greed (the love of money) also has many tools and the 'handle' used by the Bank of Italy, LLC 'counterfeiter' of US $100.00 bills was a very high-tech, state-of-the-art, extremely expensive, and brand new bank printing press. Most likely it was built in Germany, where they have the best engineers in the world, next to the US of course.

They also build a lot of these type of presses in mainland China and Indonesia, however, those are of very poor quality and the 'phony money' can be detected quite quickly.

Greed (and also power) is made so incredibly realistic in the big budget Hollywood film: "Wall Street" and its subsequent sequel: "Wall Street: *Money Never Sleeps*". It starred the famous actor, Michael Douglas, son of the even better known actor, Kirk Douglas.

Douglas played just perfectly the character of "Gordon Gekko", the epitome of greed, lust, and self absorption. Unfortunately, Michael has throat cancer and is quite ill at this time.

Old Charlie here knows him, as I worked as an extra on his movie "Black Rain" (1989). The movie was 125 minutes long and it was an action (crime - drama) picture. It was released on September 22, 1989 and was directed by the famous action director, Ridley Scott who has since made several blockbuster movies like Alien, Blade Runner, American Gangster, Body of Lies, Black Hawk Down, Gladiator, Kingdom of Heaven, and Robin Hood. Besides Mr. Douglas, the picture starred Andy Garcia, Ken Takakura (very well known Japanese movie actor), Kate Capshaw, Luis Guzman, John Spencer, and Yusaku Matsuda.

I played the part of ‘Richard Crown', a small but good role. The story line goes like this: Two New York cops get involved in a gang war between members of the Yakuza, the *Japanese Mafia*. They arrest one of their killers and are ordered to escort him back to Japan.

In Japan, however, he manages to escape. As they try to track him down, they get deeper and deeper into the Japanese mafia scene and they have to learn that they can only win by playing the game the Japanese way.

Taglines: An American Cop in Japan. Their country. Their laws. Their game. His rules.

*Some information on the film that may be of interest to you:*

Country: USA

Language: English/Japanese
Release Date: September 22, 1989 (USA)
Also know as: Lluvia Negara
Filming locations: 1000 N. Crescent Dr., Hollywood, Los Angeles, CA, USA
Budget: $30,000,000.00 (estimated)
Opening Weekend: $9,677,102 (USA) (September 24, 1989) (1610 screens)
Gross: $45,645,204 (USA)
Production Co.: Paramount Pictures, Pegasus Film Partners
Runtime: 125 minutes
Sound mix: 70 mm 6-track (70 mm prints) / Dolby SR (35 mm prints)
Color: Color (Technicolor)
Aspect Ratio: 2.35:1

It was fun working with Mr. Douglas and the whole cast during the making of the film. I know him and his wife (Catherine Zeta Jones-Douglas) but not real well. I've been thinking and praying for Mr. Douglas for about a year now.

She is drop dead gorgeous in person just like she is in the movies, and without the heavy make-up. Also as a bonus, Michael introduced me to several very influential big time movie directors/producers — and as a result I was able to work as an extra in several other big Hollywood films.

Just to name a few "Predator" (with Arnold Schwarzenegger), "Mission Impossible" (with Tom Cruise), "Transformers" (with Shia LaBeouf), "The Bourne Identity" (with Matt Damon), "Taken" (with Liam Neeson), and just recently "The Expendables (with Sylvester 'Sly' Stallone). That was great fun, I might add.

Gekko (in the movie) would do anything, and I mean anything, to make a lot of moolah (money). Lie, cheat, and steal, were just the beginning and elementary activities for him.

He would move on from there with a never ending desire for more money, more money and more money!

As you are all well aware of the World Wide Financial crisis... Liberal news media like to refer to as "the Great Recession". But in all reality it's actually the "Second *Great Depression*".

Whatever you wish to name it (i.e. whichever handle you like to use), it was a direct result of 'Greed' and the lust for more power and things.

An old saying goes (you know, another old saying): "For the love of money ($) is a root of all sorts of evil and foul deeds and some people by longing for it have wandered away from their belief in honor, decency, integrity, trustworthiness, and generosity toward others who are less fortunate than themselves in this crazy world (just to mention a few)."

In my personal opinion, it would be very intelligent as well as very prudent of people, men and women, who have been lucky to become rich (either by their own hard work, their inheritance or gifts from others) on this old planet earth: "To fix their hope *not* on the uncertainty of riches and power, but on doing good, and recalling the days gone-by when they were not in any way nearly as fortunate as they are today".

I hope that you understand this 'greed' thing (concept) that I am trying to present here? Or in Italian, I would say/ask you: "Coppice?" And, you would respond to me: "Si, capisco"...I hope, you do indeed understand what I am saying.

Of course, prior to that question, I would introduce myself to you by saying: "Mi chiamo, Charlie O'Brien". I know what you are thinking, you are saying to yourselves; "Charlie, you had better buy an 'Italian for Dummies' language book before you go to Italy". And, yes, I already had planned on doing just that. Also, by the way: "Buon giorno" to you.

For your information, here are some of the 'key players' (i.e. big hitters as I like to call them) at the *Bank of Italy, LLC*:

Chairman of the Board—Giacippi Francis Bouchilli
President and CEO (Chief Executive Officer)—Vittorio Capitolini
Office of the President—Gianni Borgia
Office of the President—Ms. Doria DePisis

Office of the President—Campo Massimiliano
Executive Vice President (Internal Offices Division)—Lorenzo Campidoglio
Executive Vice President (Corporate Loans Division)—Rudolf (Rudy) Napoli
Executive Vice President (Internal Security/Threat Division)—Luca Perugino
Executive Vice President (Retail Offices Division)—Ms. Felicia Alemanno
Executive Vice President (Information Systems Division)—Angelo Miliano
Senior Vice President (Public Relations Division)—Ms. Novana Mona Bella
Senior Vice President (Marketing Division)—Enrico Mostesano
Senior Vice President (Customer Service Division)—Ponte Farnesina

AS SOON AS I obtained the list of names from the bank, I called my friend Howard (CIA) and requested that he run a 'top secret' background check on each of these thirteen high level and highly paid individuals.

I asked just to determine if any of them could *possibly* be involved in some way to the 'phony money' scheme ($100.00 US bills). For that huge an amount of counterfeit money to be located in the secure central cash vault, I tend to believe that there had to be someone (i.e. a senior bank associate, or two) 'on the inside'. It hardly seems likely to me that just one day millions of dollars of phony cabbage (cash) just appeared 'out of nowhere'.

After all, there are normal, regular banking routines and SOP's (Standard Operating Procedures) which should have detected the counterfeit US $100.00 bills, long before they amounted to *almost one hundred* million dollars. Way, way before!

Now, following that line of thought, the question clearly becomes: 1) if it was an 'inside job', who on the inside perpetrated the 'fraud,' or 2) if it was deposited in a branch (and not the main Roma office) which one accepted it and why did they not discover it was fake?, or 3) if it was large corporate deposit, which one was it?

I like to keep things simple (remember the old saying: "KISS — Keep It Simple Stupid")?...you probably thought I was going to say something about kissing a girl, fooled you.

Also, you might say that my strategy is like that because I'm a simple-minded person, however, I prefer to think it is because I'm a logical, analytical, and clever detective (i.e. Private Investigator). Of course, you just may be more correct, after all, I admit to some bias in my favor.

I decided it was time to take another 'cruise' in my classic 1964 dark maroon Chevy Impala, two door super sport coupe. It has a 409 V-8 horsepower engine with a 4-speed stick transmission. I just love that car, I really, truly do.

It always makes me feel younger whenever I drive it, and believe me, 'old Charlie' here needs that every now and then these days. I headed down the coast on PCH (Pacific Coast Highway) to Surf City (Huntington Beach, CA) and popped in one of my favorite CD's in the after-market stereo.

Bob Dylan's "Slow Train Coming" is a favorite. It was recorded way back in the day in 1979 at CBS Records in Hollywood, California. Dylan is, of course (if you know anything about modern music at all) one of the most prolific and multi-talented Rock ‘N Roll singers (and song writers) of all time.

He seems to be able to continually, over the years, to produce and record outstanding and very relevant listening music that has a ‘message' and is also very enjoyable to listen to.

The terrific album includes:

Gotta Serve Somebody
Precious Angel
I Believe In You
*Slow Train*
Gonna Change My Way of Thinking
Do Right To Me Baby
When You Gonna Wake Up
Man Gave Names To all of the Animals

## When He Returns

It always makes me feel good whenever I play this particular CD, however, I do not play it as often as I should. I have an absolutely incredible, diverse, 'ear pleasing', and eclectic collection of three hundred CD/records.

It is impossible to listen to even my *favorite* ones as often as I would like too. I will have to try harder, much harder, to listen to the 'greatest' Rock 'N Roll (et cetera) albums of all time. I do not listen to much 'new' music, however, I like a lot of it.

Maybe that's due to the fact that I am getting older now, but I hope not. I have always liked a variety: some old (1930s), some classical, a lot of Rock 'N Roll, some oldies but goodies, some country (western), some hip hop, a lot of the blues, some soft rock (103.5 FM) and a little bit of soft core rap.

After my refreshing drive down by the absolutely beautiful (bella, in Italian), Pacific Ocean (by far one of the most exquisite oceans in the whole wide world, in my opinion at least), I started to reflect on my 'new white collar crime' case.

I usually think better after I have a nice drive and/or nice 'nap'. I wonder why that is?

Anyway, I was going to have to do a lot of research, a whole lot, on the grand old bank, "The Bank of Italy, LLC", as well as the whole country of historic Italy. Particularly the cities of *Rome* (Roma) and *Venice*.

I will need to do that before I leave for the Mediterranean to start my 'on the ground' investigation of the banks alleged money fraud.

I was in Italy in 1996. I spent a whole month there traveling around the entire magnificent country. I was taking my ex-wife on a trip of her lifetime, when all of a sudden and also at the very last minute, she cancelled her ticket, but insisted that I go anyway, since my ticket (which was very expensive back then) was non-refundable.

I found out later that she did that so she could be with her boy-friend for four weeks. Oh, well, that is a story for another time.

I was in the area, doing some research on my bank case, so I decided to drop into one of my oldest and most favorite 'kitschy' Los Angeles dining rooms: "Clifton's Cafeteria".

It was built as a furniture store in 1916. It is a restaurant dating back to the '*Great Depression*' (1931). It was founded by a great restaurateur and a great gentleman named Clifford Clinton. He combined his name for the place. It is located on the corner of Broadway and Seventh Street downtown.

It has served generations and generations of "Angelino's" and is one of the most beloved family owned eateries in LA. At one time the restaurant had eight cafeterias located in and around LA. The rest of them are closed now, due in part to the *fast food fascination* as well as the poor economy.

I first ate there in about the 60's and my parents use to eat there in the '40s and '50s. My beloved mother use to just love the place and they both could get a good, and very wholesome meal for about $2.00 a piece, believe it or not!

The dining room was designed to evoke the coastal redwoods, with multiple-mezzanine decks, a twenty-foot real waterfall, and fake redwood trees (to conceal the building support columns).

In the 1940s they served almost 10,000 customers per day. Now, it has dropped to only about one to two thousand per day.

The famous big name department stores, such as: Broadway, Bullock's, and May Company, plus several movie theatres were located close by in the good old days.

The cafeteria is now surrounded by the downtown Jewelry District. Gold is at an all time high, and as you undoubtedly know, unemployment is very high and people's income is at an all time low.

I read in the LA Times, my favorite news paper, the other day that the founder's decedent's, Robert and Don Clinton, are selling this historic eatery and also the whole building to an investor (who specializes in downtown LA properties), however, he has promised to keep the cafeteria open after a several million dollar renovation of it and as well as the four story building.

Old Charlie here was very, very happy to hear about that fact. I like to eat at places I grew up with, I don't know about you, but, it seems to make me feel somewhat stable in this fast and ever changing crazy world.

All of you who know me, already know I just love expensive watches, new fast cars, classic automobiles (especially the 1964 Chevy Impala), and beautiful women, of course.

I stopped by my favorite jewelry store in Beverly Hills, on Rodeo Drive, and checked out their latest collection of unique watches. They had several that I really liked, however, I decided to buy one that said it was *my ticket* to "Hollywood's Golden Age". It was a uniquely retro luxury timepiece. Very, very cool and you know I love to look cool!

The beautifully illustrated brochure described the magnificent watch as follows: "Hollywood got it right in 1938. Just look at the list of films released or in production that year: "Gone with the Wind," "Mr. Smith Goes to Washington," "The Wizard of Oz," "The Adventures of Robin Hood." It doesn't get any bigger or better.

And back then, screen idols created the gold standard for movie star style and celebrities have been trying to keep up ever since. Just hearing their names conjures an image of sophisticated cool: Cagney, Olivier, Garbo and Leigh. Gable, Davis, Flynn and Tracy.

We longed for that bygone era of elegance so much that we decided to build a time machine."

The Stauer 1938 *Majestic Watch* is a sleek tribute to Hollywood's Golden Age. This is the watch that the big screen's biggest stars might have flaunted at *red carpet* premieres or the Academy Awards.

After combing through hundreds of vintage watches, we found a co-star worthy of history's most popular leading men. The streamlined Art Deco design and unique display of the Majestic was inspired by a rare timepiece style of the 1930s.

Wristwatches with digital indication used rotating discs instead of hands to show the time. Finding similar vintage movements in working order is rare. And even then, it can cost you a small fortune.

But, by painstakingly reproducing the complex mechanics, we've given you a more accurate update of the stylish original. That's like getting balcony seats at the world premiere for the price of a matinee.

The easy to read dial shows the hour and minute through a triangular window in the gold-toned, stainless steel case. Powered by a precise movement, the Majestic secures with a black leather strap and is water-resistant to 3 ATMs.

Finally a Hollywood remake that gets it right!" The cost was a reasonable $5,000.00 at least I thought it was a fair price. Also, Harry Keyilian, my jeweler, gave me my usual good customer 25% discount.

# CHAPTER TWO

**JUST THE OTHER DAY, HOWARD** Wallace (CIA) said to me on the phone, "Charlie, you're an awesome PI and you are RED". My immediate response was, "What do you mean RED? I am no communist!"

He laughed, and then he laughed some more. Then he replied, "I did not mean that you're a commie pinko. I meant that your Retired and Extremely Dangerous (i.e. RED), since your retirement from the LAPD."

I smiled to myself at my 'faux pas'. Then I realized that he was giving me a compliment, I think anyway. While I would be the first to admit that I have lost a step-or-two in speed and agility during the past few years, he felt that my vast experience in law enforcement compensates for those passing years. Howard is truly a nice guy and a good friend.

I worked on the famous Wilshire Boulevard in Los Angeles, in the Travelers Insurance high rise office building. It is twelve stories tall and my office is on the tenth floor. It has a terrific view of downtown LA.

I am currently buying a very nice office/business condominium in this expensive high rise office building. Just west of down-town Los Angeles, I am located just off, north of the Santa Monica Freeway (10).

I am a nationally respected PI (Private Investigator) with con-tracts in most of the major cities in the United States. The of-fices are very expensive on Wilshire Blvd., however, they keep going up in value, even in our current economic recession (or depression, as I call it) that we find ourselves in.

Also, it is sort of a status symbol to be a PI in this professional area of LA. The only thing better for a private detective would be a Beverly Hills address like Anthony ‘the Pelican' Pelancano use to have. That was before he went away to prison for unlaw-ful detective practices, wire tapping, threats, intimidation, just to name a few of his alleged crimes.

I was thinking of moving my PI office to a high rise downtown in the city's financial district. The building is sixty-two stories tall and it is the second tallest building in all of LA.

The tallest structure is the US Bank California headquarters building which is seventy-two stories high. It is round in archi-tectural shape and is shown from the air in many Hollywood movies and TV shows. It makes for a great ‘backdrop' for a film or any production.

The suite that I am thinking about leasing (cost per month) is on the fifty-fifth floor and has a beautiful and panoramic view of both the lovely Pacific Ocean to the south and the majestic San Gabriel mountains to the north.

To the west you can see (if there is no smog, of course) Santa Monica, Century City, LAX (Los Angeles International Airport) and Beverly Hills (90210). And finally to the east, you will view the OC (splendid Orange County) and beautiful Newport Beach.

You could not find a better deal in LA (due to the current depressed lease rates) nor could you find a more breath taking view of Southern California.

The only problem I have, and the reason for my hesitation, is that this was the old headquarters building for UCB (United California Bank). That was back in the 1980's and if you lived in LA back then you will readily recall that this same building caught on fire on May 4, 1988 and five floors were destroyed as well as forty people injured and one killed.

Therefore, even though the structure was completely repaired back then, and its current inspections by the prestigious LAFD (Los Angeles Fire Department) are good, clear, and up to date, it still gives Charlie here a ‘cause to pause'.

Like I always say: "Stop, think and then act." I will let you know what I decide at a later date after doing just that.

While I was stationed at the infamous *Rampart District — Robbery and Homicide Division* (LAPD), I worked on the notorious "Grim Reaper" serial killer case (in the South Central LA area).

This was back in the 1980's to 2003 with my old friend James 'Jimbo' Bowen. Like me he is older now, but still a good golfer and great story teller.

I was a new Lieutenant back in the day and he was a *green* detective. He is the Deputy Chief of Police (LAPD) today. He has a fancy office on the top floor of the brand spanking new LAPD Headquarters in downtown LA, just off (south) of the 101 Hollywood Freeway and right by the City Hall (built in 1923) and the Walt Disney Concert Theater.

Jimbo and I, as well as the rest of our robbery and homicide team among many others we recruited to assist us, worked that case very hard regardless of what the press (i.e. Long Beach Examiner Newspaper) was quoted as saying.

Unfortunately, I am very sorry to say that we were not able to solve that particular case before I retired after putting in my *twenty*!

Even though some of the murdered women were 'allegedly' working girls (prostitutes) we put in just as much overtime, actually more, than on any of our other homicide cases at the time.

We truly did. We felt that our job was to catch the killer, not to judge the poor-defenseless victims.

Just recently an LAPD special 'cold case' squad arrested the alleged serial killer. His name was William Lonnie Jefferson. He is 67 years old and has a wife of many years and four grand children.

Jefferson faces charges of killing ten women over more than two decades. He is being held without bail, thank God.

He worked as a garbage collector for LA County for many years and lived right in the middle of the *killing zone*.

He allegedly killed seven young women between 1985 and 1988 in South Central LA. Then he supposedly resurfaced 14 years later striking three more times. The 14 year gap led to the news media giving him the nickname the "Grim Reaper".

I was watching TV the other night, a kind of mindless wasteland of nothingness I know, but good for escapism, and sometimes 'old Charlie' here needs to let his mind veg out and escape this crazy mixed up world.

There was not much worth watching, *big surprise*, and while I was 'channel surfing', I ran across a show called "Cold Case Files", not the Cold Case regular TV series, with that cutesy little blond number, WOW!

Anyway, this one was a 'real' life murder mystery investigation of old (cold) police cases throughout the country.

Then I got this bright idea. One of these days, I would get Howard Wallace and some of his associates at the CIA and big Jim Bowen, the Deputy Chief of Police, here in Los Angeles, and some of his friends, and we would investigate a 'few' of the most notorious and notable unsolved murder mysteries (i.e. Cold Cases) in Hollywood's very, very shady past.

The *first* case I want to look into happened in 1922. The handsome and debonair movie director, "William Desmond Taylor". He was found slain in his fashionable bachelor pad near the corner of Fourth and Alvarado Streets (LA, California).

Today, that area is full of drug dealers and gang bangers. But, back then it was quite nice. Just down the street from the lovely Mac Arthur Park. His butler and one of his many girlfriends 'spread' the word of his premature demise, and before the police (LAPD) arrived, there appeared to be a '*party going*' on at his bungalow. Paramount studio actors — actresses — as well as movie executives were rummaging through bedroom drawers and closets.

The butler was washing dishes and an unnamed movie extra was walking out the front door with a case of 'bootleg gin'. Everyone there seemed to be looking for something, except for the host, Mr. Taylor, who was neatly laid out on the living room floor with a bullet hole in the *middle* of his back.

It was said that some of the lovely Hollywood leading ladies were looking for love letters that they had written to Mr. Taylor, and to no one's' surprise some of these gorgeous women were married.

At the time, the LAPD had several 'persons of interest' (i.e. suspects): an actress with a big crush on Taylor, and a very jealous type supposedly; an actresses mother (different actress, of course), who also was enamored with him; a separate actresses drug dealer; a thieving valet (who was secretly Taylor's brother); a wife who he had deserted on the East Coast; and a soldier from his wartime days who he had court marshaled for theft many years prior.

The police were pretty sure that the butler did *not* do it, but they were not quite certain who actually *did* do it?

The *second* one occurred in 1932. In "Deadly Illusions", authors Samuel Marx and Joyce Vanderveen argue that director Paul Bern did not shoot himself in 1932, as the coroner had ruled.

They contend that an ex-lover did it in Bern, who was the husband of blond *bombshell* actress Jean Harlow.

In the *third* case, the body of the wild and beautiful actress Thelma Todd was discovered in December 1935 in her Lincoln

Phaeton convertible (a fabulous car even by today's standards) in a garage near her café in Pacific Palisades. I read once that the cocktail drink,

"Hot Toddy" was named after Thelma, as she had invented it in the 1930s when she was known to drink more than just a little. She was married at the time to the flamboyant actor Pat Di-Cicco. The coroner ruled she died of carbon monoxide poisoning after turning on the ignition and striking her head on the steering wheel.

But others theorized she may have been killed by a film director or an abusive ex-husband or even minions of Lucky Luciano, Costra Nostra ( or Bugsy Siegel, a mob hit man) who she had angered by refusing to allow casino gambling on her property.

Todd's death followed a series of show-business scandals, and "The studio bosses were worried that many Americans who paid to see movies wouldn't tolerate yet another." wrote authors Marvin Wolf and Katherine Mader in "Fallen Angels". An official finding of death by her own hand, accidental, or otherwise, put an end to speculation about murder... A neat and tidy solution.

Several days after Hollywood publicist Ronni Chasen was found shot to death in her Mercedes-Benz, a friend voiced the hope to KNBC-TV news that the case wouldn't turn into "another Black Dahlia", the *fourth* case I would like to investigate.

The friend was referring to the 1947 slaying of aspiring actress Elizabeth Short, which has never been solved. The Times' attributes fascination with the Black Dahlia case to the fact that the killing was a "gruesome, unsolved murder of an attractive victim with a *haunting* nickname."

SHE PICKED UP the nickname because of her black outfits and black hair and because a movie of that era was titled "the Blue Dahlia." Old Charlie here was told by his now deceased mother (who lived in the LA area at that time) that Ms. Short was a prostitute who wanted to become an actress.

Short's mutilated body was found January 15, 1947, in a vacant lot on Norton Avenue in the Leimert Park area. More than 50 delusional characters confessed. No one was ever arrested. Over the years, the villain has variously been identified as a pipe salesman, a doctor, a cop, another mobster, a café owner or an actor. Or a big time movie producer's relative who was a UCLA medical school dropout.

The *fifth* case occurred in 1959, the case of George Reeves the TV "Superman," who died not by jumping out a window — as one urban myth has it - but by gun shot. I remember watching "Superman" as a kid. And I recall being very sad one day when another kid told me at school that Superman was dead and had committed suicide. I am not even sure that I knew what suicide was at the time.

It was ruled a suicide and connected to Reeves' inability to land serious roles after his "Superman" days. But in the book, "Hollywood Kryponite", authors Sam Kashner and Nancy Schoenberger assert that he may have been killed on orders of a studio executive whose wife was having an affair with Reeves. The producer's name was Mannix.

In 1978 the *sixth* one happened. No one of course, thought the bludgeoning death of Bob Crane — the star of TV's "Hogan's Heroes" — in a Scottsdale, Arizona apartment was anything but *murder*.

In 1994, John Henry Carpenter, a friend of Crane's and a longtime suspect, was tried for the slaying but acquitted. Prosecutors alleged that Carpenter, who was with Crane the night before the killing, had had a falling out with the actor.

I remember reading, and it was reported in the press, that Crane and Carpenter were involved in the 'pornography' business. If this was true, I am sure they knew several very shady perps (perpetrators) and dangerous characters.

Their case hinged in part on a photograph of a speck found on the door of Carpenter's rental car, which prosecutors said was fatty matter from Crane's skull. Unfortunately, the speck was lost before the trial started. "What was the speck?" asked the jury foreman later. Officially, the case remains unsolved.

And *finally*, just recently in 2010 the most current Hollywood murder mystery demise occurred. It is too soon to predict the outcome of the investigation into the slaying of Ronni M. Cohen-Chasen.

But, as the above cases illustrate all too brutally, not every Hollywood story has a happy ending. And some have no ending at all. And, those we call *cold cases*.

Have no fear, while these cases are still yet unsolved, I will soon be on the cold case. And, you know when on an investigation, I am like a dog *after a bone* — I do not quit. I will keep you posted of any developments and/or progress in these cases.

Late last evening, I jerked myself awake in the middle of the night. It was out of a completely sound sleep, I believe that I was snoring very loudly and I shot straight up in bed like a poker.

I was totally wet and soaked all over. Sweat ran down my face into my eyes, my nose, ugh, and down the back of my neck. My hair felt like I just got out of the shower, it was so damp, and my legs were shaking, and my feet twitching.

I was not sure that I could even stand up without falling flat on my face. And, my ulcer, it was so upset, "forget about it!"

I had just had another horrible nightmare, I finally realized. No, it was not a terrifying nor disturbing (i.e. Disturbia — the movie) dream about almost being killed on previous investigations and assignments in: a) Los Angeles, California, b) San Diego, California, c) Russia (Siberia), d) Kazakhstan (Eastern Europe), e) Mexico City, f) Vera Cruz, Mexico (one of the most lovely cities in all of Mexico by the way), nor g) others I will not bother to name.

I was having another of those heinous and horrifying 'nightmares' about my *ex-wife*. That was much worse than the bad dreams that I have occasionally about almost losing my simple and dangerous life. Actually much worse than the other types, trust me on that!

Immediately, the theme song I have dedicated to my *ex-spouse* for the past ten (10) years (since she left me after 30 years of marriage), came 'crystal clear' to rest on my mind.

Some of you older men and women readers may remember: "WHAM" — the 1980's British Pop singing duo. It was very famous at the time in the USA as well as in England and Europe. It was made up of Sir George Michaels and his singing partner Andrew Ridgeley. Both had all kind of 'Big Hair' (i.e. remember the musical 'Hair' on Broadway way back then?) what kick it was. Well it was the 1980's after all.

Even old Charlie here had a lot hair back then, way over my ears, shirt collar and jacket. I wish it would have laid flatter like a lot of men's, however, mine was very wavy, which I did not like but the girls seem to go crazy over it. They liked to 'play' in it, and of course you know that I just hated them doing that,...Right!

Sir George Michaels went on to become a very successful Solo Act, however, I don't know what happened to his old partner. Do you?

There are a lot of great songs about unfaithfulness, disloyalty, cheating, gold digging, deserting, et cetera, ex-wives. However, of all of them this one by 'WHAM' best fits my lovely former spouse.

Well, that is unless I were to write one myself with the assistance of my good friend Howard (CIA). I sincerely hope that the lyrics do not upset or offend any nice sweet women who *are* working hard, have two jobs, take care of the kids, take out the trash, home school their children, plant a vegetable garden, go to night school to advance her career, and on and on!

Most women are smarter than most men. Also, they can endure nine times as much physical pain as most men (i.e. child birth). There are just a few women like my ex-wife (and Howard's ex-spouse from what he tells me) and a few others who are...let's just say disloyal, mean spirited, untrustworthy, slanderers, libelous, et cetera, to be polite (politically correct).

Well anyway, here goes my "song of divorce". Please let me know if any of you men out there in bookstore land, recognize any women after you read the lyrics to this inspirational song, at least it was helpful to old Charlie here! The song is entitled:

"Everything She Wants"

Oh yeah...

Work...work...

Somebody told me,

Boy, everything she wants is everything she see's...

I guess I must have loved you once

Cause I said you were the perfect girl for me,

Maybe...

But now we're six months older... (ten years in my' case)

And everything you want and everything you see,

Is out of reach...not good enough

I don't know what the hell you want from me but boy...

La la la

Somebody tell me

Won't you tell me...

Why I work so hard for you?

All to give you money

All to give you money...

## THE MONEY CHANGER

Some people work for a living

Some people work for fun

Girl, I just work for you!

They told me marriage was a give and take,

Well, you showed me you can take now you've got some

Giving to do. I'll tell you that I'm happy if you want me to

One step further and my back will break,

If my best isn't good enough

Than how can it be good enough for two?

I can't work any harder than I already do

Somebody tell me

Won't you tell me

Why I work so hard for you?

All to give you money

All to give you money

Oh...

Why do I do the things I do?

I'd tell you if I knew

I don't even think that I love you

Won't you tell me

Tell me...tell me...tell me...

How could you settle for a boy like me

When all I could see was the end of the week

All the things we sign

And the things we buy

Ain't gonna keep us together...

It's just a matter of time

My situation

Never changes

Walking in and out of that door!

Like a stranger

But with wages

I give you all and you say you want more

And all I can see is the end of the week

All the things we sign

And the things we buy

Ain't gonna keep us together

Because no matter what I do

Or how hard I work

Or how much money I give you

It's never good enough for you!

The song pretty much says it all, don't you think? Please don't get me wrong, I dearly love women. I truly do. All shapes, sizes, hair colors, eye colors, tall and short figures, nationalities, et cetera. I do, however, have a small problem with just a few women who I have had the misfortune to run across in my long and sometimes frustrating dating life. I hope you women understand that I clearly do not have a bias against women in general, only a handful.

# CHAPTER THREE

**THE OTHER DAY, I WENT** to see my therapist on Rodeo Drive in Beverly Hills, up in the high rent district. His name is Curt Roundtable (no relation to the Pizza Family). Yes, I have a counselor.

Just about everyone in La La Land (LA, California) has one, even a tough PI like myself (well, I like to *think* I am tough anyway). When you work 'life and death' cases as yours truly does, it sometimes help to 'unpack' and get some of the garbage of this crazy and violent world off of your shoulders and also out of your head. At least that is what I tell myself to justify going to a shrink.

He said to me: "Charlie, one of your *many* problems, is that you are a bonafide *hopeless* romantic. You keep thinking that you will find the perfect woman. Due to your dysfunctional childhood (et cetera) you are attracted to women who are needy, broke, and controlling (albeit very nice looking, instead of caring, strong, and independent women".

I thought to myself...paused...and then replied to him: "You know doc, I think you just may be on the right track here. These circumstances certainly apply to my ex-wife and most of the women I have dated for very long periods".

I think I will be much more careful in selecting and dating girlfriends in the future. Maybe the guy is worth the $400.00 per hour that I pay him.

He gives me a discount so I should not complain, he usually brings down $800.00 per hour. But, to 'the rich and famous' of Hollywood, that is peanuts.

The other day I decided to buy an investment (rental) property since the interest rates are at an all time low and home prices are still at 'depressed' levels. I found a home the real estate agency posted on the internet:

**"A Bond Pad For A Charlie's Angel".** Even for Los Angeles, it's an impressive cast. Roger Moore owned the Beverly Hills Post office Spanish hacienda in the 1980s and 90s, then Candice Bergen bought it, and then Cameron Diaz (current owner).

The property was quietly shopped around to agents as a '*pocket listing*' for $10.25 million. Occupying about three acres in a gated community, the compound has a 5,000 square-foot main house with three bedrooms and four bathrooms and a 2,000 square-foot guesthouse with three bedrooms and two bathrooms, according to the marketing pitch.

Brick defines the alfresco dining area and surrounds the swimming pool and spa. Sweeping stairs lead down to an expansive lawn. There are fruit trees, a tennis court and gazebo beside a stream.

Moore, 82, secret agent 007 in seven of the James bond films, owned the estate for about a decade. When Bergen, 64, bought the property from him in 1996 for $3.4 million, it had 1.5 acres of land.

The Emmy-winning actress, star of "Boston Legal" (2004-2008) and "Murphy Brown" (1988-1998), expanded the property and renovated the 1949 estate, which was featured in Architectural Digest. Diaz, 37, whose purchase follows her star turns in "Knight and Day" with mega movie star Tom Cruise (2010) and "My Sister's Keeper" (2009).

I was told by a friend of mine who is a real estate broker in Beverly Hills (the lovely Mary Lucas, sister of movie producer George Lucas) that I could pick the beautiful property up for about $8.25 million. And then could probably sell it in five years $15 million. Once the current recession (depression) is finally over (if ever).

Just when I was about to put the famous and lovely 'Bond Pad' home into a short 30 day escrow, with a minimum deposit of $100,000.00, I received a rushed cell phone call (on my Blackberry) from a good real estate broker friend of mine.

He told me that there was a 'buy of a lifetime' that just came out on the real estate MLS (multiple listing service). He heard a rumor that I was in the market for an exceptional property with a matching exceptionally low price.

It was the *palatial* mansion of 'William Randolph Hearst' (the world renown newspaper owner and publisher Barron), and his infamous mistress and famous actress of Hollywood, Ms. Marion Davies.

The current owner, I was told by my friend (Jim McVie) just filed for Chapter 7 bankruptcy, only yesterday, like so many millions of other homeowners across California (as well as the whole nation).

The loss of homes by the poor, middle class and even the wealthy was caused by man's Greed, Deceit, Secrecy and Lack of Government oversight and proper regulations. Due to man's '*Love of Money*' the housing market and foreclosures are rampant all over the entire globe (not just in the USA).

The world famous home and lavish compound, which was listed for sale at $165 million dollars three years ago, is now back on the extremely depressed real estate market for *only* $95 million dollars.

This may sound like a lot of money, however, to old Charlie here it looks like a very good buy that in about five to seven years should be worth $150 million dollars. Of course, it could take up to ten years.

I cannot afford this big a purchase by myself naturally, however, I know of a very wealthy real estate investment consortium, a real estate limited liability partnership, and real estate joint venture corporation who one or all may clearly be interested in this spectacular opportunity.

You see, I like to say "Charlie, your opportunity is just around the corner. Right over the horizon". In addition, I have some good friends at the 'First Interstate Bank' in Los Angeles, California, that probably would finance the purchase if I was involved in it.

I assisted them on my last case down in Mexico and they are very grateful for what a good job I and my team did for the bank. If I make an offer on the magnificent mansion, *and if* it is accepted, I will get in touch with them for more information, rates terms, et cetera. My friend feels that I could pick up the property for about $85 million, which sounds about right to me.

The 50,000-plus-square-foot mansion sits on 3.7 flat acres on a hilltop above the Beverly Hills Hotel and comes with staff accommodations, a security cottage, a separate two-bedroom apartment and a two-story four-bedroom gatehouse.

Built by banker Milton Getz, the H-shaped Mediterranean main home was designed by Gordon Kaufmann and retains its original landscaping design by Paul Thiene.

Despite the property's sumptuous features and storied history, the price reduction isn't all that surprising given the condition of the housing business. Median home prices in Southern California have declined 43% since the 2007 peak, according to

MDA Data Quick, matching the price drop reflected on the new listing.

Called *Beverly House*, the 1920's era mansion has had fairytale moments. John (JFK) and Jacqueline Kennedy spent part of their honeymoon there. The estate also has a lurid side, including a movie career highlighted by the famous scene from "The Godfather" in which a horse's head is found in a character's bed.

The home's fourth owner, bought Beverly House more than 30 years ago. During his ownership he refurbished the structure, expanded the living space by more than 20,000 square-feet and reacquired adjacent property that had been sold off.

Most of the individuals shopping in the $95 million price range are *international* buyers, Century 21 Realtors represented the buyer in the $50 million sale several months ago of a 2.2 acre French chateau estate in Bel Air, which set the record as the highest-priced US residential sale this year. The property had been listed at $85 million.

Local buyers are more likely to be looking at the $20 million to $30 million range. Los Angeles County has just *29 billionaires* in residence, according to the Los Angeles Business Journal, the lowest number in five years.

Hearst was attracted by the same features that the modern-day ultra-rich crave: Hearst refused other houses in Beverly Hills because he wanted seclusion, privacy and views, which all came together at Beverly House.

Davies wanted to keep the appearance of separate residences, even though the couple had been living together for more than 30 years, previously in Santa Monica and at the Hearst Castle in San Simeon.

THE TERRA-COTTA stucco structure blends Spanish and Italian styles. The interiors feature intricately carved ceilings, paneled walls, French doors, balconies and floor-to-ceiling windows. Cascading waterfalls lead to a swimming pool and Venetian columns beyond the pool house.

The main level has a 50-foot entry hall with a loggia, a living room with 22-foot high arched ceiling and a library with hand-carved woodwork. The billiard room retains its herringbone parquet floors and a carved stone fireplace mantle originally from Heart's San Simeon mansion.

Other features include an Art Deco nightclub, a wine cellar, a gym and two projection rooms. Will it be enough to attract a buyer in a market with estates priced as high as $150 million? I do not think so.

Have you ever noticed that just when you think you have this silly ‘single' life all figured out, SLAM — BAM!...something, or someone, hits you right in the face. I was just driving out of a potential PI client's office structure on Rodeo Drive in Beverly Hills (i.e. 90210—the TV show) close to Sunset Blvd. I was felling OK about being single and not having a girlfriend at the present time. Although, I felt a little bit lonely sometimes, especially at night. If you are a man, you know what I mean.

When all of a sudden, this woman, ran right into my bumper. I was very upset, to say the least, because the car was a brand new BMW and only had 1,000 miles on it. I got out of my car, went back to the lady (driver), to tell her ‘what's what'.

All of a sudden, another sudden, I saw her close up and went ‘WOW'—luckily I did not say it out loud. She had ravishing long red hair, tied up in a cutesy pony tail, and big bright and beautiful emerald green eyes. They had Irish ‘pixy' dust in them, I kid you not. OMG.

I swallowed hard, I felt very light headed, a ‘twinge' in my ulcer, I swallowed again, and tried my best to calm my old heart down. I do not need to have a heart attack right in front of this lovely Irish lass, at least she looked Irish.

I asked her what her name was and she replied: "My name is Mary St. Cloud-O'Connell" then added; "I am from Dublin, Northern Ireland. I just got to the States (USA) recently and I am having *trouble* driving in all of this world famous, or infamous, LA traffic."

I started to tell her 'trouble' was my middle name (kind of like Elvis Presley use to do), however, I decided that would sound like a little bit too much for an old PI like myself.

Remember his classic old song "Trouble"? They just do not make songs like "the King" use to make, these days. We do have a lot of great recording artists of course, however, there will never be another "King", let's face it. I've revised the lyrics a little to better fit Charlie, of course.

"If you're looking for trouble

You came to the right place

If you're looking for trouble

Just look right in Charlie's face

I was born standing up

And talking back

My daddy was a green-eyed farmer and mountain jack

Because I'm evil, my middle name is Kennedy

Well I'm evil, so don't you mess around with me

*Charlie* never looked for trouble

But I've never ran

I don't take no orders

From no kind of man

I'm only made out

Of flesh, blood and bone

But if you're gonna start a rumble

Don't you try it on alone

Because I'm evil, my middle name is *Kennedy*

Well I'm evil, so don't you mess around with me

I'm evil, evil as can be

I'm evil, evil as can be

So don't mess around, don't mess around, don't mess around with me

I'm evil, I'm evil

So don't mess around, don't mess around with Charlie!

I'm evil, I tell you!"

The original Elvis song was written by the truly dynamic song writing team of Leiber and Stoller of Barry Gordy's Motown (Detroit) fame. I am not really that tough and I most certainly am not that evil, however in my line of work (Private Investigator) it always help to have a good tough image (rep, reputation) and I think I will make this my new advertising theme song. What do you think?

Then I asked, "May I call you Mary?". To which she replied: "After hitting the bumper of your beautiful new BMW, you can call me anything you want. You could even call me for dinner if you would like."

Yeah, like what man in his right mind would not want to have dinner with a 'real live' Irish Princess? She was 39 years old by the way, and I am...well older than that, a lot older.

After she made her kind offer, she smiled with absolutely perfect, gleaming white teeth. My old heart 'skipped' a beat, or *perhaps*, two or three, I told her I would have my insurance company take care of the damage to my BMW as well as her little VW Passat. It was a bright red convertible of course, what else?

Two days later, I picked Miss Mary up from her condominium in Marina Del Ray. That is where all of the single flight attendants from LAX (airport) live.

Why would she want to live anywhere else? I took her to dinner at the famous 'House of Blues' on *Sunset Boulevard*, in Hollywood. Great, even better than great music, if you like the blues. And, I really, truly do! I have some blues CD's that would 'knock your socks off'.

ONE OF MY most prized blues CD's and iTunes is "Robert Johnson — The Complete Recordings." Johnson was the founder of modern blues! It is a two disc set:

| | |
|---|---|
| Kind Hearted Woman Blues | (2:49) |
| Kind Hearted Woman Blues (2) | (2:31) |
| I Believe I'll Dust My Broom | (2:56) |

| | |
|---|---|
| Sweet Home Chicago | (2:59) |
| Ramblin' On My Mind | (2:51) |
| Ramblin' On My Mind (2) | (2:20) |
| When You Got A Good Friend | (2:37) |
| When You Got A Good Friend (2) | (2:50) |
| Come On In My Kitchen | (2:47) |
| Come On In My Kitchen (2) | (2:35) |
| Terraplane Blues | (3:00) |
| (an all-time blues favorite for over 70 years) | |
| Phonograph Blues | (2:37) |
| Phonograph Blues (2) | (2:32) |
| 32-20 Blues | (2:51) |
| They're Red Hot | (2:56) |
| Dead Shrimp Blues | (2:30) |
| Cross Road Blues | (2:30) |
| Cross Road Blues (2) | (2:39) |
| Walkin' Blues | (2:28) |
| Last Fair Deal Gone Down | (2:39) |

And on disc two are these fabulous songs:

| | |
|---|---|
| Preachin' Blues (Up Jumped The Devil) | (2:50) |
| *If I Had Possession Over Judgment Day* | *(2:34)* |
| Stones In My Passway | (2:27) |

| | |
|---|---|
| I'm A Steady Rollin' Man | (2:35) |
| From Four until Late | (2:23) |
| Hell Hound On My Trail | (2:35) |
| Little Queen Of Spades | (2:11) |
| Little Queen Of Spades (2) | (2:15) |
| Malted Milk | (2:17) |
| Drunken Hearted Man | (2:24) |
| Drunken Hearted Man (2) | (2:19) |
| Me And The Devil Blues | (2:37) |
| Me And The Devil Blues (2) | (2:29) |
| Stop Breakin' Down Blues | (2:16) |
| Stop Breakin' Down Blues (2) | (2:21) |
| Traveling Riverside Blues | (2:47) |
| Honeymoon Blues | (2:16) |
| Love In Vain Blues | (2:28) |
| Love In Vain Blues (2) | (2:19) |
| Milkcow's Calf Blues | (2:14) |
| Milkcow's Calf Blues (2) | (2:20) |

Some very memorial quotes by some extremely well known recording artists, about these very special CD's are:

"You want to know how good the blues can get? Well this it." — Keith Richards (Rolling Stones — second best Rock-N-Roll band in history)

"He is the most important artist in the blues..all blues seem to revolve around

Robert Johnson." — Keb' Mo' (a very well known contemporary country-blues guitarist)

"...I have never found anything more deeply soulful than Robert Johnson."

Eric Clapton (one of the best guitarists in the whole wide world. Nicknamed — "Slow Hand")

"He had such an old soul for someone so young." — Robert Cray (fabulous young and well respect blues guitarist. Learned from Albert King; B.B. King; Stevie Ray Vaughn; amongst others)

Also, another extremely valuable collectors CD is my "Billie Holiday". There is no better blues/jazz singer in history better than "Blue Billie". The incomparable songs included in this CD are listed here and are absolutely breathtaking!

Easy Living

What Is This Thing Called Love?

Solitude

You're My Thrill

Them There Eyes

No More

God Bless the Child

My Man (Mon Homme)

Don't Explain

There Is No Greater Love

Tain't Nobody's Bizness If I Do

You Better Go Now

Big Stuff

Good Moring, Heartache

I Loves You Porgy (from Porgy and Bess, musical on Broadway)

Guilty

Lover Man (Oh, Where Can You Be?)

Crazy He Calls Me

That Ole Devil Called Love

The original recordings were made between 1944 through 1950. Oops!, I got off track again. It is getting to be a habit with old me.

Now back to my tale about *Little Miss Mary*. We had a delicious dinner. She preferred Italian to Cajun food. She ordered linguini with extra parsley, parmesan cheese, with tomatoes and olives. I believe it was called "Linguini con Dongle Biance." Plus a side of "tortoni"; a little 'pasta con pesto' with lots of spices on everything she ate of course.

She drank red wine. The house wine was quite good, she added. Then she had a sample of "Conard au Pierre" (duck) at the insistence of the chef, who had noticed she was the only patron who was eating Italian instead of Southern cooking.

When she ordered dessert, I almost choked. She cannot possibly have any room left in that lovely little body of hers. And trust old Charlie here, she does have a terrific body.

How could this lovely 'little' Irish Lass eat so much? I said to myself, not out loud luckily. I think she gained five pounds, but it looked good on her, as a matter of fact, everything looked good on her.

I started out with a huge shrimp cocktail. Fresh from the cleaned up New Orleans Harbor. Then I had Kentucky Chicken wings with 'mild' dipping sauce — have to watch that 'hot' sauce — due to the old stomach. I put on one of their big Bar B-Q 'bibs' because I knew I would make a mess and did not want to ruin my new suit I wore for my 'hot' date with Mary.

I ate original country Bar B-Q ribs, simmered over a big smoke grill, with hush puppy potatoes, fries, special-made house Bar B-Q beans (hope I don't not get gas later), greens, corn bread, the way my beloved Mama use to make it, and a lot of ice cold milk for my GERD (i.e. ulcer).

For dessert, I had eight layer German chocolate cake with lots of chocolate chips. It must have had 7,500 calories in it! Well, maybe just a few less than that but, plenty, trust me on that.

We cruised Hollywood (or Holly*wierd*, as some call it) Boulevard. She had never seen anything like the people out 'after dark' on "the Boulevard".

Then, I drove my lovely Irish Princess to Signal Hill (overlooking Long Beach, California) and we watched the big red ball (the sun), come up over the magnificent Pacific Ocean.

You could see the well known and even more hated oil drilling rig towers in the Harbor with their fake palm trees.

I called my friend Howard Wallace (CIA), to tell him the good news. That I had, at least I hoped that I had, a new woman (w.o.m.a.n.) in my life! Possibly the new 'love of my life'. That would be quite nice, would it not?

You women are going to hate me when I tell you this, however, while I was talking to Howard, on his encrypted satellite cell phone, I asked him a little personal favor.

I requested that he do a background check on Miss Mary from Ireland. I did not want to get involved with a member of the Shin Finn (branch of the IRA, Irish Republican Army).

That is just what I do not need at my ripe old age. Even if she is 'drop dead gorgeous'. And by the way, she is!

A guy, or gal, cannot be too careful these days with the "war on terror" and such going on all around the world, as that old saying goes, and you will recall that I just love old sayings: "*The world is going to Hell in a hand basket*".

My friend Howard gets the biggest bang out of that saying. He had never heard it before I told him it years ago. He says he hears it all the time now.

You will be glad to know that when he called back, after only two hours, that he gave Mary a 'thumbs up' and an 'all clear'. Then added "Go for it old man!"

I was very elated with the results, however , he could have skipped the 'old man' *reference*. Anyway, it was very thoughtful of him to use his CIA connections, to collect the information for me. He is one of my best friends in this 'topsy turvy' world but I would never tell him, he might just get a big head.

# CHAPTER FOUR

SINCE I WILL SOON BE traveling to Italy on my new "Bank of Italy, LLC" investigation, I needed to do some in depth research of that country. The information just may be helpful to me when my 'boots hit the ground'. And it may save my life. The obvious place to start was with some old historical facts about Italy, for the case record.

Italy, officially the Italian Republic (Republica Italiana), is a country located partly on the European Continent and partly on the Italian Peninsula in Southern Europe and on the two largest islands in the Mediterranean Seal, Sicily and Sardinia.

Italy shares its northern, Alpine boundary with France, Switzerland, Austria and Slovenia. The independent states of San Marino and the Vatican City are enclaves within the Italian Peninsula, and *Campione d'Italia* is an Italian exclave in Switzerland.

With 60.2 million inhabitants, it is the sixth most populous country in Europe, and the twenty-third most populous in the world.

The land known as Italy today has been the cradle of European cultures and peoples, such as the Etruscans and the Romans.

Italy's capital, Rome, was for centuries the political center of Western civilization, as the capital of the *Roman Empire*.

After its decline, Germanic tribes such as the Lombard's and Ostrogoths, to the Normans and later, the Byzantines, among others. Centuries later, Italy would become the birthplace of the Renaissance, an immensely fruitful intellectual movement that would prove to be integral in shaping the subsequent course of European thought.

Through much of its post-Roman history, Italy was fragmented into numerous kingdoms and city-states (such as the Kingdom of Sardinia, the Kingdom of the Two Sicilians and the Duchy of Milan), but was unified in 1861, a tumultuous period in history known as the "*Risorgimento*".

In the late 19th Century, through World War I, and to World War II, Italy possessed a colonial empire, which extended its rule to Libya, Eritrea, Italian Somaliland, Ethiopia, Albania, Rhodes, the Dodecanese and a concession in Tianjin, China.

Italy plays a prominent role in European and global military, cultural and diplomatic affairs, and it is affiliated with worldwide organizations such as the Food and Agriculture Organization, World Food Programme, International Fund for Agricultural Development, Global Forum, and the NATO Defense College, which are headquartered in Rome.

The country's European political, social and economic influence make it a major regional power, alongside the United Kingdom, France, Germany, and Russia, and Italy has been classified in a study, measuring hard power, as being the eleventh greatest worldwide national power.

The country has a high public education level, high labor force, is a globalised nation, and also has 2009's sixth best international reputation.

Italy also has the world's nineteenth highest life expectancy, and in 2000 its healthcare system was ranked the second best in the world by the *World Health* Organization Report.

In 2007 it was the world's fifth most visited country, with over 43.7 million international arrivals, and boasts a long tradition in the arts, science and technology, including the world's highest number of UNESCO World heritage Sites to date (44).

The origin of the term Italia, from Latin, is uncertain. According to one of the more common explanations, the term was borrowed through Greek from the Oscan Viteliu, meaning "land of young cattle".

The bull was a symbol of the southern Italian tribes and was often depicted goring the Roman wolf as a defiant symbol of free Italy during the Samnite Wars. The name Italia originally applied only to a part of what is now Southern Italy — according to *Antiochus of Syracuse*, the southern portion of the Bruttium peninsula (modern Calabria).

But by his time Oenotria and Italy had become synonymous, and the name also applied to most of Lucania as well. The Greeks gradually came to apply the name "Italia" to a larger region, but it was not until the time of the Roman conquests that the term was expanded to cover the entire peninsula.

Excavations throughout Italy reveal a modern human presence dating back to the Paleolithic period, some 200,000 years ago. In the 8$^{th}$ and 7$^{th}$ centuries BC Greek colonies were established all along the coast of Sicily and the southern part of the Italian Peninsula became known as Magna Graecia.

Ancient Rome was at first a small agricultural community founded circa the 8$^{th}$ Century BC that grew over the course of the centuries into a colossal empire encompassing the whole *Mediterranean Sea*, in which Ancient Greek and Roman cultures merged into one civilization.

This civilization was so influential that parts of it survive in modern law, administration, philosophy and arts, forming the ground that Western civilization is based upon.

In its twelve-Century existence it transformed itself from monarchy to republic and finally to autocracy. In steady decline since the 2$^{nd}$ Century AD, the empire finally broke into two parts in 285 AD: the Western Roman Empire and the *Byzantine Empire* in the East.

The western part under the pressure of Goths finally dissolved, leaving the Italian peninsula divided into small independent kingdoms and feuding city states for the next 14 centuries, and leaving the eastern part sole heir to the Roman legacy.

In the sixth Century AD the Byzantine Emperor Justinian re-conquered Italy form Ostrogoths. The invasion of a new wave of Germanic tribes, the Lombard's, doomed his attempt to resurrect the Western Roman Empire but the repercussions of *Justinian's* failure resounded further still.

For the next thirteen centuries, while new nation-states arose in the lands north of the Alps, the Italian political landscape was a patchwork of feuding city states, petty tyrannies, and foreign invaders.

For several centuries the armies and Exarchates led by the *Exarchate of Ravenna*, Justinian's successors, were a tenacious force in Italian affairs — strong enough to prevent other powers such as the Arabs, the Holy Roman Empire, or the Papacy form establishing a unified Italian Kingdom, but too weak to unify and control the region.

Italy's regions were eventually subsumed by their neighboring empires with their conflicting interests and would remain divided up to the 19$^{th}$ Century. It was during this vacuum of authority that the region saw the rise of the Signoria and the Comune.

In the anarchic conditions that often prevailed in medieval Italian city-states, people looked to strong men to restore order and disarm the feuding elites.

In times of anarchy or crisis, cities sometimes offered the *Signoria* to individuals perceived as strong enough to save the state, most notably the Della Scala family n Verona, the Visconti in Milan and the Medici in Florence.

During the late Middle Ages Italy was divided into smaller city-states and territories: the kingdom of Naples controlled the south, the Republic of Florence and the Papal States the center, the Genoese and the Milanese the north and west, and the Venetians the east.

The unique political structures of late Middle Ages Italy and its dynamic social climate and florescent trade allowed the emergence of a unique cultural efflorescence. Italy never regained the unity it once had in the days of the Roman Empire.

The renaissance was so called because it was a "rebirth" of many classical ideas that had long been buried in the chapters of classical Antiquity.

One could argue that the fuel for this rebirth was the rediscovery of ancient texts that had been almost 'forgotten' by *West-*

*ern civilization*, but were preserved in some monastic libraries or private libraries of powerful and wealthy patrons.

Some would argue that there were translations of Greek and Arabic texts into Latin from the Islamic world that found their way into Italy and contributed to the Italian/European Renaissance.

However, most of the manuscripts were either already in the Italian Peninsula or in 'Greece' and were taken to Italy in the centuries preceding the Renaissance by the Italians themselves (by the traders who traveled regularly to the Eastern Mediterranean, including Greece) and by Byzantine Greeks who migrated to Italy during the onslaught of the Ottoman Empire, against the Byzantine Empire in the 1400's and specially after 1453, once the Ottomans had conquered by Byzantine capital, Constantinople.

These Byzantines fled the Turks, sometimes carrying preciou8s manuscripts and their knowledge (Greek and Ancient Greek) and while fixating themselves in Italy made a discreet but crucial contribution to the Renaissance.

The *Black Death* pandemic in 1348 left its mark on Italy by killing one third of the population. However, the recovery from the disaster of the Black Death led to a resurgence of cities, trade and economy.

This growth greatly stimulated the successive phase of the Humanism and Renaissance (15th - 16th Centuries), when Italy again returned to be the center of Western civilization, strongly influencing the other European countries with Courts like Este in Ferrara and De Medici in Florence.

ROME WAS ALSO a city particularly affected by the Renaissance. This period of reform changed the city's face dramatically, with works like the Pieta by Michelangelo and the frescoes of the Borgia Apartment.

Rome reached the highest point of splendor under Pope Julius II (1503-1513) and his successors Leo X and Clement VII, both members of the *Medici family*.

In this twenty-year period Rome became one of the greatest centers of art in the world. The old St. Peter's Basilica built by Emperor Constantine the Great, was re-built mainly by Michelangelo, who in Rome became one of the most famous painters of Italy creating frescos in the Cappella Niccolina, the Villa Farnesina, the Raphael's Rooms, plus many other famous paintings.

Michelangelo started the decoration of the ceiling of the Sistine Chapel and executed the famous statue of the Moses for the tomb of Julius.

Rome lost in part its religious character, becoming increasingly a true Renaissance city, with a great number of popular feasts, horse races, parties, intrigues and licentious episodes.

Its economy was rich, with the presence of several Tuscan bankers, including Agostino Chigi, who was a friend of Raphael and patron of arts. Before his early death, Raphael also promoted for the first time the preservation of the ancient ruins.

After a Century where the fragmented system of Italian states and principalities were able to maintain a relative independence and a balance of power in the peninsula, in 1494 the French king Charles VIII opened the first of a series of invasions, lasting half of the sixteenth Century, and a competition between France and Spain for the possession of the country.

Ultimately Spain prevailed (*the Treaty of Cateau-Cambresis* in 1559 recognized the Spanish possession of the Duchy of Milan and the Kingdom of Naples) and for almost two centuries became the hegemon in Italy.

The holy alliance between Hapsburg Spain and the Holy See resulted in the systematic persecution of any Protestant movement, with the result that Italy remained a Catholic country with marginal Protestant presence.

Due to its long rule on Italy, the Spanish Empire systematically spoiled the country and imposed heavy taxation. It interfered and held a tight grip over the affairs of the Vatican. Moreover,

Spanish administration was slow and inefficient, and its social consequences in the long term, in Southern Italy, where Spanish rule was effective, have lasted till the current age.

Austria succeeded Spain as hegemon in Italy after the Peace of Utrecht (1713), having acquired the State of Milan and the Kingdom of Naples.

The Austrian domination, thanks to the Enlightenment embraced by *Habsburgic emperors*, somewhat improved the situation. The northern part of Italy, under the direct control of Vienna, gained economic dynamism and intellectual fervor.

The main Italian cities, such as Milan, Rome, Turin, Venice, Florence and Naples become fertile grounds for intellectual discussion and thought, and several Italian philosophers and literary figures were active at the time, such as the Milanese Cesare, Marquis of Beccaria-Bonesana, better known as Cesare Beccaria, or Antonio Genovesi.

Leopold I, Grand Duke of Tuscany or also known as Leopold II of the Holy Roman Empire, abolished the death penalty and torture in the Grand Duchy of Tuscany.

The French Revolution and the Napoleonic Wars (1796-1815) stirred the ideas of equality, democracy, laws and nation which many in Italy endorsed and even supported as the basis on which they could and eventually would build a national unity in

Italy. This unity, or creation of modern Italy was yet to come in the second half of the nineteenth Century.

The plague repeatedly retuned to haunt Italy throughout the 14th to 17th Centuries. Italy's last major epidemic occurred in 1656 in Naples. In northern Italy, a report of 1767 noted that there had been famine in 111 of the previous 316 years and only sixteen good harvests. Italy's population between 1700 and 1800 rose by about one-third, to 18 million.

The creation of the Kingdom of Italy was the result of efforts by Italian nationalists and monarchists loyal to the House of Savoy to establish a united kingdom encompassing the entire Italian Peninsula.

In the context of the 1848 liberal revolutions that swept through Europe, an unsuccessful war was declared on Austria.

Giuseppe Garibaldi, popular amongst southern Italians, led the Italian republican drive for unification in southern Italy, while the northern Italian monarchy of the Kingdom of Piedmont-Sardinia whose government was led by *Camillo Benso*, conte di Cavour, had the ambition of establishing a united Italian state under its rule.

The kingdom successfully challenged the Austrian Empire in the Second Italian War of Independence with the help of Napoleon II, liberating the Lombardy-Venetia. It established Turin as its capital of the newly formed state. In 1865 the capital was moved to Florence.

In 1866, Victor Emmanuel II aligned the kingdom with Prussia during the Austro-Prussian War, waging the Third Italian War of Independence which allowed Italy to annex Venice.

In 1870, as France during the disastrous *Franco-Prussian* War abandoned its positions in Rome, Italy rushed to fill the power gap by taking over the papal State from French sovereignty.

Italian unification finally was achieved, and shortly afterwards Italy's capital was moved from Florence to Rome. While keeping the monarchy, the government became a parliamentary system, run by liberals.

In 1935, Mussolini invaded Ethiopia. This resulted in international alienation and along with other factors, led to Italy's withdrawal from the *League of Nations*.

A first pact with Nazi Germany was concluded in 1936, and a second in 1938. Italy strongly supported Franco in the Spanish civil war. The country was opposed to Adolf Hitler's annexations of

Austria, but did not interfere with it. Italy supported Germany's annexation of Sudetenland, however. In April 1939, Italy occupied Albania, a *de facto* protectorate for decades, and entered World War II in 1940, taking part in the late stages of the Battle of France.

Mussolini, wanting a quick victory like Hitler's Blitzkriegs in Poland and France, invaded Greece in October 1940 via Albania but was forced to accept a humiliating defeat after a few months.

At the same time, Italy, after initially conquering *British Somalia*, saw an allied counter-attack lead to the loss of all possessions in the Horn of Africa. Italy was also defeated by British forces in North Africa and was only saved by the urgently dispatched German Africa Corps led by Erwin Rommel.

Italy was invaded by the Allies in June 1943, leading to the collapse of the fascist regime and the arrest of Mussolini. In September 1943, Italy surrendered.

The country remained a battlefield for the rest of the war, as the allies were moving up from the south as the north was the base for loyalist Italian fascist and German Nazi forces. The whole picture became more complex by the activity of the Italian partisans.

The Nazis left the country on April 25, 1945 and the remaining Italian forces eventually disbanded. Nearly half a million Italians (including civilians) died between June 1940 and May 1945.

An estimated 200,000 partisans took part in the Resistance, and German or fascist forces killed some 70,000 Italians (including both partisans and civilians) for Resistance activities. At least 54,000 Italian prisoners of war died in the Soviet Union.

This is all very interesting historical information however, I am not quite sure that it will assist me with my investigation. But, you never know.

And, I have found out from experience over the years that when in a foreign country, the more you know about it the better prepared for the unexpected you are.

# CHAPTER FIVE

AFTER I READ AND RECORDED the aforementioned historical information, I wanted to know a little 'modern' history of Italy.

In addition, I wished to know something about their Islands, mountains, and borders, their climate, the military and police, and last but certainly not least — their language.

I was going to have to get an "Italian for Dummies" book at 'Barnes and Noble' bookstore right away. And, study it well before leaving on my 'next' big adventure.

Italian Republic (1946 - present): In 1946, Victor Emmanuel III's son, Umberto II, was forced to abdicate. Italy became a republic and a referendum held on June 2, 1946, a day celebrated since as Republic Day.

This was also the first time in Italy that Italian women were entitled to vote. The Republican constitution was approved and come into force on January 1, 1948.

Under the *Paris Peace Treaties* of 1947, the eastern border area was lost to Yugoslavia, and later, the free territory of Trieste was divided between two states.

Fears in the Italian electorate of a possible Communist takeover proved crucial for the first universal suffrage electoral outcome on April 18, 1948 when the Christian Democrats, under the leadership of *Alice De Gasper*, won the election with 48 percent of the vote.

In the 1950's Italy became a member of NATO and allied itself with the United States.

The Marshall plan helped revive the Italian economy which, until the 1960's, enjoyed a period of sustained economic growth commonly called the "Economic Miracle".

In 1957, Italy was a founder member of the European Economic Community (EEC), which became the European Union (EU) in 1993.

From 1992 to 2009, Italy faced significant challenges, as voters, disenchanted with past political paralysis, massive government debt and extensive corruption (collectively called Tangentopoli after being uncovered by *Mani pulite* — "Clean hands"), demanded political, economic, and ethical reforms.

The scandals involved all major parties, but especially those in the government coalition: between 1992 and 1994 the Christian Democrats underwent a severe crisis and was resolved, splitting up into several pieces, while the Socialists and the other governing minor parties also dissolved.

Italy is located in Southern Europe and comprises the boot-shaped Italian Peninsula and a number of islands including the two largest, Sicily and Sardinia.

Although the country occupies the Italian peninsula and most of the southern Alpine basin, some of Italy's territory extends beyond the Alpine basin and some islands are located outside the Eurasian continental shelf.

These territories are the *comuni* of: Livigno, Sexten, Innichen, Toblach (in part), Chiusaforte, Tarvisio, Graun im Vinschgau (in part), which are all part of the Danube's drainage basin, while the Val di Lei constitutes part of the Rhine's basin and the island commune of Lampedusa e Linosa is on the African continental shelf.

Including the islands, Italy has a coastline and border on the Adriatic, Ionian, Tyrrhenian seas, and borders shared with France, Austria, Slovenia, and Switzerland; San Marino and Vatican City, both enclaves, account for the remainder.

The *Apennine Mountains* form the peninsula's backbone, the Alps form its northern boundary. The Po, Italy's longest river, flows from the Alps on the western border with France and crosses the Padan plain on its way to the Adriatic Sea. The five largest lakes are:

Garda (142 sq mi)

Maggiore (82 sq mi)

Como (56 sq mi) — The famous actor George Clooney as well as several very wealthy people own vacation home here.

Trasimeno (48 sq mi)

Bolsena (44 sq mi)

The country is situated at the meeting point of the Eurasian Plate and the African Plate, leading to considerable seismic and volcanic activity. There are 14 volcanoes in Italy, three of which are active: Etna, Stromboli and Vesuvius.

Vesuvius is the only active volcano in mainland Europe and is most famous for the *destruction of Pompeii* and Herculaneum. Several islands and hills have been created by volcanic activity, and there is still a large active caldera, the Campi Flegrei north-west of Naples.

The climate of Italy is highly diverse and can be far from the stereotypical Mediterranean climate, depending on location. Most of the inland northern regions of Italy, for example Piedmont, Lombardy and Emilia-Romagna, have a continental climate often classified as humid subtropical.

The coastal areas of Liguria and most of the peninsula south of Florence generally fit the *Mediterranean stereotype*. Conditions on peninsular coastal areas can be very different from the interior's higher ground and valleys, particularly during the winter months when the higher altitudes tend to be cold, wet, and often snowy.

The coastal regions have mild winters and warm and generally dry summers, although lowland valleys can be quite hot in summer.

The Italian armed forces are under the command of the Supreme Defense Council, presided over by the President of the Italian Republic. In 2008 the military had 186,798 personnel on active duty, along with 114,778 in the national Gendarerie.

As part of NATO's nuclear sharing strategy Italy also hosts 90 United States nuclear bombs, located in Torre and Aviano air bases. The Italian armed forces are divided into four branches:

The Italian Army (Esercito Italiano) is the ground defense force of the Italian Republic. It has recently become a professional all-volunteer force of active-duty personnel, numbering 109,703 in 2008.

Its best known combat vehicles are the Dardo infantry fighting vehicle, the Centauro tank destroyer and the Ariete tank, and among its aircraft the mangusta attack helicopter, recently deployed in UN missions. The Esericito Italiano also has at its disposal a large number of Leopard 1 and M113 armored vehicles.

The Italian Navy (Marina Militare) in 2008 had a strength of 43,882 and ships of every type, such as aircraft carriers, destroyers, modern frigates, submarines, amphibious ships, and other smaller ships such as oceanographic research ships.

The Marina Militare is now equipping itself with a bigger aircraft carrier, (the Cavour), new destroyers, submarines and multipurpose frigates. In modern times, Italian troops (in connection with NATO) have operations around the world, including Afghanistan and Iraq.

The Italian Air Force in 2008 has a strength of 43,882 and operates 585 aircraft, including 219 combat jets and 114 helicopters. As a stopgap and as replacement for leased Tornado ADV interceptors, the AMI has leased 30 F-16A Block 15 ADF and for F-16B Block 10 Fighting Falcons, with an option for more.

The coming years also will see the introduction of 121 EF2000 Euro fighter typhoons, replacing the leased F-16 Fighting Falcons. Further updates are foreseen in the tornado IDS/IDT and AMX fleets. A transport capability is guaranteed by a fleet of 22 C-130Js and Aeritalia G.222s of which 12 are being replaced with the newly developed G.222 variant called the C27J Spartan.

AN AUTONOMOUS CORPS of the military, the *Carabinieri* are the gendarmerie and military police of Italy, policing the military and civilian population alongside Italy's other police forces. While the different branches of the Carabinieri report to separate ministries for each of their individual functions, the corps reports to the Ministry of Internal Affairs when maintaining public order and security.

At the Sea Islands Conference of the G8 in 2004, the Carabinieri were given the mandate to establish a Center of Excellence for Stability Police Units (CoESPU) to spearhead the development of training and doctrinal standards for civilian police units attached to international peacekeeping missions.

Italy's official language is Italian. Ethnologue has estimated that there are about 55 million speakers of the language in Italy and a further 6.7 million outside of the country. However, between 120 and 150 million people use Italian as a second or cultural language, worldwide. Italian, adopted by the state after the unification of Italy, is based on the Florentine variety of Tuscan and is somewhat intermediate between the Italo-Dalmatian languages of the South and the Gallo-Romance *Northern Italian languages*.

Its development was also influenced by the Germanic languages of the post-Roman invaders. Unlike most other Romance languages, Italian has retained the contrast between short and long consonants which exist in Latin. As in most Romance languages, stress is distinctive. Among the Romance languages, Italian is considered to be the closest to Latin in terms of vocabulary.

The Mafia, Italy only (called La Cosa Nostra in USA. A completely separate organization) originates from Sicily and its influence is widespread in Italian society, directly affecting 22% of Italians and 14.6% of Italy's GDP, while even Prime Minister Rudolf Bertinelli has long been accused of links with organized crime.

*Note*: In the United States organized crime families are known as the "La Cosa Nostra". In Italy and Sicily, the syndicates are referred to as "the Mafia" and in the old days "the black hand".

It is entirely possible that the Mafia may, quite possibly have had something to do with the "Bank of Italy, LLC" fraud counterfeit case.

The fight against the Mafia has cost the lives of many, including the high profile assassinations of judges Giovanni Falcone and Paolo Borsellino.

There are four separate *Mafias* controlling territory and business activities in four Southern Italian regions: *Cosa Nostra* in Sicily, *Camorra* in Campania, *'Ndrangheta* in Calabria and *Sacra Corona* Unita in Puglia, exerting influence over 13 million Italians.

Their business involvement reaches European and global scale. Businesses, entrepreneurs, shopkeepers, and craftsmen in these regions are expected to pay a "*pizzo*", or protection money, to crime syndicates controlling their area.

There rarely is possibility of escaping payment, and persons not complying find their business premises and their lives at risk. Those not able to meet demands might find their business partly or completely taken over by organized crime.

Italy has the 47th highest murder rate in the world, in a sample of 63 countries.

The first form of televised media in Italy was introduced in 1939, when the first experimental broadcasting began. However, this lasted for a very short time: when fascist Italy entered World War II in 1940 all the transmissions were interrupted, and were resumed in earnest only nine years after the end of the conflict, in 1954.

There are two main national television networks responsible for most viewing: state-owned RAI, funded by a yearly mandatory license fee and Media set, commercial network founded by current *Italian Prime* Minister Silvio Berlusconi. While many other networks are also present, both nationally and locally, these two alone account for 80% of the TV ratings.

As with all the other media of Italy, the Italian television industry is widely considered both inside and outside the country to be overtly politicized.

The public broadcaster RAI is, unlike the BBC which is controlled by an independent trust, under direct control of the government; the most important commercial stations in the country are, in turn, owned by the current prime minister.

According to a December 2008 poll, only 24% of *Italians trust* television news programs, comparing unfavorably to the British rate of 38% , making Italy one of only three examined countries where online sources are considered more reliable than television ones for information.

Along with Turkey, Italy has one of the lowest levels of press freedom in Europe, even falling behind some ex-communist countries, such as Poland and the Czech Republic.

This background information will be a lot more helpful to me than the previous research on Italy's history. Of particular interest, was the information on the Italian Armed Forces, especially the "Carabinieri" (the Gendarmerie) Police.

Not to mention a lot of 'potentially' very useful information on the "Italian Mafia". Mainly the 'Camorra' and 'Sacra Corona Unita' organized crime families in Southern Italy.

# CHAPTER SIX

I FEEL MUCH MORE COMFORTABLE now that I know a lot more about the country of Italy since I will be there very soon. I did, however, want to know just a few more 'minor' things about this beautiful land.

A little about its architecture, historical landmarks, the opera (I think old Charlie here could use a 'little more class'), some of its famous citizens and corporations, and, of course, its *cuisine*.

I do not go anywhere without knowing about the food at my planned destination. It is one of the few rules that I actually have. As you recall "The Transporter" (movie) Jason Strathan has a lot of rules.

Italy boasts a long period of different architectural styles, from Classical Roman and Greek, Gothic, Renaissance, Baroque, Neo-Classical, Art Nouveau to Modern.

The nation contains several architectural *monuments*, such as the Pantheon, the Coliseum, *the Leaning Tower of Pisa*, the Piazza del Campo, Milan Cathedral, Florence Cathedral, the Palladian Villas of the Veneto, the Basilica di Santa Maria Maggiore, Villa Olmo and the Pirelli Tower.

Italy has also been home to numerous famous architects, some who even changed the course of architectural history, such as Andrea Palladio, Filippo Brunelleschi, Bernini and Reno Piano.

Italian architecture began with Ancient Greece, Ancient Rome and Etruscans, when both civilizations built temples, basilica, columns, for a, palaces, aqueducts, walls and public baths.

Roman architecture had great influence on that of Italy and the Western world. Because the Roman Empire extended over so great an area and included so many urbanized areas, Roman engineers developed methods for civic development on a grand scale, including the use of concrete. Massive buildings like the *Pantheon* and the *Coliseum* could never have been constructed with pre-existing techniques.

Though concrete had been invented a thousand years earlier in the Near East, the Romans extended its use from fortifications to their most impressive buildings and monuments, capitalizing on the material's strength and low cost.

In Roman architecture, a wall's concrete core was covered with a plaster, brick, stone, or marble veneer, and decorative polychrome and gold gilded sculpture was often added to produce a dazzling effect of power and wealth.

Italy of the 15$^{th}$ Century, and the city of Florence in particular, was home to the Renaissance. It is in Florence that the new architectural style had its beginning, not slowly evolving in the way that *Gothic* grew out of *Romanesque,* but consciously brought to being by particular architects who sought to revive the order of a past "Golden Age".

The scholarly approach to the architecture of the ancient coincided with the general revival of learning. A number of factors were influential in bringing this about.

Italian architects had always preferred forms that were clearly defined and structural members that expressed their purpose. Many *Tuscan* Romanesque buildings demonstrate these characteristics, as seen in the Florence Baptistery and Pisa Cathedral.

In the 20$^{th}$ Century, Italy too saw the construction of several significant edifices, starting in the Art Nouveau architectural style, which in Italy was called, Liberty architecture.

Rationalist-Fascist architecture developed in Italy during the Fascist era, lasting until the 1940s. During that period Italy built the fiat's Lingotto, at the time the world's *biggest automobile* factory.

In the 1950s and 60s several skyscrapers were built across the country, the Pirelli Tower and the Torre Velasca being the most notable. The 21$^{st}$ Century most notable Italian buildings are the Fiera Milano exposition center in Rho, just outside Milan, and the new plans for the Expo 2015 to be held in Milan too, where three new skyscrapers called "lo storto", "il curvo" and "il diritto" will be constructed by foreign architects such as Zaha Hadid, Arata Isozaki and Kaniel Libeskind.

This will also be a project or urban redevelopment, called "City-Life", where new pedestrian areas, parks, green spaces, lakes and waterways will be constructed, in the North-Western part of Milan.

Italy boasts a wide variety of palaces, in various cities, mainly Rome, Florence, Venice, Milan, Turin, Bologna and Naples, built in a wide variety of different styles, from Roman, Byzantine, Romanesque, Medieval and Gothic, to Renaissance, Baroque, Rococo, Neo-Classical and Fascism. In Italian, the word "Palazzo" is more broadly used in Italy than its English equivalent "palace".

In Italy, a palazzo is a grand building of some *architectural* ambition that is the headquarters of a family of some renown or of an institution, or even what the British would call a "block of flats" or a tenement. In Venice, most palaces are referred to as a "Ca", which is short for "Casa", meaning "house" in Italian.

Over the centuries, Italian art has gone through many stylistic changes. Italian painting is traditionally characterized by a warmth of color and light, as exemplified in the works of Caravaggio and Titian, and a preoccupation with religious figures and motifs.

Italian painting enjoyed preeminence in Europe for hundreds of years, from the Romanesque and Gothic periods, and through the Renaissance and baroque periods, the latter two of which saw fruition in Italy.

Notable artists who fall within these periods include Michelangelo, Leonardo da Vinci, Donatello, Botticelli, Fra Angelico, Tintoretto, Caravaggio, Bernini, Titian and Raphael.

Italian theater can be traced back to the Roman tradition which was heavily influenced by the Greek; as with many other literary genres, Roman dramatists tended to adapt and translate from the Greek. During the 16$^{th}$ Century and on into the 18$^{th}$ Century, commedia dell'arte was a form of improvisational theatre, and it is still performed today.

*Travelling troupes* of players would set up an outdoor stage and provide amusement in the form of juggling, acrobatics, and more typically, humorous plays based on a repertoire of established characters with a rough storyline, called canovaccio.

Italy's most famous composers include the Renaissance composers Palestrina and Monteverdi, the baroque composers Alsessandro Scarlatti, Corelli and Vivaldi, and the Classical composers Paganini and Rossini, and the Romantic composers Verdi and Puccini.

Modern Italian composers such as Berio and Nono proved significant in the development of experimental and electronic music. While the classical music tradition still holds strong in Italy, as evidenced by the fame of its innumerable opera houses, such as *La Scala of Milan* and San Corlo of Naples, and performers such as the pianist Maurizio Pollini and the late tenor Luciano Pavarotti, Italians have been no less appreciative of their thriving contemporary music scene.

Italy is widely known for being the birthplace of opera. Italian opera was believed to have been founded in the early 1600s, in Italian cities such as Mantua and Venice.

Later, works and pieces composed by native Italian composers of the 19$^{th}$ and early 20$^{th}$ centuries, such as *Rossini, Belini, Bonizetti, Verdi,* and *Puccini*, are amongst the most famous operas ever written and today are performed in opera houses across the world.

La Scala opera house in Milan is also renowned as one of the best in the world.

THE HISTORY OF Italian cinema began a few months after the Lumiere brothers began motion picture exhibitions. The first Italian film was a few seconds long, showing Pope Leo XIII giving a blessing to the camera. The Italian film industry was born between 1903 and 1908 with three companies: the *Societa Italiana Cines*, the *Ambrosio Film* and the *Itala Film*.

Other companies soon followed in Milan and in Naples. In a short time these first companies reached a fair producing quality, and films were soon sold outside Italy.

Cinema was later used by Benito Mussolini, who founded Rome's renowned Cinecitta studio for the production of Fascist propaganda until the end of World War II.

After the war, Italian film was widely recognized and exported until an artistic decline around the 1980s. Notable Italian film directors from this period include Vittorio De Sica, Federico Fellini, Sergio Leone, Pier Paolo Pasolini, Michelangelo Antonioni and Dario Argeto.

Movies include world cinema treasures such as La dolce vita, Il buono, il brutto, IL cattivo and Ladri di biciclette. In recent years, the Italian scene has received only occasional international attention, with movies like La vita e bella directed by Roberto Benigni and Il postino with Massiomo Troisi.

Through the centuries, Italy has given birth to some notable scientific minds. Amonst them, and perhaps the most famous polymath in history, *Leonardo da Vinci* made several contributions to a variety of fields including art, biology, and technology.

*Galileo Galilei* was a physicist, mathematician, and astronomer who played a major role in the Scientific Revolution. His achievements include improvements to the telescope and consequent astronomical observations, and support for Copericanism.

The physicist *Enrico Fermi*, and Nobel Prize laureate, was the leader of the team that built the first nuclear reactor and is also noted for his many other contributions to physics, including the co-development of the quantum theory.

A brief overview of some other notable figures includes the astronomer Giovanni Domenico Cassini, who made many important discoveries about the Solar System; the physicist Alessandro Volta, inventor of the electric battery; the mathematicians Lagrange, Fibonacci, and Gerolamo Cardano, whose Arts Magna is generally recognized as the first modern treatment on mathematics, made fundamental advances to the field; Marcello Malpighi, a doctor and founder of microscopic anatomy.

The sport with the highest spectator attendance and number of registered players is football (soccer), the Series A being one of the most famous competitions in the world.

Italy's national football team is the second-most-successful team in the world, with four World Cup victories, the first one of which was in 1934. Other popular sports include basketball, volleyball, water polo, Rugby Union, Rugby League, cycling, fencing, ice hockey (mainly in Milan, Trentino-Alto Adige and Veneto), roller hockey, motor racing and swimming.

Winter sports are most popular in the northern regions, with Italians competing in international games and Olympic venues. Turin hosted the 2006 *Winter Olympic Games*.

Italian fashion has a long tradition, and is regarded as one of the most important in the world, along with French, American, British, and Japanese fashion.

Milan, Florence and Rome are Italy's main fashion capitals, however Naples, Turin, Venice, Bolgna, Genoa and Vicenza are other major centers. According to the 2009 Global Language Monitor, Milan was nominated the true fashion capital of the world, even surpassing other international cities, such as New York, Paris, London and Tokyo, and Rome came $4^{th}$.

Major Italian fashion labels, such as Gucci, Prada, Versace, Valentino, Armani, Dolce & Gabbana, Missoni, Fendi, Moschino, Max Mara and Ferragamo, to name a few, are regarded as amongst the finest fashion houses in the world. Also, the fashion magazine *Vogue Italia*, is considered the most important and prestigious fashion magazine in the world.

Italian cuisine has evolved through centuries of social and political changes, with its roots reaching back to the $4^{th}$ Century BC. Significant change occurred with the discovery of the *New World*, when vegetables such as potatoes, tomatoes, bell peppers, and maize became available.

However, these central ingredients of modern Italian cuisine were not introduced in scale before the 18th Century. Ingredients and dishes vary by region. However, many dishes that were once regional have proliferated in different variations across the country.

*Cheese and wine* are major parts of the cuisine, playing different roles both regionally and nationally with their many variations and Demoninazione di origine controllata (regulated appellation) laws. Coffee, and more specifically espresso, has become highly important to the cultural cuisine of Italy. Some *famous* dishes and items include pasta, pizza, lasagna, focaccia, and gelato.

Once again, this background information was very interesting, especially the parts about the famous 'Spaghetti Westerns' movie directors, "Sergio Leone" and "Federico Fellini". Also, Leonardo da Vinci, Michelangelo, and Donatello. Not to mention, something of a real importance to me, information concerning Italian cuisine (food)! A subject near-and-dear to my heart, as you all know by now.

# CHAPTER SEVEN

THE COUNTERFIET $100.00 BILLS located in the vault at "The Bank of Italy, LLC" could have far reaching effects to the world financial community, especially the United States.

Howard Wallace got permission from the Director of the CIA (Chan Mean), and approval from the head of the NSA (National Security Agency) to come join me in Italy with a team of CIA "white collar" (*bank fraud*) experts. The crack team that Howard brought with him included the following seven members:

Manny Murrieta who spoke Spanish fluently, English, and Italian. The languages, he said, are quite similar. He is a very close friend of Howard's and is very strong and very quick with a knife. He has assisted me on several prior investigations in LA, California as well as in Mexico.

Besides Howard, he is the person I want to have 'watch my back' when a situation goes south (i.e. bad). He is a distant relative of the infamous Mexican bandito "*Juaquin Murrieta*" (1849).

His voice was like a husky whisper. He did not believe in playing by civilized rules. He felt that it took too long and was a waste of time. Although, since he worked for the CIA — he had to follow some rules — he had a great deal of flexibility with his protocol, unlike the high strung and constantly watched FBI personnel.

He could be a 'warm and fuzzy' type man, which he was normally, but when necessary he had nerves of steel *and* ice water for blood!

Chealy Te, a karate and mixed martial arts expert. He speaks English, Chinese, Cambodian, French, Spanish and some (a little) Italian. He is also a specialist in explosives (C-4, et cetera) and close hand to hand combat.

He was educated in Cambodia, Australia and the United States. His eyes could shoot daggers when he needed them to. The rest of the time, they just remained very clear and focused.

Always shifting back and forth like a lion (although this is the year of the tiger). His stare could pierce through people as if he had x-ray vision and could examine their insides to see what made them tick.

And, whether they were good or bad people. In the field, when he spoke, it was in a low, snarling growl — and immediately got the attention of the perp — that he was talking to (questioning).

Luigi Guttuso will run the control center (i.e. the war room), as he was a surveillance, computer and internet expert. He has an

MBA (master in Business Administration) from Yale in International Banking.

He was born in Italy (Rome), speaks fluent Italian, French as well as English. One of the foremost experts within the CIA, and the world in *ferreting out* white collar crimes.

He worked on the infamous Bernard 'Bernie' Madoff investment fraud case in the USA. Even when young, he was wise, charming, articulate, and acutely aware of others and the world around him, mentally incisive, athletically gifted, physically beautiful, flawlessly polite and agonizingly shy. He tested at 160 on the Stanford-Binet IQ test they gave him.

The results embarrassed him. He's pushing six feet tall. My score on that same test when I was in community college (Cerritos College), was 135. Obviously Luigi's mind was more intelligent than mine. And, he's also probably a lot stronger since he was quite a bit younger than I. At that college, I'd studied accounting and economics. It was a great school, very small at the time I attended. It is quite large today and one of the best two year colleges in California. Anyway, I digress, (as usual).

AS AN ASIDE, I have never had anybody be attacked and die or be murdered in my family, but when it comes to the financial devastation of my family (and also some close friends) it is about as bad as you can get. It was a *financial mass murder*.

As a result of the huge Bernie Madoff 'Ponzi' scheme, my family and many others (including several whole foreign countries) were major victims of Madoff (and his two sons') fraud. One of his son's (Mark) just committed suicide recently (two years to the date Bernie was arrested) due to his guilt feelings over his involvement in the fraud perpetrated with his father. Now to continue:

Giovanni Colonna is an expert in organized crime (including counterfeiting) in Italy. He was born in Sicily and schooled at Harvard. His father was a high ranking Capo member of the "Cosa Nostra".

One of the four leading "mafias" controlling crime in southern *Italy and Sicily*. He got out of 'the life' when he was twenty, when his father wanted a better life for his only son. He sent Giovanni to live with relatives in the United States. The relatives just happened to work secretly for the CIA.

His expertise in counterfeiting, as well as his family contacts, will be invaluable in our investigation. His body was an efficient and highly trained *lethal* weapon. His very dark brown eyes were all cool and shadowed. His mind was sharp as a knife. When he was in his work (CIA) mode, his words would sneer, as his thick lips curled into a ferret of a smile. He did not care about money, fame, or fortune, just getting the bad guys around the world. This was probably due to his family background in the Italian Mafia. He was definitely not a bureaucrat and was at the top of his game.

Maria Gabbana Lombardi is an expert in working with CI's (confidential informants). She was born in Napoli (Naples), Italy. She speaks Italian — slang — which is used by most locals in Rome (Roma).

She looks like a model, long legs, which should be of assistance in gathering intelligence from the Italian bankers and others. I can honestly tell you that if she were to pump me for information, I would tell her 'everything' I knew, and, probably very quickly.

A very classy creature if I do say so myself. As naturally attractive as she was, and trust me on this, she was extremely pretty, when on the job for the CIA, she could exude a voice as cold as a Siberian winter. And folks, I am here to tell you, that - that is cold, real cold!

You cannot date fellow co-workers, while on assignment for the CIA. At least, you are not supposed to. If I were to make an exception, however, to that silly rule, it would be with Maria. Those legs just never stop and as you already know, I am a leg man.

Angel Ortega Bermudez is an expert at running the internal control panel for the 'Reaper' and 'Rapture' surveillance drones. She speaks fluent Italian as well as Spanish and English.

She is young, only 25, but wise beyond her years. She worked with me in Mexico. Very sharp lady and pretty too, a nice bonus. She was very smart. She was very brave, quite possibly, too brave for her own good. An extremely strong woman.

Angel was the only other female on this op (operation) and no petite miss at five-eight. She could more than handle herself in hand-to-hand combat, cool as an ice cube under pressure. Few men would suspect the trim woman packaged with all those lush curves to be so lethal, but she was one tough babe from the short, sandy brown hair to the mile of legs...to the AK-47 rifle strapped across her camo suit when in the field.

Carlo Piacentini is a former investigator with the famous *Interpol Agency* in France. Now he is working with the CIA as the foremost expert in counterfeit currency (paper money). He is consulted by governments, banks, and financial institutions from all over the world.

His expertise will be of 'great' assistance in our current investigation of "The Bank of Italy, LLC" fraud case. He will be able to determine which $100.00 bills are real and which ones are counterfeit. Also, probably where they were printed (which country), and even which type of printing equipment was used in the creation of the 'bogus bills'.

And if we are lucky, real lucky, he might even be able to find some leads to who the culprits are in this difficult case. He is six feet-four inches tall, and his body is all lean planes, angles, and very hard muscle.

He was born in Italy, however, he was raised and educated at prestigious private schools in France. That was where he went to work for the renowned Interpol, prior to being recruited by Howard Wallace (Assistant Director of the CIA). Interpol was a little bit upset with Howard for doing that, however, they could not match the salary — plus benefits — offered to him.

I was already in Rome when Howard and his seven member CIA TAC (Tactical) team arrived. I booked a 'suite' at the well known five star "Palatine Hill Hotel and Casino", located close to the famous Roman Coliseum in the oldest part of town. It was just a magnificent old hotel (built in 1850) and just recently completely renovated in 2010 at a cost of three hundred million (US) dollars.

My suite consisted of a large drawing room, full kitchen, three large bedrooms, three bathrooms, a pool table room, separate sauna room, and a full balcony with an unbelievable and just breathtaking view of most of Rome.

The cost of my very glamorous suite was $5,000.00 per night. A lot of money for me, old Charlie, however, "The Bank of Italy, LLC" was picking up the tab.

My professional services contract with the bank included my regular daily rate/fee 'plus' all expenses. The CIA would not charge the bank for Howard's and his team's services. The US taxpayers, you and I, are going to pay for their expenses.

The other day while I was walking around Rome looking for some great Italian restaurants — I just love real Italian food (I must be part Italian) there are more than you can count, by the way — I noticed that the natural *dress code* in Italy was the same as it was in the United States.

Namely, jeans (blue or black), t-shirts with names of products, companies, rock bands, or pictures of famous or infamous people, and new expensive or well worn athletic shoes.

Some of the lovely Italian women, and there were too many of them to count, wore high heels with red soles, very sexy. Please do not be upset with me America, however, they have the most gorgeous women in the whole world in Italy, they truly do.

They are in the open-air markets, the department stores, the restaurants, the cinemas, the hotels, the supermarkets and even the taxis.

Everywhere you look, I think I may have to buy some real thick and dark sun glasses or I might have a stroke before I can even begin to investigate my fraud case.

I am going to get out my 'Italian for Dummies" language book, so I can figure out what to say to pretty women and flirt with them, just in case they do not speak English. Luckily for me, a lot of people in Rome (at least) speak a little English. Probably as a result of so many tourists visiting their fair city every year.

Believe it or not, there are a lot of natural blondes with green or blue eyes in Italy. They are from the Northern part of the country, closer to Switzerland and Austria.

A pretty blonde Italian woman with emerald green and sparkling gold eyes, a real nice figure, a mouth full of gleaming white teeth, makes my old *heart pump hard*, even skip a beat (or two or three), I grow two or three inches taller, raise my IQ about 10 - 15 points, and turn my grey hair jet black like it use to be — smile.

I must be honest and admit I am a hopeless romantic and I still believe that the "love of my life" is out there somewhere. Maybe on the internet, maybe on eHarmony, maybe at CCI or maybe, just maybe here in the City of Love, Rome.

You know how Charlie here just loves old sayings. One of my favorite romantic ones is: "When a man quits wanting to make *love* to a beautiful woman (Italian or otherwise)...he is *almost* dead.

And, when a man quits *looking* at gorgeous women, he *is* dead!" Good and true statement is it not? Almost all men from all around the world would agree. I want all of you good folks to know, for sure, that I am neither almost dead *nor* really dead. And you can "take that to the bank" as they like to say in the banking and PI business.

I believe that the greatest gift under the sun, or heaven, is a lovely woman to look at. And for a moment, just a brief moment, to feel a little bit younger, a little bit better looking, and a little bit more virile.

In case you were curious, for my wardrobe, I took along my usual dress/work clothes. Remember, I *always* say: "You must dress for success."

*I took to Italy:*

Grey Glen plaid all wool year round suit (no vest), ideal to wear to work.

Classic navy blue all wool year round blazer with antique brass buttons, wine lining to wear with a pair of medium grey slacks.

Classic camel hair sport jacket with brown leather buttons. Wear with a pair of dark brown wool slacks.

Grey herringbone tweed spot jacket with black leather button (British cut), with charcoal grey flannel slacks for casual wear.

Solid navy blue all wool year round suit with vest, to wear at formal occasions.

Medium grey stripe all wool year round suit with vest, to wear for business meetings.

Solid dark grey all wool year round suit with vest, to wear at meetings and "courtroom" trails, if there are any.

Tan gabardine all wool year round suit (no vest), great for spring and summer. Very pleasant looking and ideal to wear to work, at the bank.

You should have at least a dozen 100% cotton or cotton/polyester custom made shirts in your wardrobe. Mine are monogrammed with my initials — C.O'B. on left sleeve...a must.

Plus my accessories: Black wing-tip shoes, brown wing-tips, black penny loafers, Doc Martins, New Balance athletic shoes (3 pairs — black, brown and white), and two pair of well broke in army ranger jump boots (for when I am in the field on assignment).

Also, just for good measure, I took a pair of my favorite black Acme cowboy boots with snake skin trim. Everyone in Italy (and Europe) think all Americans are cowboys. Yes, Charlie here wears ‘boxers', not briefs. So I took several, and many socks, ties, belts and t-shirts and sweat shirts.

I could always buy anything else that I might need and charge it to the bank, therefore, I was not worried if I forgot something. I have always dressed very professionally ever since I was a policeman. I always wore a clean, freshly pressed police uniform. And when I made Detective, I always wore nice suits or sport jackets/slacks.

THE OTHER DAY, I had to make a quick trip down to the Hotel store/market and I just happened to pass the gift shop. There in the window, a lovely ring called out to me.

Well, it did not actually speak to me verbally you understand, let's just say it caught my attention. The sign above the ring said: "He invented infamous". Being that I know a lot of famous, as well as infamous people, I was very intrigued.

The beautifully crafted and gold lettered brochure stated the following (written in Italian, English, German and French): "Benvenuto Cellini was one of Italy's most celebrated goldsmiths.

During the Golden Era of the Old Masters, he competed with Michelangelo, Titian, and Donatello for greatness. But as a Renaissance bad boy, he had all of them beat.

From blood feuds and scandalous affairs to embezzling the Pope's gem collection, Cellini knew how to get into trouble (kind of like me, Charlie).

If you want to look into the details, we recommend his autobiography, a sprawling account of *romance,* skullduggery and outrageous behavior.

But if you want to see how his work continues to inspire jewelry designers, look no further than our 14K Gold Vermeil Florence Ring.

A shining example of the metal smith's craft, the ring features an ornate "cage" of swirled sterling silver, layered in lustrous 14K gold. It projects all the weighty opulence of a *Medici* treasure, while sitting surprisingly light on the finger.

It's the perfect way to capture the elegance of the Italian Renaissance with a unique, artistic flair."

The cost was $1,000.00 (US dollars) but, it was supposedly on sale. You know me, I simply never pass up a great sale. Besides, it will look great with some of the cool watches I wear when I dress up now and again.

I said to myself (out loud, again) thank God I was alone at the time: I am going to have to stop doing that or someone, possibly one of my arch enemies (from prior cases, my ex-wife, et cetera) are going to have me arrested and committed to the 'nut house', or a retirement community. Just what I need.

They have only older pretty women in those places, however, I have seen some knockouts in a few I have visited in the past (they looked younger than me in some cases).

However, nothing like the women who play women's volleyball on the sand, who walk on the pier, or who walk right in front of my house (Hermosa, beautiful in Spanish), just off the 'Strand' close to the beautiful old and very historic pier.

They have the most beautiful, sensual, and tan women between my house and the famous Santa Monica Pier, than anywhere else in the whole wide world, with the exception of Italy (and Roma).

Yes, Parisian women are rated up there as are Brazilian women, Swedish models, women from Dallas, Texas (with their Southern drawl accent — I just love a Southern accent, it drives me wild and if the lovely lady has a nice figure to go with the accent, I am just G.O.N.E — gone!)

Now, where was I? Oh, yes: "Giusto een cura io incontraare uno bello donna" (i.e. translation from Italian, just in case you meet a beautiful Roman woman or goddess).

"Lei avere ad sapere qualcosa ad dire ad lei" (i.e. I have to know something in Italian to say to her). Otherwise she will think I am a stupid tourist and will walk away in those beautiful red soled high heel shoes that I like so well.

And then add: "Qualcosa piacere lei alcuno bello, suo biondo capelli sta piacere oro". (i.e.: You are so beautiful and your blonde hair is like gold) Good opening line would you think? I know it would work in Hollywood and LA, however, not quite so sure if it will work here in Italy.

Let us continue with our lesson: "Come' ferita lei piacere ad andare ad il opera' con mi note?" (i.e.: How would you like to go to the opera with me tonight?)

Now you are getting the idea, Charlie, you are on a roll, I thought. Bless that little yellow language book: "Italian for Dummies".

Now the most important part, ‘closing the deal ‘as the Americans like to say. "Ed dopo il opera" forse noi latta andare schiena ad mio mettere' per dei vino per lei ed dei latte per vecchio, et al, Charlie?" (i.e.: "And after the opera maybe we could go back to my place" (with a little smile, of course), "For some wine (red — of course) for you and some milk for me?”

Now, I told myself (out loud) if you are lucky, really lucky, and the nice Italian Lady with beautiful long legs and a perfect (killer) smile, says: "Si" (i.e. yes), then probably the rest of the evening you will be able to communicate quite nicely without any, or very little, Italian or English for that matter, "Capise" (understand?)

I needed to rent some wheels (transportation) so I could get around Roma while I was here. You can't take the bus when you're a PI. I wanted to rent something "way cool", of course, since I always travel *in style*. Especially when the client is picking up the tab.

I contemplated renting a new "Maybach" just for the fun of it. Hip-hop mogul Diddy gave his son a $360,000 Maybach for his 16$^{th}$ birthday. Madonna, Jay-Z, and Samuel L. Jackson have all owned one.

The storied German marquee, revived by Mercedes-Benz in the early 2000s, has become synonymous with super-wealth and the $463,000 Maybach 62S won't change that.

For the price of a family home, buyers get options like personalized motifs on the chauffer partition screen, sterling silver wheels, a perfume atomizer, and a cinema screen. But I decided that it would stand out too much, for a private eye.

Then I thought about a "Rolls", Rolls-Royce, the British brand beloved of royalty for over a Century and, more recently, by rock stars and rappers (The Who's Keith Moon famously drove one into a pond).

The company's flagship Phantom ($380,000 for a 2011 model) offers outrageous options including 44,000 color choices, a special power reserve dial and a retractable "Spirit of Ecstasy" hood ornament.

Each car takes 720 hours to build, including seven hours alone of hand polishing. Rolls-Royce production topped 300 cars a month for the first time in the summer of 2010, mostly thanks to the booming Asian marketplace. They just love Rolls-Royce's in Hong Kong (China). Too ostentatious for Charlie, I had to pass.

Maybe a European master vehicle would work: the latest in a long line of Mercedes-Benz supercars, the SLS AMG ($185,750) — the first-ever car designed and developed from the ground up by the company's AMG high performance division is set apart by its roof hinged "gull wing" doors.

Though aesthetically echoing the company's classic 300SL of the 1950s and 60s, the SLS AMG is *sublime and sinister*, with a throaty 563-horsepower V-8, a spoiler that automatically deploys at high speeds and cabin that's rich in leather and aluminum or, for a few grand more, carbon fiber.

No, I said to myself, I think the "Gull wing" doors would be so very cool, but this is not Germany, it is Italy, right?

Could a James Bond car, the famed "Aston Martin" fit the bill? Aston Martin is *quintessentially* British. The company is displaying its breathtaking DB9 coupe ($187,615) at this year's auto show.

Timeless beauty, fastidious built quality and heart-racing performance of zero to 60 mph in 4.6 seconds have made DB9 owners out of celebrities like Ryan Seacrest and Adam Carolla.

Maybe, but no. Therefore, I finally made up my mind. I decided to go with a "BMW". One of my all time favorite cars and also one of the finest *road production* vehicles in the whole world!

The BMW Alpina B7 Sedan ($122,875) has only restrained exterior enhancements to set it apart from a regular 7 series, under the hood it's a different story.

The Alpina B7's bestial V-8, taut steering and exceptional handling place it on my list, but the company's new A8L W12 long-wheelbase sedan ($130,000 estimated) would be right at home in a head of state's motorcade or in mine.

At over 17 feet long, it could probably swallow an entire royal family. The 12-cylinder A8L gives even the Rolls-Royces of this world a run for their money with its Valcona leather interior, ambient lighting, and heated/ventilated seats with remote-controlled air bladders to massage the lucky passengers, and a date if you are lucky and have one.

When the folks at German manufacturer Alpina get their expert hands on a BMW, the transformation goes well beyond mere aesthetics. I said to myself, after the two week lease is up I am going to switch my leased vehicle to a "Ferrari" or a "Lamborghini", after all, this is Italy!

And you would look so very suave and cool driving a hot ‘red' Ferrari around Roma. Just think of how many lovely Italian chicks you could date.

I also needed to rent two additional vehicles. One for Howard and one for his CIA TAC team to use. Since cost was not an object, as "The Bank of Italy, LLC" was paying for them, I picked out a Porsche 911 Speedster for Howard.

I picked out a red one of course, he will look real good cruising around Roma in this hot set of wheels. The 2011 Porsche 911 Speedster ($204,000), one of a plethora of 911 variants now available, chops the coupe's windshield by two inches, does away with the miniscule rear seats and adds a distinctive double-bubble tonneau to house the folding top.

In a nod to Porsche's original production model - the 356 - only that number of 911 Speedsters is planned. After a week or two, I am going to get Howard a "Maserati" to drive, unless he wants to keep the *tire burning* 911.

For his team's ride, I picked a brand new Range Rover (Land Rover) SUV. This vehicle will go anywhere and under any driving conditions with its four-wheel drive high ground clearance and its under-carriage skid plates.

Land Rover (Range Rover) Autobiography Black ($117,950) should soon be a regular backdrop in paparazzi pics. Marketing the Range Rover's 40$^{th}$ anniversary the Autobiography comes in a unique Barolo Black finish set off by 20-inch diamond-turned alloy wheels and an array of aluminum, chrome and titanium flourishes.

Range Rovers have become vehicles of choice for celebrities including Charlize Theron, Pete Wentz and Kate Walsh. I had the leasing company (Europcar) install (at extra cost of course): bullet proof glass; bullet proof tires, and steel plates in all four doors.

# CHAPTER EIGHT

WHEN HOWARD AND HIS TEAM (Manny, Chealy, Luigi, Giovani, Maria, Angel, and Carlo) arrived in Rome we spent a few days planning and discussing various issues and eating pasta, lots of pasta, of course.

This is Italy after all, right? Next, we went to the bank's headquarters in their beautiful old building constructed in 1621. It has been remodeled and refurbished several times since then, naturally.

We met in the office of the President, his secretary/assistant was ‘drop dead gorgeous', I kid you not. Her name was Anna Gigi Sordi. She was 5'8", natural blond, emerald green eyes, and legs that just did not stop.

"I think I'm in love", I said to myself — *luckily not out loud*, like normal. In attendance were the following bank VIPs:

Mr. Giacippi Francis Bouchilli, Chairman of the Board

Mr. Vittorio Capitolini, President and CEO

Ms. Doria DePisis, Office of the President

Mr. Luca Perugino, Director of Internal Security, Threats, Employee kidnappings, and counterfeiting.

Ms. Novana Mona Bella, Sr. VP of Public Relations and

Mr. Nino Proietti, the banks top legal counsel and advisor.

There were two big and armed security guards at the door. The first thing out of the mouth of the bank's attorney (Nino), even before we got a chance to sit down was:

"You gentlemen/women understand that this information is top secret and highly confidential, coppice?" Everyone looked at me, so old Charlie, said in my broken Italian: "Si - si, Senor Proietti."

Each and every one of us completely realized the immense secrecy needed in this *in house* investigation. As soon Nino heard our responses, he became more relaxed, but you know attorneys, whether they are Italian or American, they never relax very much. It is just part of their nature.

Please do not tell anyone or you will get old Charlie here in trouble, but I just hate attorneys. I always have and I always will. It seems to me that all they do is lie, cheat, intimidate others, and then after doing that for years, they become congressmen/women?

Then the Chairman, Mr. Bouchilli, welcomed us and spoke a little and then quickly turned the leadership of the meeting over to Mr. Luca Perugino, the bank's Internal Security Director.

He use to work for the 'Carabinieri' (they are the gendarmerie and military police of Italy).

He carries a Glock 40 Caliber automatic in his shoulder holster (under his expensive Italian designer suit) and a small light weight 9 MM Beretta in a leg holster on his left ankle (under his long slacks).

He told me that in his desk he keeps a 5.62 bullet, sub Italian military issue machine gun, just in case something heavy goes down at the bank (i.e. a total take over/hostage taking for ransom or regular armed robbery, or a terrorist attack).

After Luca spoke about the counterfeit $100.00 US bills, ($100,000,000.00 worth) located in the main underground vault, located four stories beneath this very building, our Maria and Angel were so enamored by Luca they started to flirt with him by pretending to ask him questions about the investigation.

Only a fool would not notice and we are definitely not fools. He looked like a Greek tri-athlete or a Roman warrior. He was 6' 2", dark long wavy hair, with black, very neatly trimmed and groomed, black, jet black eyes, wearing an Armani suit (of course), you could see your reflection on his shiny Italian shoes.

His tie was pure silk, custom made, with a 100% pure Egyptian cotton dress shirt which looked like it was glued to his body.

As discretely as I possibly could, I got Maria and Angel to back off by requesting that they do some research on the executive/top floor that we were on.

Now I had the same problem as they did, except it was with the secretary just outside the door, Gigi, unfortunately I could see almost all of her legs as she was working the computer on her desk, OMG.

I have never seen legs like that in my whole life. Yes, she was truly "uno bella donna" (one beautiful woman). Try to calm down, I told myself. And as if that was not bad enough, Doria and Mona looked like they both just walked off an Italian fashion 'catwalk', in Milan, or somewhere else in Italy...WOW!

They both had on designer business suits and matching blouses and black small bow ties, 5" or 6" heels (with red soles, designer *Christian Louboutin* shoes) I started to drool and then grabbed my kerchief and pretended I was going to cough. Sly dog that I am.

I decided if I was going to be able to concentrate on the case at all, I would have to dismiss them for now, anyway. Mr. Capitolini (the President and CEO) and Nino (the attorney), said very little and seemed very distracted, or worried, or guilty?

Of course, you have to remember that all attorneys look guilty...that is because they usually are! And, bank presidents usually look worried these days because they get fired about every year or two due to this world wide economic depression (not recession).

When Mr. Capitolini, Doria and Mona moved out that just left Mr. Bouchilli, Luca and Nino from the bank.

And then Howard, Manny, Chealy, Luigi, Giovani, and Carlo from the CIA plus myself.

You could easily tell how absolutely *terrified* the Chairman was that some horrible problem was going to befall his beloved bank.

He had started working here in 1950 and worked his way up from a real estate loan officer trainee. He is 82 now and became Chairman when his father (Giuseppe Bouchilli) retired in 1985.

Luca was also worried because this fraud took place on his watch and if it was not resolved, and resolved quickly, he would be out in the cold without a job.

A very well paying job might I add. Howard, Luca and I took a small table in the corner. It was away from the others. We wanted to put together some sort of 'preliminary' plan to discover who was behind the large bank fraud.

The Presidents secretary (Gigi), yes, the one with the gorgeous legs *and* beautiful long hair, came over to our little table and very politely asked if I wanted "coffee, tea or me?" (I mean her). Then she gave me a big eye popping smile and said: "Just kidding, the choice is only coffee or tea, it doesn't include me. I was so terribly disappointed, but said tea since I am English and Irish.

Then I said to her: "Thank you very much and please re-consider the ‘me' offer." She smiled and laughed. I thought to myself, she probably said to herself, "What a handsome devil Charlie is, tall, dark, and handsome." Right. In my dreams.

A moment later, after I watched Gigi walk away and ... while we were talking, Luca got an urgent cell phone call from one of his internal security staff members (Enrico) located in the bank's central cash vault where the "counterfeit" money was located.

He told Luca that an employee, named "Celio Virabilli" had just committed suicide by hanging himself in his office in the central cash department. It was located four stories below the bank.

LUCA, HOWARD AND I went down the elevator to investigate this event. When we entered the office, we found him still hanging from the ceiling fan with his own belt.

On his desk was a computer written note saying that he was involved in the exchanging of the ‘counterfeit' bills for the good ones that were now missing.

We notified the local *Carabinieri* (police) who came and re-moved the body. Of course, we did not divulge the confidential information about the counterfeit bills nor the bank fraud investigation to the local police.

Mr. Luca Perugino told the homicide/police detectives that "Celio" had been depressed lately because his beautiful wife (and ex-model) had run off with an executive at the Lamborghini automobile factory in Milan.

After the "carabinieri" left, the three of us returned to the President's office on the top floor of the bank building. As we entered and passed the desk of Gigi, I accidently tripped over an exquisite Persian rug, while I was starring at her legs.

Charlie, I told myself, not out loud, "you have to get a grip", "she is just a beautiful Italian woman and there are lots of them around." Yeah, right.

Anyway, we sat back down at our little corner table. Mr. Bouchilli, Manny, Chealy, Luigi, Giovani, and Carlo had all left and we were now all alone with the exception of the still present scent of Gigi's *Channel No. 5 perfume*.

That made it a little bit hard for me to concentrate on the business at hand. It is just perfume I told myself, and I was finally able to think clearly again, well almost anyway.

Luca was friends with most of the Bank executives, and many employees, and did not feel any of them would be involved in anything as bad as the fraud and embezzlement.

He did admit that some 'padded' their expense accounts, used the *banks fleet* of airplanes, helicopters and yachts for 'personal' use, had girlfriends (mistresses) who worked at the bank (a BIG no-no), and/or gave loans to friends/relatives at reduced interest rates. These

actions Luca pointed out were very common in most banking institutions around the world and not just in his bank or other Italian banks.

Upon further questioning he finally did 'fess' up his suspicion of one individual, Mr. Vittorio Capitolini, the Bank President and CEO .

Luca confided in us and then swore us to top secrecy that Vittorio (President and CEO) had three mistresses. One was a top Italian model, another was a famous Italian clothing designer, and the third a senior Vice President at the bank.

Yes, he added all three looked like Roman goddesses. Of course they do, I said to myself, silently. Also, he owned an exclusive home here in Rome, an estate in the fabulous wine country in *Tuscany*, as well as an ancient mansion on famous *Lake Como* in Northern Italy.

George Clooney, Sylvester Stalone, and many famous actors, actresses, and many famous and wealthy people have vacation homes located there.

I took a scenic boat cruise on Lake Como in 1996 while on vacation in Italy. It is just an absolutely magnificent locale, but very, very cold and foggy.

I was also in beautiful Tuscany, where the delicious Italian wine comes from. It is miles and miles of vineyards with rolling hills, coble stone walls and streets, and wonderful people, many farmers and growers.

In addition, Vittorio owned a stable of automobiles (as well as a stable of race horses). He owned two Ferraris, two Maseratis, a Rolls Royce, a Bentley, a Maybach, a Lotus, an Alpha Romeo sports car, and a ‘fleet' of Fiats for his kids and family.

He was also a close personal friend of the *Prime Minister* of Italy. They went on double dates together with their mistresses and sometimes with their wives. Hope they kept them straight — could be very embarrassing if they got them mixed up.

Luca, being an ex-carabinieri and detective, felt that Vittorio's life style could very well have gotten him involved in the bank fraud as a way out of his terrible financial mess.

He makes a *million dollars* (USD) a year, big money in Italy — however, his expenditures were in the one and a half million per year. His expenses were fifty per cent higher than his income. Technically, you see, he was bankrupt.

And besides his large cash flow problems, his liabilities were larger than his assets. That, as you know is the definition of bankruptcy.

Howard said he would do a discreet check on Vittorio through the CIA in Langley, Virginia and also at Interpol in Lyon, France. Off the record, Luca told us that he did not like Nino Proietti, the top bank legal counsel, because, like me, he did not like, nor trust most lawyers either.

Then he added, while he disliked Nino, he did not feel that Nino had anything to do with the 'counterfeiting' case.

Now at last we had one good viable suspect, Mr. Vittorio Capitolini, the bank President and CEO. In some of my prior-early-research, it appeared that due to the size and enormous scope of the fraud, there had to be several bank employees involved as well some very big hitters (criminals) outside of the bank to make and pass the counterfeit $100.00 bills. Possibly, very possibly, some facet of the Italian Mafia.

You cannot date suspects, or even their company employees, when you are working on a case. You should not even contemplate doing such a thing. Therefore, I said to myself (to myself this time and not out loud):

"Charlie, what in the heck are you thinking about? Asking out Novana Mona Bella (the banks senior Vice President who was in charge of the press releases, promotions, transfers, acquisition notices, TV interviews and, all of the most important public relations for "the Bank of Italy, LLC", as well as (and equally important) the public activities of all of the bank's senior management team.

From the Chairman of the Board down to the other two Senior Vice Presidents, plus a few other important power players/brokers that worked at the banks headquarters.

Anyway, as I was saying, Novana, who went by her middle name, Mona (kind of like "Mona Lisa"), whose last name was Bella, not Bello (which in Italian translates to 'beautiful').

However, her last name should have been Bello and her whole name should be "Ms. Mona Lisa Bello". For she truly was just like her name sake, the beautiful and never aging, "Mona Lisa" shown in Leonardo da Vinci's exquisite, famous and priceless painting (pittura). I saw this magnificent art work in person at the famous Louvre Museum in Paris, France in 1991.

I then said: "Ella vespa giusto bello in verita!" Meaning: She (Mona) was just beautiful (and breathtaking) indeed! And added: "Ella veramente qualcoso ad vedere." Meaning: she is really something to see. And she really, truly was.

I said to myself once again: "I don't care if she is the real "Mona Lisa", the most beautiful woman in the world, you still can't date her, Charlie, period, end of report."

But, then I responded to myself, I am sure that any woman that exquisite just could not be involved in anything remotely dishonest. Oh, yeah, how about Cleopatra, Matta Hari, Marie Antoinette (Queen of France), and my ex-wife."

Here is a question for you Charlie. Now my unconscious mind was even getting into the conversation between me, myself, and I. "Perche fare signori sempre caduta tutto sopra loro stessa per uno bello donna?" Which roughly translates: Why do grown men always fall all over themselves for a beautiful woman?

And, the answer is, I have NO idea. After all, they are just blood, flesh and bone, just like the rest of us — yeah right. To be completely candid with you folks, I think that it is the 'flesh' that does us in. I for one, do not like blood (especially my own), and do not like skinny or bony women.

So you can easily see my dilemma, right? I should not ask "Mona" out on a date because she works for the bank (banco) I am working for (and getting paid by), and she herself is a suspect in my investigation.

As a matter-of-fact; *everyone* (ognuno) who works for the bank (banca) is a suspect as well as everyone (ognuno) who does not work for the bank. In plain English (inglese) that means that everybody except Howard, his CIA team, and myself (Charlie) are suspects (sospetto) at least in theory anyway!

I will have to ponder this question (domanda) some more. I may never, ever meet another Roman goddess like 'Mona' again.

Another question, Charlie: "Keh ferita avere il palla ad tirare speso uno cuocere compito questo grande?" A lass, my Dio: "Who would have the balls (guts) to pull off a criminal job this big?"

Answer: 1. Someone who was desperate for cash, that worked at the bank, and also had access to cash money and had a lot of power, 2. Someone inside the Italian Government at the highest level, 3. A high level employee at the Italian FDIC, and/or 4. A big time criminal organization (i.e. the Italian Mafia).

# CHAPTER NINE

SINCE I WAS GOING to be spending most of my time on the "*Bank of Italy, LLC*" investigation, in Rome (i.e.: Roma), I decided that I should do some in detail examinations of its history, the Roman Empire, government, and its territories.

After all, and since, I had already researched and studied in depth the country of Italy as a whole, now I wanted to look at the key component: the capital city, Rome, Italy.

Rome (Roma) is the capital of Italy and the country's largest and most populated municipality (central area), with over 2.7 million residents in 496.3 square miles.

While the population of the urban area was estimated by *Eurostat* to have been 3.46 million in 2004, the metropolitan area of Rome was estimated by OECD to have had a population of 3.7 million no later than 2006.

The city of Rome is located in the central-western portion of the Italian Peninsula, on the Tiber River within the Lazio region of Italy. Rome's history spans over *two and a half thousand* years.

It was the capital city of the Roman Kingdom, the Roman Republic and the Roman Empire, which was a major political and cultural influence in the lands bordering the Mediterranean Sea for over seven hundred years from the $1^{st}$ Century BC until the $7^{th}$ Century AD.

Since the $2^{nd}$ Century AD Rome has been the seat of the Papacy and after the end of Byzantine domination, in the 8th Century it became the capital of the Papal States, which lasted until 1870. In 1871

Rome became the capital of the Kingdom of Italy, and in 1946 that of the Italian Republic. Since 1929 it is also the site of the Vatican City, an independent city-state presided over by the Pope.

After the Middle -Ages, Rome was ruled by popes such as Alexander VI and Leo X, who transformed the city into one to the major centers of the Italian Renaissance, along with Florence. The current-day version of St. Peter's Basilica was built and the Sistine Chapel was painted by Michelangelo.

Famous artists and architects, such as Bramante, Bernini and Raphael resided for some time in Rome, contributing to its Renaissance and Baroque architecture.

The city hosted the 1960 Olympic Games, and is also an official candidate for the 2020 edition of this event. In 2007 Rome was the $11^{th}$-most-visited city in the world, $3^{rd}$ most visited in the EU, and the most popular tourist attraction in Italy.

The city is one of Europe's and the world's most successful city brands, both in terms of reputation and assets. Its historic center is listed by UNESCO as a World Heritage Site.

Monuments and museums such as the Vatican Museums and the Coliseum are amongst the world's 50 most visited tourist destinations (the Vatican Museums receiving 4.2 million tourists and the *Coliseum* receiving 4 million tourists every year).

There is archaeological evidence of human occupation of the Rome area from at least 14,000 years, but the dense layer of much younger debris obscures Paleolithic and Neolithic sites.

Evidence of stone tools, pottery and stone weapons attest to at least 10,000 years of *human presence*. The power of the well known tale of Rome's legendary foundation tends also to deflect attention from its actual, and much more ancient, origins.

Rome's early history is shrouded in legend. According to Roman tradition, the city was founded by Romulus on April 21, 753 BC. The legendary origin of the city's name is the traditional founder and first ruler. It is said that *Romulus* and *Remus* decided to build a city.

After an argument, Romulus killed his brother Remus. Then he named it after himself, Rome. More recently, attempts have been made to find a linguistic root for the name Rome. Possibilities include derivation from Greek language meaning bravery, courage, possibly the connection is with a root *rum-, "teat", with possible reference to the totem wolf that adopted and suckled the cognately named twins Romulus and Remus.

Etruscan give us the word Rumach, "from Rome", from which Ruma can be extracted. Its further etymology, as with that of most Etruscan words, remains unknown.

The Basque scholar Manuel de Larramendi though that the origin could be related to the Basque language word Roma (modern Basque kirreal), "wall".

Archaeological evidence supports the view that Rome grew form pastoral settlements on the Palatine Hill built in the area of the future Roman Forum. While some archaeologists argue the Rome was indeed founded in the middle of the 8th Century BC, the date is subject to controversy.

The original settlement developed into the capital of the roman Kingdom (ruled by a succession of seven kings, according to tradition), and then the Roman Republic (from 510 BC, governed by the Senate), and finally the *Roman Empire* (from 27 BC, ruled by an Emperor).

This success depended on military conquest, commercial predominance, as well as selective assimilation of neighboring civilizations, most notably the Etruscans and Greeks. From its foundation Rome, although losing occasional battles, had been undefeated in war until 386 BC, when it was briefly occupied by the Gauls.

According to the legend, the Gauls offered to give Rome back to its people for a thousand pounds of gold, but the Romans refused, preferring to take back their city by force of arms rather than ever admitting defeat, after which the Romans recovered the city in the same year.

The Roman Empire had begun in a more formalized way when Emperor Augustus (63 BC - AD 14; also known as *Octavian*) founded the participate in 27 BC, which was a monarchy system which was headed by an emperor holding power for life, rather than making himself dictator like *Julius Caesar* had done, which had resulted in his assassination on March 15, 44BC.

At home, Emperor Augustus started off a great program of social, political and economic reform and grand-scale reconstruction of the city of Rome. The city became dotted with impressive and magnificent new buildings, palaces, and basilica. He became a great and enlightened patron of the arts, and his court was surrounded by Virgil, Horace and Propertius.

His rule also established the Pax Romana, a long period of relative peace which lasted approximately 200 years. Following his rule were emperors such as Caligula, Nero, Trajan, and Hadrain, to name just a few.

Roman emperor Nero was well-known for his extravagance, cruelty, tyranny, and the myth that he was the emperor who "fiddled while Rome burned" during the night July 18 to 19, 64 AD.

With the reign of Constantine I, the 'Bishop of Rome' gained political as well as religious importance, eventually becoming known as the Pope and establishing Rome as the center of the Catholic Church.

After the Sack of Rome in 410 AD by Alaric I and the fall of the Western Roman Empire in 476 AD, Rome alternated between *Byzantine and Germanic* control. Its population declined to a mere 20,000 during the Early Middle Ages, reducing the sprawling city to groups of inhabited buildings interspersed among large areas of ruins and vegetation.

Rome remained nominally part of the Byzantine Empire until 751 AD, when the Lombard's finally abolished the Exarchate of Ravenna. In 756, Pepin the Short gave the pope temporal jurisdiction over Rome and surrounding areas, thus creating the Papal States. In 846, Muslim Arabs invaded Rome and looted St. Peter's Basilica.

Rome remained the capital of the Papal States until its annexation by the Kingdom of Italy in 1870; the city became a major pilgrimage site during the Middle Ages and the focus of struggles between the Papacy and the Holy Roman Empire starting with *Charlemagne*, who was crowned its first emperor in Rome in 800 by Pope Leo III.

Apart from brief periods as an independent city during the Middle Ages, Rome kept its status as Papal capital and "holy city" for centuries, even when the Papacy briefly relocated to Avignon (1309 - 1377).

The latter half of the $15^{th}$ Century saw the seat of the Italian Renaissance move to Rome from Florence. The Papacy wanted to equal and surpass the grandeur of other Italian cities and to this end created ever more extravagant churches, bridges, squares and public spaces, including a new *Saint Peter's Basilica*, the Sistine Chapel, Ponte Sisto (the first bridge to be built across the Tiber since antiquity), and Piazza Navona.

The Popes were also patrons of the arts engaging such artists as Michelangelo, Perugino, Raphael, Ghirlandaio, Luca Signorelli, Botticelli, and Cosimo Rossselli.

The Italian Renaissance in Rome more or less began when the end of the French captivity came in 1377, and the return of the papacy to Rome. Pope Martin V (1417 - 1431), planned to renew the Roman Catholic Church, and pursue new spiritual and political reforms. Martin V and his successors began to follow these new instructions, and Pope Nicholas V (1447 - 1455) really began to plan out much of the Renaissance-style urban re-development of the city.

IN THE BEGINNING of the sixteenth Century the Church began also a secular struggle against the Reformation, which subtracted a great part of Christendom to the papal authority.

The revenge of the church started with the Council of Trent, and with the great Popes of the counter-Reformation (from Pius IV to Sixtus V). Under them Rome became the center of the reformed Catholicism, and thanks to them the City was adorned with monuments which celebrated the restored greatness of the Papacy.

During the seventeenth and the beginning of the eighteenth centuries the Popes continued the tradition of Counter-reformation, enriching the city's landscape with Baroque buildings, erected by the Popes themselves or by their Cardinal-nephews.

During the *Age of Enlightenment* the new ideas reached also the Eternal City, where the Papacy supported Archeological Studies and improved the people's welfare. However, at the same time the Popes had to fight against the anti-church policy of the great European powers which, among others, forced them to suppress the Jesuits.

The rule of the Popes was interrupted by the short-lived Roman Republic (1798), which was built under the influence of the French Revolution.

During *Napoleon's reign*, Rome was annexed into his empire and was technically part of France. After the fall of Napoleon's Empire, new states were created in Italy through the Congress of Vienna of 1814.

The Kingdom of the Two Sicily's (Naples and Sicily) under Bourbon Ferdinand IV, the restored Papal States, and the Kingdom of Piedmont-Sardinia under King Charles-Albert. The two regions of Venetia and Lombardy were given to the Austrians under their direct control for some time.

Rome became caught up in the nationalistic turmoil of the 19th Century and twice gained and lost a short-lived independence. Rome became the focus of hopes of Italian reunification when the rest of Italy was reunited under the *Kingdom of Italy* with a temporary capital at Florence.

In 1861, Rome was declared the capital of Italy even though it was still under the control of the Pope. During the 1860s, the last vestiges of the Papal State were under the French protection napoleon III.

And it was only when this was lifted in 1870, owing to the outbreak of the Franco-Prussian War, the Italian troops were able to capture Rome through Porta Pia. Afterwards, Pope Pius IX declared himself as prisoner in the Vatican, and in 1871, the capital of Italy was moved from Florence, to Rome.

Soon after World War I, Rome witnessed the rise to power of Italian Fascism guided by *Benito Mussolini,* who marched on the city in 1922, eventually declaring a new Empire and allying Italy with Nazi Germany.

The interwar period saw a rapid growth in the city's population, that surpassed 1,000,000 inhabitants, but this trend was abruptly halted by World War II, during which Rome was damaged by both Allied forces bombing and Nazi occupation.

After the execution of Mussolini and the end of the war, a 1946 referendum abolished the monarchy in favor of the Italian Republic.

Rome grew momentously after the war, as one of the driving forces behind the "Italian economic miracle" of post-war reconstruction and modernization.

It became a fashionable city in the 1950s and early 1960s, the years of la dolce Vida, ("the sweet life"), with popular classic films such as Ben Hur, Quo Vadis, Roman Holiday and La Dolce Vita, being filmed in the city's iconic *Cinecitta Studios.*

A new rising trend in population continued until the mid-1980s, when the commune had more than 2,800,000 residents; after that, population started to slowly decline as more residents moved to nearby suburbs.

Being the capital city of Italy, Rome hosts all the principal institutions of the nation, like the Presidency of the Republic, the government (and its single Ministry), the Parliament, the main Judicial Courts, and the diplomatic representatives of all the countries for the states of Italy and the Vatican City (curiously, Rome also hosts, in the Italian part of it territory, the Embassy of Italy for the *Vatican City*, a unique case of an Embassy within the boundaries of its own country).

Many international institutions are located in Rome, notably cultural and scientific ones — such as the American Institute, the British School, the French Academy, the Scandinavian Institutes, the German Archaeological Institute — for the honor of scholarship in the Eternal City, and humanitarian ones.

Rome, also hosts major international and worldwide political and cultural organizations, such as the International Fund for Agricultural Development (IFAD), World Food Program (WFT), the NATO Defense College and ICCROM, the International Center for the Study of the Preservation and Restoration of Cultural Property.

Rome has a growing stock of contemporary and modern art and architecture, The national Gallery of Modern Art has works by Ballad, Miranda, Pirandello, De Chirico, De Isis, Guttuso, Fontana, Burris, Mastroianni, Turcato, Kandisky, and Cezanne on permanent exhibition.

2010 sees the opening of Rome's newest arts foundation, a contemporary art and architecture gallery designed by acclaimed Iraqi architect Zaha Hadid. Known as Maxxi National Museum of Rome.

Twenty-first Century Art and Architecture it restores a dilapidated area with striking modern architecture. Maxxi features a campus dedicated to culture, experimental research laboratories, international, exchange and study and research.

It is one of Rome's most ambitious modern architecture projects alongside Renzo Piano's Auditorium Parco della Musica and Massimiliano Fuksas' Rome Convention Center, Centro Congressi Italia EUR, in the EUR district, due to open in 2011.

The Convention Center features a huge translucent container inside which is suspended a steel and Teflon structure resembling a cloud and which contains meeting rooms and an auditorium with two piazzas open to the neighborhood on either side.

Rome is the national capital of Italy and is the seat of the Italian Government. The official residences of the President of the Italian Republic and the Italian prime Minister, the seats of both houses of the Italian Parliament *and* that of the Italian Constitutional Court are located in the historic center.

The state ministries are spread out around the city; these include the Ministry of Foreign Affairs, which is located in Palazzo della Farnisina near to Olympic stadium.

Rome constitutes one of Italy's 8,101 communes, and is the largest both in terms of land area and population. It is governed by a mayor and a city council.

The seat of the commune is in on the *Capitaoline Hill* the historic seat of government in Rome. The local administration in Rome is commonly referred to as "Campidoglio", the name of the hill in Italian.

Rome is divided into 20 administrative areas, called municipal or municipalities. They were created in 1972 for administrative reasons to increase decentralization in the city.

Each municipality is governed by a president and a council of four members who are elected by the residents of the municipality every five years. Them municipalities frequently cross the boundaries of the traditional non-administrative divisions of the city.

Rome is located in the Lazio region of central Italy on the Tiber river (Italian: Tevere). The original settlement developed on hills that faced onto a ford beside the Tiber Island, the only natural ford of the river.

*The Rome of the Kings* was built on seven hills: the Aventine Hill, the Caelian Hill, the Capitoline Hill, the Esquiline Hill, the Palatine Hill, the Quirinal Hill, and the Viminal Hill. The city is also crossed by another river the Aniene which joins the Tiber north of the historic center.

Although the city center is about 15 miles inland from the Tyrrhenian Sea, the city territory extends to the shore where the south-western district of Ostia is located.

The altitude of the central part of Rome ranges from 43 feet above sea level to 456 feet. The Commune of Rome covers an overall area of about 496 square miles, including many green areas.

Throughout the history of Rome, the urban limits of the city were considered to be the area within the city walls. Originally, these consisted of the Servain Wall, which was built twelve years after the Gaulish sack of the city in 390 BC.

This contained most of the Esquiline and Caelian hills, as well as the whole of the other five. Rome outgrew the Servian Wall, but no more walls were constructed until almost 700 years later, when, in 270 AD, Emperor Aurelian began building the Aurelian Walls.

These were almost 12 miles long, and were still the walls the troops of the Kingdom of Italy had to breach to enter the city in 1870. Modern Romans frequently consider the city's urban area to be delimited by its ring-road, the Grande Raccordo Anulare, which circles the city center at a distance of about 6 miles.

The Commune of Rome, however, covers considerably more territory and extends to the sea at Ostia, the largest town in Italy that is not a commune in its own right. The commune covers an area roughly three times the total area with the Raccordo and is comparable in area to the entire provinces of *Milan and Naples*, and to an area six times the size of the territory of these cities.

It also includes considerable areas of abandoned marsh land which is suitable neither for agriculture nor for urban development. As a consequence, the density of the Commune is not that high, the communal territory being divided between highly urbanized areas and areas designated as parks, nature reserves, and for agricultural use. The Province of Rome is the largest by area in Italy. At 2.066 square miles, its dimensions are comparable to the region of Liguria.

More very informative research information. Especially the early "Roman Empire", the recently discovered archaeological evidence, and, "Julius Cesar". Also, Virgil, Horace, and Propertius. As well as Emperors such as Caligula, Tyrannical Nero, and Trajan.

# CHAPTER TEN

I DID SOME DETAILED RESEARCH at the Library of Congress (in Washington DC) via the internet and discovered some absolutely fascinating details which I want to share with you.

Counterfeit money is currency that is produced without the legal sanction of the state or government to resemble some official form of currency closely enough that it may be confused for genuine currency. Producing or using counterfeit money is a form of fraud.

Counterfeiting is probably as old as *money* itself. Before the introduction of paper money, the most prevalent method of counterfeiting involved mixing base metals with pure gold or silver.

A form of counterfeiting is the production of documents by legitimate printers in response to fraudulent instructions. During World War II, the Nazis forged British pounds and American dollars.

Today some of the finest counterfeit banknotes are called *Super dollars* because of their high quality, and likeness to the real US dollar.

There has been a considerable amount of counterfeiting of Euro banknotes and coins since the launch of the currency in 2002.

Some of the ill-effects that counterfeit money has on society are: a reduction in the value of real money, increase in prices (inflation) due to more money getting circulated in the economy — an unauthorized artificial increase in the money supply, a decrease in the acceptability of paper money, and losses, because companies are not reimbursed for counterfeit money which is detected and confiscated by banks and credit unions.

Traditionally, anti-counterfeiting measures involved including fine detail with raised intaglio printing on bills which allows non-experts to easily spot forgeries. On coins, *milled* or *reeded* (marked with parallel grooves) edges are used to show that none of the valuable metal has been scraped off.

The history of counterfeiting is as old as money itself. Coinage of money began in the *Greek city of Lydia* around 600 BC.

A common practice was to "shave" the edges of a coin. This was known as "clipping". While not itself counterfeiting, the exponents were able to use these precious metal shaving to create counterfeits.

A *fourree* is an ancient type of counterfeit coin, in which a base metal core has been plated with a precious metal to resemble its solid metal counterpart.

Rulers often dealt very harshly with the *perpetrators* of such deeds. In 1162, Emperor Gaozong of Song had promulgated a decree to punish the counterfeiter of Huizi to death and to reward the informant.

The English couple Thomas and Anne Rogers were convicted on October 15, 1690 for "Clipping 40 pieces of Silver." Thomas Rogers was hanged, drawn and quartered while Anne Rogers was burnt alive.

Evidence supplied by an informant led to the arrest of the last of the English Coiners "King" David Hartly, who was executed by hanging in 1770.

The extreme forms of punishment were meted out for acts of treason against state or Crown, rather than simple crime.

Both in the United States, and England, counterfeiting was once punishable by death.

Paper currency printed by *Benjamin Franklin* often bore the phrase "to counterfeit is death." The theory behind such harsh punishments was that one who had the skills to counterfeit currency was considered a threat to the safety of the State, and had to be eliminated.

Another explanation is the fact that issuing money that people could trust was both an economic imperative, as well as a (where applicable) Royal prerogative — therefore counterfeiting was a crime against the state or ruler itself, rather than against the person who received the fake money.

Far more fortunate was an earlier practitioner of the same art, active in the time of the Emperor Justinian. Rather than being executed, when Alexander the Barber was apprehended, the Emperor chose to employ his talents in the government's own service.

Modern counterfeiting begins with paper money. Nations have used counterfeiting as a means of warfare. The idea is to overflow the enemy's economy with fake bank notes, so that the real value of the money plummets.

Great Britain did this during the *Revolutionary War* to reduce the value of the Continental Dollar. Although this tactic was also employed by the United States during the American Civil War, the fake Confederate currency it produced was of superior quality to the real thing.

A form of counterfeiting is the production of documents by legitimate printers in response to fraudulent instructions.

An example of this is the Portuguese Bank Note Crisis of 1925, when the British banknote printers Waterlow and Sons produced *Banco de Portugal* notes equivalent in value to 0.88% of the Portuguese nominal Gross Domestic Product, with identical serial numbers to existing banknotes, in response to a fraud perpetrated by Alves dos Reis.

Similarly, in 1929 the issue of postage stamps celebrating the Millennium of Iceland's parliament, the Althing, was compromised by the insertion of "1" on the print order, before the authorized value of stamps to be produced.

In 1926 a high-profile counterfeit scandal came to light in Hungary, when several people were arrested in the *Netherlands* while attempting to procure 10 million francs worth of fake French 1000-franc bills which had been produced in Hungary; after 3 years, the state-sponsored industrial scale counterfeit operation had finally collapsed.

The League of Nations' investigation found Hungary's motives were to profit from the counterfeiting business to boost a militarist, border-revisionist ideology. *Germany and Austria* had an active role in the conspiracy, which required special machinery. The quality of fake bills was still substandard however, owing to France's use of exotic raw paper material imported from its colonies.

During World War II, the Nazis attempted to implement a similar plan (Operation Bernhard) against the Allies. The Nazis took Jewish artists in the Sachsenhausen concentration camp and forced them to forge *British pounds and American dollars*.

The quality of the counterfeiting was very good, and it was almost impossible to distinguish between the real and fake bills. The Germans could not put their plan into action, and were forced to dump the counterfeit bills into a lake. Most of the bills were not recovered until the 1950s.

The source of the "*Super notes*" is disputed, with North Korea being vocally accused by US authorities. Recently, on May 23, 2007, the Swiss government has raised some doubt as to the ability of North Korea to produce the "Superdollers".

*Bulgaria and Colombia* are also significant sources of counterfeit currency. The amount of counterfeit United States currency is estimated to be less than $3 per $10,000, with less than $3 per $100.00 difficult to detect.

There has been a rapid growth in the counterfeiting of Euro banknotes and coins since the launch of the currency in 2002. In 2003, 551,287 fake euro notes and 26,191 bogus euro coins were removed from EU circulation. In 2004, French police seized fake 10 euro and 20 euro notes worth a total of around €1.8 million from two laboratories and estimated that 145,000 notes had already entered circulation. In the early years of the 21st Century, the United States Secret Service has noted a substantial reduction in the quantity of forged US currency, as counterfeiters turn their attention towards the Euro.

At the same time, in countries where paper money is a small fraction of the total money in circulation, the macroeconomic effects of counterfeiting of currency may not be significant. The microeconomic effects, such as confidence in currency, however, may be large.

Traditionally, anti-counterfeiting measures involved including fine detail with raised intaglio printing on bills which would allow non-experts to easily spot forgeries.

On coins, milled or reeded edges are used to show that none of the valuable metal has been scraped off. This detects the shaving or clipping of the rim of the coin.

However, it does not detect sweating, or shaking coins in a bag and collecting the resulting dust. Since this technique removes a smaller amount, it is primarily used on the most valuable coins, such as gold.

In early paper money in Colonial North America, one creative means of deterring counterfeiters was to print the impression of a leaf in the bill. Since the patterns found in a leaf were unique and complex, they were nearly impossible to reproduce.

In the late twentieth Century advances in computer and photocopy *technology* made it possible for people without sophisticated training to copy currency easily.

In response, national engraving bureaus began to include new more sophisticated anti-counterfeiting systems such as holograms, multi-colored bills, embedded devices such as strips, micro-printing and inks whose colors changed depending on the angle of the light, and the use of design features such as the "EURion constellation" which disables modern photocopiers.

Software programs such as Adobe Photoshop have been modified by their manufacturers to obstruct manipulation of scanned images of banknotes. There also exist patches to counteract these measures.

For US currency, anti-counterfeiting milestones are as follows:

1996 $100 bill gets a new design with larger portrait

1997 $50 bill gets a new design with larger portrait

1998 $20 bill gets a new design with larger portrait

2000 $10 bill and $5 bill get a new design with larger portraits

2003 $20 bill gets a new design with no oval around Andrew Jackson's portrait and more colors

2004 $50 bill gets new design with no oval around Ulysses S. Grant's portrait and more colors

2006 $10 bill gets a new design with no oval around Alexander Hamilton's portrait and more colors

2008 $5 bill gets a new design with no oval around Abraham Lincoln's portrait and more colors

2010 $100 bill gets new design with no oval around Benjamin Franklin's portrait and more colors

The redesigned $100 bill was unveiled on April 21, 2010, and the Federal Reserve Board began issuing the new bill on February 10, 2011. The Treasury had made no plans to redesign the $5 bill using colors, but recently reversed its decision, after learning some counterfeiters were bleaching the ink off the bills and printing them as $100 bills.

The new $10 bill entered circulation on March 2, 2006. The $1 bill and $2 bill are seen by most counterfeiters as having too low of value to counterfeit, and so they have not been redesigned as frequently as higher denominations.

In the 1980s counterfeiting in the Republic of Ireland twice resulted in sudden changes in official documents: in November 1984 the £1 postage stamp, also used on savings cards for paying television licenses and telephone bills, was invalidated and replaced by another design at a few days' notice, because of widespread counterfeiting.

Later, the £20 Central Bank of Ireland Series B banknote was rapidly replaced because of what the Finance Minister described as "the involuntary privatization of banknote printing".

In the 1990s, the portrait of Chairman Mao Zedong was placed on the banknotes of the People's Republic of China to combat counterfeiting, as he was recognized better than the generic designs on the renminbi notes.

In 1988 The Reserve Bank of Australia, released the world's first long lasting and counterfeit resistant polymer (plastic) banknotes with a special Bicentennial $10 note issue, the problems discovered were addressed and in 1992 a problem free $5 not was issued.

In 1996 Australia became the first country to have a full series of circulating polymer banknotes.

On May 3, 1999 the New Zealand Reserve Bank started circulating polymer banknotes printed by Note Printing Australia Limited. The technology developed is now used in 26 countries.

Note Printing Australia is currently printing polymer notes for 18 countries. The Swiss National bank has a reserve series of notes for the Swiss Franc bill, in case widespread counterfeiting were to take place.

Some well-known counterfeiters are:

*Eric "Klippling" V* — The King of Demark (1259 - 1286). The king's nickname refers to "clipping" of the coin.

*King Philip the Fair* of France (1268 - 1314) caused riots and was known as "the counterfeiting king" for emitting coinage that was debased compared to the standards that had been prevalent during the half Century previous to his reign.

*Anatasios Arnaouti* — A British counterfeiter of more than £2.5 million in fake money, sentenced in 2005.

*Abel Buell* — American colonialist who went from altering five-pound note engraving plates to publishing the first map of the new United States created by an American.

*Mary Butterworth* — a counterfeiter in colonial America

*William Chaloner* — A British counterfeiter convicted by Sir Isaac Newton and hanged on March 16, 1699.

*Alves dos Reis* — by the end of 1925, Reis had managed to introduce escudo banknotes worth £1,007,963 at 1925 exchange rates into the Portuguese economy, which was equivalent to 0.88% of the Portugal's nominal GDP at the time.

*Stephen Jory* — Great Britain's most renowned counterfeiter started his career by selling cheap perfume in designer bottles. He later established his own illegal printing operation to produce and distribute an estimated five billion pounds in counterfeit currency throughout the United Kingdom.

*"King" David Hartley* — was the leader of the Cragg Vale Coiners of rural 18th Century England. Producing fake gold coins, he was eventually captured and hanged at Tyburn near York on April 28, 1770 and buried in the village of Heptonstall, W Yorks. His brother, Isaac, escaped the authorities and lived until 1815.

*Catherin Murphy* was convicted of coining in 1789 and was the last woman to suffer execution by burning in England.

*Samuel C. Upham* — The first known counterfeiter of Confederate money during the American Civil War. His activities began or became known in early July 1862.

*Edward Mueller* — Documented in Mister 880, he was possibly the longest uncaught counterfeiter in history. For ten or more years he eluded government authorities while he printed and spent fake $1 bills in his New York neighborhood.

*Wesley Weber* — Was sent to prison for counterfeiting the Canadian hundred-dollar bill.

*Albert Talton* — Was sent to prison for counterfeiting the one hundred US dollar bill and the twenty US dollar bill. Produced over 7 million dollars in counterfeit US currency using standard inkjet printer. Convicted and sent to prison in May 2009.

Arthur Williams — was sent to prison for counterfeiting the one hundred US dollar bill.

Mike DeBardeleben — was sent to prison for counterfeiting the twenty US dollar bill.

AFTER ALL OF that information, I wanted to learn just a *few* more items about Roma prior to my arrival. Something about its parks and geography, airports (for fast escapes if necessary), as well as the bus and train network.

And, last but certainly not least, I wanted to read up again about the famous and intriguing catacombs. I was there in 1996, however, with my 'gray' memory, I do not recall much, except that it was a little bit claustrophobic for me.

Public parks and nature reserves cover a large area in Rome, and the city has one of the largest areas of green space among European Capitals. The most notable part of this green space is represented by the large number of villas and landscaped gardens created by the Italian aristocracy.

While many villas were destroyed during the building boom of the late 19th Century, a great many remain. The most notable of these are Villa Borghese, Villa Ada, and Villa Doria Pamphili. Villa Doria pamphili is west of the Gianicolo hill comprising some 1.2 square miles. Also on the Gianicolo hill there is Villa Sciarra, with playgrounds of children and shaded walking areas.

In the nearby area of Trastevere the Orto Botanico (Botanical Garden) is a cool and shady green space. The old Roman hippodrome (*Circus Maximus*) is another large green space but the main attraction is the ancient site of Chariot racing and it has few trees.

Nearby is the lush Villa Celimontana, close to the gardens surrounding the Baths and Rose Garden ('roseto comunale'). The Villa Borghese garden is the best known large green space in Rome, with famous art galleries among its shaded walks.

It is close to the Spanish Steps and Piazza del Popolo. Rome also has a number of regional parks of much more recent origin including the Pineto Regional Park and the *Appian Way* Regional Park. There are also nature reserves at Marcigliana and at Tenuta di Castelporziano.

Rome is a city famous for its numerous fountains, built in all different styles, from Classical and Medieval, to Baroque and Neoclassical. The city has had fountains for more than two thousand years, and they have provided drinking water and decorated the piazzas of Rome.

During the Roman Empire, in 98 AD, according to Sextus Julius Frontinus, the Roman consul who was named curator aquarum or guardian of the water of the city, Rome had nine aqueducts which fed 39 monumental fountains and 591 public basins, the water supplied to the Imperial household, baths and owners of private villas. Each of the major fountains was connected to two different aqueducts, in case one was shut down for service.

During the $17^{th}$ and $18^{th}$ Century the Roman popes reconstructed other ruined Roman aqueducts and built new display fountains to mark their termini, launching the golden age of the Roman fountain.

The fountains of Rome, like the *paintings of Rubens* were expressions of the new style of Baroque art. They were crowded with allegorical figures, and filled with emotion and movement.

In these fountains, sculpture became the principal element, and the water was used simply to animate and decorate the sculptures. They, like baroque gardens, were "a visual representation of confidence and power."

Rome is well known for its statues but, in particular, the talking statues of Rome. These are usually ancient statues which have become popular soapboxes for political and social discussion, and places for people to (often satirically) voice their opinions. There are two main talking statues: the Pasquino and the Marforio, yet there are four other noted ones: il Babuino, Madame Lucrezia, il facchino and Abbot Luigi.

MOST OF THESE statues are ancient Roman or classical, and most of them also depict mythical gods, ancient people or legendary figures; il Pasquino represents Meneaus, Abbot Luigi is an *unknown* Roman magistrate, il Babuino is supposed to be Silenus, Marforio represents Oceanus, Madame Lucrezia is a bust of Isis, and il Facchino is the only non-Roman statue, created in 1580, and not representing anyone in particular.

They are often, due to their status, covered with placards or graffiti expressing political ideas and points of view. Other statues in the city, which are not related to the talking statues, include those of the Ponte Sant'Angelo, or several monuments scattered across the city, such as the two Giordano Bruno in the Campo de'Fiori.

The city contains eight ancient Egyptian and five ancient Roman obelisks, together with a number of more modern obelisks; there was also formerly (until 2005) an ancient Ethiopian obelisk in Rome.

The city contains some obelisks in piazzas, such as in Piazza Navona, St. Peter's Square, Piazza Montecitorio, and piazza del Popolo, and others in villas, thermae parks and gardens, such as in Villa Celimontana, the Baths of Diocletian, and the Pincian Hill. Moreover, the center of Rome, Trajan's and Antonine Column, two ancient Roman columns with spiral relief.

CATACOMBS: Rome has an extensive amount of ancient catacombs, or underground burial places, under or near the city, of which there are at least forty discovered only in recent decades.

Though most famous for Christian burials, they include pagan and Jewish burials, either in separate catacombs or mixed together. The first large-scale catacombs were excavated from the 2$^{nd}$ Century onwards. Originally they were carved through 'tuff', a soft volcanic rock, outside the boundaries of the city, because Roman law forbad burial places within city limits. Currently, maintenance of the

catacombs is in the hands of the Papacy, which has invested in the Salesians of Don Bosco, the supervision of the Catacombs of St. Callixtus on the outskirts of Rome.

I visited the ancient and fascinating catacombs in 1996. I was in the country for a 30 day vacation. I took a guided tour in a brand new Mercedes Benz diesel bus that went all around the old and beautiful country of Italy for a whole month.

Rome is at the center of the radial network of roads that roughly follow the lines of the ancient Roman roads that began at the Capitoline Hill and *connected Rome* with its empire. Today Rome is circled, at a distance of about 6 miles, by the ring-road (the Grande Raccordo Anulare).

Due to its location in the center of the Italian peninsula, Rome is a principal railway node for central Italy. Rome's main train station, Termini, is one of the biggest train stations in Europe and the most heavily used in Italy, with around 400 thousand travelers passing through every day. The second-largest station in the city, *Roma Tiburtina,* is currently being redeveloped as a high-speed rail terminal.

Rome is served by three airports. The intercontinental *Leonardo Da Vinci* International Airport is Italy's chief airport and is commonly known as "Fiumicino Airport", as it is located within the nearby Comune of Fiumicino, south-west of Rome.

The older Rome *Ciampino* Airport is a joint civilian and military airport. It is commonly referred to as "Ciampino Airport", as it is located beside Ciampino, southeast of Rome. A third airport, the *Roma-Urbe* Airport, is located about 4 miles north of the city center, which handles most helicopter and private flights.

Above-ground public transport in Rome is made up of a bus and tram network. This network is run by Trambus SpA under the auspices of ATAC SpA (which originally stood for the Bus and Tram Agency of the Commune, Azienda Tranvie ed Autobus del commune in Italian). The bus network has in excess of 350 bus lines and over 8 thousand bus stops, whereas the more-limited tram system has 25 miles of track and 192 stops. There is also one trolleybus line, opened in 2005, and additional trolleybus lines are planned.

Did not find much in this research section that was really obviously a benefit to my investigation like I said before, however, sometimes you never know what information will come in handy later on when 'out-in-the field'. It is always better to be 'prepared than deterred' I like to say!

# CHAPTER ELEVEN

ONE DAY I NOTICED THAT Howard had on a very nice dress wrist watch — one for the office at the CIA and functions in Langley and Washington DC. I decided that since he was a good friend and frequently assists me in my private investigation business adventures and cases, I should buy him a watch. One that he could really use on a mission and/or assignment here in Italy.

I found just the perfect watch for him. It was the official watch of the US Navy SEAL's. You could read the time on it 'even' in zero light-nighttime with no moon.

The very graphic illustrated brochure that I read, described the SEALs as "The World's Baddest Good Guys." Then it went on to say: "When the most elite fighting force in the United States military asks you to build a watch for them, you'd better get it right.

That's why when the Navy SEALs requested a special timepiece from our friends at Luminox, the watchmakers spared no expense. Since 1994, the original (and official) Navy SEALs Watch has been worn on the wrists of the nation's highest-skilled, combat soldiers and tested under the world's most extreme conditions.

The verdict? Mission accomplished.

When the stakes are literally *life and death*, timing is critical. Covert operations are synchronized to the second and every one of those seconds count when you're dealing with drop-offs and pick-ups behind enemy lines or the setting of explosives. And part of what makes the Luminox such an invaluable tool to the SEALs is the remarkable illumination system that keeps the hands and markers powered micro-gas lights that don't need to be "charged" by an external light source. Even after days in the field, the glowing face brightly displays the exact time.

The Navy SEAL Fast strap Watch features a rugged, PC carbon reinforced case with a bold white-on-black design. The luminescent night vision tubes and watch face are protected by hardened mineral glass.

The lightweight black nylon strap features a stylized Navy SEAL insignia and fastens with Velcro and brushed steel buckle. The Luminox is water-resistant up to 20 ATMs and ready for action whenever you are." Quote.

It set me back $3,000.00(US dollars), which was not bad for a buddy and someone who *risks his life* for his country (USA) everyday working for the CIA. Also it may, just possibly, save his or my own life some day.

It was now time to set up our operation center, or 'War Room' as Howard liked to call it, at the bank. *Luigi Guttuso*, will be in charge of the War Room. He is a surveillance, computer and internet expert and speaks Italian fluently.

Luigi took a corner of the war room for himself and immediately installed six HP (Hewlett-Packard) lap top computers. These were not your ordinary garden variety computers as they included the latest high tech spy software available anywhere in the world. He also installed a direct-encrypted satellite phone line to CIA headquarters in Langley, Virginia.

This way he could keep in touch with them at a moment's notice and vice versa. You do not want to wait around on hold or with an operator when you are investigating a case and an agent is in a 'life or death' situation.

Information is very necessary in a criminal investigation and instant resources are power, real-time power.

The war room was trying out a brand new, high tech, state-of-the-art surveillance robotic plane (i.e. drone). It is called the "Global Hawk" and it can hover more than eleven miles above Rome and snap images so crystal clear that our CIA TAC team can make out the cars and pickup trucks (parked nearby a residence and/or business of interest) and even their license plate numbers.

The 'Hawk' is made by "Raytheon International, Inc." located in El Segundo, close to Long Beach Harbor, California. The pilotless 'spy plane' is larger than a regular drone.

The sensors on the new plane, enable our CIA team to 'listen in' on cell phone conversations and also pinpoint the location of the caller on the ground in Rome.

It can also 'smell' the air and 'sniff' out chemical plumes emanating from a potential underground laboratory or printing factory. The plane will give us an 'unblinking' eye over all of Roma (Rome).

I read that the drone industry now generates three billion dollars in revenue each year, and that is expected to double to six billion dollars in the next eight years.

More than 7,000 drones ranging from the small, hand-launched Raven to the massive Global Hawk are currently deployed in Iraq and Afghanistan.

Though some have been outfitted with laser guided bombs or missiles — grabbing most of the new headlines — all are equipped with sensors for reconnaissance and surveillance work.

The most advanced cameras and sensors are on the Global Hawk, a long endurance, high-altitude drone that can fly for 30 hours at a time at more than 60,000 feet, out of range of most antiaircraft missiles and undetectable to the human eye.

The latest detectors not only can pick out a person from a crowd, but know when that person may have fired a rifle. Such sensors can detect the heat from the barrel of a gun and estimate when it was fired.

Many of the sensors have been developed by Raytheon engineers in El Segundo, where the company has had a long history of developing spy equipment, including those found on the famed *U-2 spy plane*.

Some of the more advanced cameras can cost more than $15 million and take 18 months to make. Raytheon develops the cameras in a humidity-controlled, dust free laboratory to ensure that they are free of blemishes. Each basketball-sized camera must be perfect, if it isn't it is putting lives at risk.

Raytheon has begun to face stiff competition as other aerospace contractors vie for its business. Sparks, Nevada based Sierra Nevada Corp., which is known for its work on developing parts for spy satellites, also developed a sensor system named the "Gorgon Stare that widens the area that drones can monitor from 1 mile to nearly 3 miles.

Named for the creature in *Greek Mythology* whose gaze turns victims to stone, the sensor system features twelve small cameras — instead of one large one. It is to be affixed to Reaper drones before the end of 2010.

With the multiple cameras the operator can follow numerous vehicles instead of just one, the US Air Force's director of intelligence, surveillance and reconnaissance. But, with an increase in the number of drone patrols and new sensor technology, the Air Force will be drowning in data. That means we're going to need a lot more people looking at computer screens, he added.

The Pentagon has said that drones last year took so much video footage that it would take someone 24 years to watch it all. By the end of 2011 the Air Force expects to have almost 5,000 people trawling through the images for intelligence information.

That's up from little more that 1,200 nine years ago. The reconnaissance work that is being done now takes seconds, where it used to take days before.

Inside the war room, and close to Luigi's corner office, *Angel Ortega Bermudez* was in charge of the one "Global Hawk" unmanned spy plane.

Also, she said that she may use some pilotless "Reaper" or "Rapture" US Air Force spy drones.

Howard had got a hold of a few from the Pentagon since he was the Assistant Director for the whole CIA. They were very expensive (ten $10 Million each) but if one were lucky, real lucky, we would be able to return all of them in one piece.

As long as the Mafia, the Italian Air Force, or someone else, does not shoot them down of course.

She had several state of the art - large desk top computers used to operate the "Hawk" and the drones. And to observe the planes cameras she had three wall screen monitors.

Sitting next to Angel was *Giovanni Colonna*, our resident Italian Mafia expert. He had only one lap top computer and five phones on his desk.

All five had different numbers and they were all satellite encrypted with a new CIA software protection program.

In the opposite corner from Luigi, sat *Maria Gabbana Lombardi*. She also had five phones with different numbers in order to work her CI's (confidential informants).

She was born in Napoli (Naples), Italy and knew her way around Roma like the back of her hand.

Sitting right in the middle of the war room (operations center) was *Carlo Piacentini*. He was a former detective for the famed Interpol.

Also, he is one of the foremost 'counterfeit' experts in the world. While he was with Interpol, he helped crack several very high profile 'phony money' cases around the globe.

Just to name a few: Dubai, UAE (United Arab Emirates), Hong Kong, China, Los Angeles, California, Moscow, Russia, Tijuana, Mexico, and the largest in the history of Interpol, Abuja, Nigeria. The last one involved three hundred-thirty-three million dollars of *weird cabbage* (counterfeit money).

Carlo's first assignment was to determine how many $100.00 dollar US bills in "The Bank of Italy, LLC" central cash vault were *counterfeit*. The bank's internal auditors stated about one hundred million dollars worth, however, it is possible, quite possible actually, that the figure could be higher, much higher.

His second job was to determine what type of equipment was used to print the supposedly 'almost' perfect "*Ben Franklin green*". And, his third task would be to figure out, if at all possible, what country the 'bogus bills' came from.

Off to the side were two smaller desks, with just one phone on each, and one lap top on each. These were for *Manny Murrieta* and *Chealy Te*. Both of these seasoned CIA operatives would be out of the office most of the time 'beating the pavement' in Roma (and the nearby cities) looking for any leads which may assist our team in solving our bank fraud case.

They were both very likeable with charming manners, but their other side was fast and very lethal.

*Howard* had a private office across the hall from the war room. It was filled with all of the latest, and high tech electronic surveillance equipment. Plus ten secure phone lines, each with different phone numbers.

THE OTHER DAY, while working with a CI (confidential informant) the lovely and quite talented secret operative (Maria Gabbana Lombardi) on Howard's CIA TAC team got some very interesting, tantalizing and not to mention surprising confidential information.

The CI swore her to secrecy and said to just tell your CIA boss that: "You heard it through the grape vine!" (Remember that great, classic old *Motown hit* by the incomparable Marvin Gay) and never, ever mention my name or the mafia (Camorra) will have me 'sleeping with the fish' before night fall".

He went on to tell her that, he had heard that a "Ms. Doria De Pisis, the assistant to the chairman of the board (at "The Bank of Italy, LLC") and, part of the office of the Presidents three person staff, was spending a lot of money and traveling around the world frequently. A lot of money.

She was said to be visiting high end casinos on the French Rivera in the south of France; Monte Carlo in the Mediterranean Sea, Macow (Hong Kong), Lima, Peru, the Cayman Islands and Panama.

She was also supposedly dropping 'bundles of cash' at most of these casinos, while only *occasionally* winning. Also, she was seen in the company of some very nefarious, suspicious *and* even possibly connected criminal male admirers.

She was just good enough, just dangerous enough, that if Charlie made a move on her too soon, he might (just maybe) might end up with some extra ventilation holes in his body, which would spoil his rep for being lucky.

And, if he was wrong about her, then he would have to go back to finding another suspect by using his computer, CI's, surveillance as well as his great deductive reasoning.

She clearly had access and sufficient influence (power) at "The Bank of Italy, LLC" to pull it off, as well as the technical know-how to switch the counterfeit $100.00 bills for the real bills. She may have even been doing it for years, of course, with the assistance of someone in the central cash vault.

She was now added to the list of our possible perps for the one-hundred million dollar 'counterfeit' embezzlement case.

I will be the first to tell you, when you go hiking, you need to wear the right boots with a good fit and thick 100% cotton socks.

Also, carry a very well equipped Nike back pack, equipped with some food, flashlights and a lot of batteries, both warm and cold weather clothing, et cetera. Now, when you go hunting for a *counterfeit* organization in a foreign country — possibly the *Italian Mafia* — you will need special equipment as well.

I asked Howard to call his assistant in charge of the Armory at CIA headquarters in Langley, Virginia and order our TAC team some supplies. Sort of like you would order camping gear through Sears and Roebuck (Sears) in the States.

The only difference was that instead of goods to save your life while hiking, these special goods might be necessary to take a life, if it came down to that.

I ordered the following hardware; just in the event that we needed it. And if we did not use some of them, all the better.

Three Remington sniper rifles with night scopes and silencers.

Nine AK-47's (Russian made, not Chinese); this is one of the best and most dependable assault weapons ever made.

Eighteen Glock 9mm pistols with 15 shot clips. Two of them for each of us and with leg and shoulder holsters.

Two razor sharp machetes. I would probably cut my foot off if I tried to use one.

Six Remington assault shotguns with a bandolier for extra shells.

Nine Kimber-Crimson model no. 1911, a .45 ACP automatic pistol with a 3" barrel and light for this kind of serious duty. Weighs only 25 ounces and hits like a bull. These will go on the back of our belts for backups. Just because.

Nine .38 caliber Smith and Wesson LT five shot revolvers for our ankles. You never know when you will have to reach down and grab it to save your life, or someone else's.

One H&K (Heckler & Koch) XM-8 just for me. It is a new version, possible replacement for the aging M-16 marine machine gun. I have never shot one but, I heard that it was a fathomable weapon. This might, just might be an excellent time to try it out. I will let you know how well it plays-out after my mission. That is, if I am still alive after it is all over.

Eighteen hand grenades, not new but look like they should do the job and make a Big Bang. I'm thinking two apiece. We will see.

Six bar's of C-4 plastique explosives. These were for Manny and Chealy. C-4 (or Semtex) plastique was much safer to handle than dynamite or nitro (nitroglycerin). It is also more stable. It was very powerful and required a detonator to go 'KA-BOOM!' Once again, I would probably blow up all of us if I was in charge of the explosives, I smile, but a truism.

Almost done, boy is the 'bank' going to love me when they get the CIA bill.

Nine new ultra lightweight bullet-proof vests. Hope we do 'not' need these, of course. Again, one for each of us.

Nine infrared 'night' vision zoom binoculars. Help to see during the day as well as at night. Everyone needs these.

Nine Hi-Tech satellite, extra light weight, Nextel radios, with extra back up batteries. One each.

Nine sets of cammo (camouflage) clothes. Plus Army Ranger jump boots with steel toes. Pair for each member.

Nine heave duty Nike back packs to carry all of our 'toys' in.

Nine high powered stun guns, with extra batteries. You never know when you are going to need one of these little beauties. For 'up close and personal' contact.

Nine Marine K-bar knives, with 14 inch blades and razor sharp. Also, they will cut wire fencing and concertina razor wire fences. One for all of the TAC personnel.

I do not know the price tag for all of these 'toys' (I would estimate $50,000.00) however, Howard told me that the CIA was going to bill "The Bank of Italy, LLC" for their cost. Also, he was going to give them a discount since this investigation could possibly benefit the United States Federal Reserve System.

# CHAPTER TWELVE

WHILE I WAS THINKING ABOUT my complex investigation into "The Bank of Italy, LLC" fraud case, something just 'popped' into my little brain (as you know that is not an uncommon occurrence for me). Before I left LA (Hollywood, La La Land), I had driven past an old-condemned drive-in theater. And it made me think and even became a little bit 'nostalgic'. Imagine that, waxing nostalgic!

When I was a kid 'back in the day' I used to just love going to the drive-in movies. Not that I went there just to make out with my dates, of course not. I went there to see great films and enjoy the fresh air, yeah right.

People who grew up in the 1950s and '60s often wax nostalgic about the drive-in theaters of their youth. Younger folk, raised with high-tech entertainment devices, might not see the appeal of a fuzzy screen, poor sound, and a long evening spent in the car with their parents.

But those who lived in LA in the 1930s and '40s might remember the Pico Drive-In Theater at Pico and Westwood boulevards in Los Angeles — California's *first* drive-in movie theater — which opened September 9, 1934.

America's first drive-in theater open in Camden, New Jersey, in June *1933*. Inventor Richard Holingshead reasoned that even during the Great Depression, people wouldn't give up on their cars or stop going to the movies.

Thanks to Hollingshead, drive-in theaters sprang up across the country, and, except for some technical improvements, their basic elements remained unchanged throughout the following decades.

Dubbed "ozoners," these open-air theaters reached the zenith of their popularity during the suburban boom of the 1950s, ‘60s and ‘70s. Piling the kids in the car made for a cheap family night out and drive-ins were a favorite hangout for teens who'd recently gotten driver's licenses (kids like me).

But the competing lures of shopping malls and television, and the increase in land values brought on by encroaching development, spelled the end for most outdoor theaters.

Only 19 operating drive-ins remain in California (as of 2011). The Pico drive-in relocated a few miles away to a site on Olympic Boulevard — where it was fittingly renamed the Olympic Drive-In — in the late 1940s, and closed for good in 1973.

The Westside pavilion — containing a modern cinema complex — now stands at Pico and Westwood, where rows of cars once bathed in the eerie glow of the big screen under starry night skies. And teenagers, some on their first dates, got their first hugs and kisses from their high school sweethearts (just like me).

After my little trip down 'memory lane' and recalling my early days at the wonderful drive-in theaters, I glanced at a copy of the LA Times, my favorite newspaper.

I still prefer printed news to internet news, guess I am still old school about that among everything else. As usual there was no good news '*above or below*' the fold.

I did, however, find a very interesting article on the back page (A30). It was entitled: "High-profile Murder with a Historical Twist". The police chief who first sought funds for cameras in LA became a victim in a crime-scene photo.

It's a grim irony tucked away in the files of the LAPD (Los Angeles Police Department). The first request for funding to buy photographic equipment for the department was made by Chief Walter Auble in 1905. And the oldest crime scene photos in the LAPD's possession are of Auble's murder on September 9, 1908.

Auble, who had resumed his old job as captain after finishing his term as chief, remains LA's highest-ranking officer to be murdered in the line of duty. He was shot to death by one of two burglary suspects that he and another captain had trailed to the corner of 9th Street and Grand Avenue. "Just the idea, a couple of captains pounding ground to find burglars — those days are long gone," said an executive director of the Los Angeles Police Historical Society.

The Auble murder will be one of many Los Angeles cases exhibited this week at the annual training conference of the California Homicide Investigators Association in Las Vegas, Nevada. Included will be evidence never seen in public, including the bullet-riddled getaway car from the *1997 North Hollywood shootout* between police and two bank robbers wearing body armor.

Also on display was the rifle carried by kidnapped heiress *Patty Hearst* during a *1974* bank robbery with the SLA (Symbioses Liberation Army) guerrilla group. The coat she wore won't be there, though; it's at an FBI exhibit in Washington, DC.

The homicide get-together is a real chance "to figuratively step behind the crime-scene tape." The displays will involve such names as mobsters Benjamin "Bugsy" *Siegel* and Johnny *Stompanato*, the *Manson family*, serial killer *Richard Ramirez* and *Elizabeth Short* (the murder victim in the *Black Dahlia* case).

The historical society's gruesome evidence has been omitted. "It’s not a ghoul show, but an effort to show how a homicide detective goes about solving a case", which is similar to how I as a Private Investigator solve a case.

One exhibit spotlights Helen Golay and Olga Rutershmidt, two septuagenarians who were convicted in *2008* of taking out insurance policies on homeless men whom they later ran over and killed, I am sure you saw this on the news.

Their display includes a check that Golay wrote to the Auto Club for her membership fee. It was pertinent because the Auto Club was summoned for a tow after Golay damaged the car near where one victim was run down. The dead man's DNA was found on the undercarriage of the car.

A few of the cases, including the Black Dahlia's', have never been solved. But the killer of Captain Auble did not elude capture a Century ago. He was Carl Sutherland, a 26-year-old small-time hood, and he lived in a downtown rooming house on Georgia Street with a cohort, Fred Horning, 21.

Their landlady, suspicious of the duo, contacted police a few days before the murder. While the men were away, Auble and another captain, Paul Flammer, searched their room and found "a burglar's kit," a "dope fiend outfit," false whiskers and mustaches, two revolvers, and a letter spelling out plans to burglarize two upscale residences.

The next day, the officers followed the men to a shop at 9$^{th}$ and Grand, then decided to arrest them. Neither officer brandished a firearm, apparently because they believed they had disabled the duo's weapons during their search of the rooming house.

Flammer grabbed Horning and subdued him as the two fell into the shop. But Sutherland shot Auble three times. A fourth bullet tore into the hand of the killer as the two men struggled. Sutherland fled. News of the Auble murder "spread amazingly fast," and "officers from every department in the city and county donated their services."

There were cries for a posse in Los Angeles, which was not so many years removed from being a frontier town. "Old cattlemen who have spent recent years of their lives within the city, but whose eyes can still squint dangerously down the barrels of a gun, came trooping into the station with their Winchesters resting in the hollows of their arms."

Exits from the city were sealed. Officers, using bloodhounds, followed the trail of Sutherland's blood. The gunman was found "on a lonely country road" near 77th Street about eight hours after the murder. Before he could be arrested, he gulped a bottle of cyanide and died. Very unusual way to commit suicide back in those days.

His partner Horning was sentenced to 14 years in Folsom State Prison. Auble, nearing death a few hours before Sutherland's suicide, regained consciousness long enough to shake the hands of his physicians.

Now, where was I? Oh, yes I remember now. I took a quaint old train from Roma and headed south toward Napoli (Naples). The built-in overhead speaker was playing *Ms. Cecilia Bartoli.* Her new CD entitled, "Sacrificum", (meaning — come to Naples) was just delicious like ear candy.

She is a famous Italian mezzo-soprano and she sings 'Arias' written in the seventeenth and eighteenth Century Europe. On the wall of the coach were paintings by *Luca Giordano* (an Italian) and *Jusepe de Ribera* (a Spaniard who lived most of his life in Italy). The lovely train was designed by the famous architect *Ferdinando Sanfelice*.

After Ms. Bartoli CD —they played one by "the great Farinelli". He sang in the 1720's and is said to have sung away the sever depressions of King Phillip V of Spain.

He had a seamless range of three octaves and could perform chains of trills' for a *full minute* without taking a breath. I do not know much, about opera, or operatic singers, however, when I get back to LA, I am going to make a concentrated effort to attend the operas at the Disney Concert Hall (downtown), and the Dorothy Chandler Music Pavilion. I need a little more sophistication and class in my life, don't you agree?

THE MAGNIFICENT AND enchanting opera house, Teatro San Carlo, is Italy's oldest functioning operatic showcase. If it is indeed true that certain places have a *genius loci* (i.e. presiding spirit), then Teatro San Carlo, in Naples, is the baroque and clearly does.

I stayed at the "Hotel Costantinopoli", a very chic spot in a nineteenth Century villa set around a quiet courtyard with a swimming pool and just down the street from the National Archaeological Museum.

It had a magnificent view of the *Bay of Naples*. The rates were very reasonable, only $1,000.00 per night including breakfast. After my wonderful brunch at the lovely hotel, I had lunch at *Ciro A Santa Brigida*, an old and famous Naples institution located near Teatro San Carlo and also the Galleria Umberto I.

Lunch only cost $100.00, not including the wine, of course. I had dinner at a fabulous restorante on the *Piazzetta Matilde Serao*, the La Chiacchierata, cost was $200.00 per person, quite reasonable, I thought for the excellent cuisine.

Then, I went to the majestic Teatro San Carlo for an opera, naturally. It was beyond words, just absolutely sublime. Everything in this part of town seems to speak of Neapolitan kings.

Most of them were foreigners who gained the throne of the Kingdom of the *Two Sicily's* (encompassing southern Italy and the island of Sicily) by conquest, treaty or war and then had to face the even greater challenge of ruling rambunctious Naples.

Nevertheless, the city developed a fondness for its kings, voting 10 to 1 in favor of retaining the monarchy during the popular referendum of 1946 when the rest of Italy chose to become a republic.

The wide, sloping Piazza del Plebiscito is decorated with equestrian statues of two great $18^{th}$ Century kings descended from a tangled web of Spanish, French, and Italian royal families.

Carlo di Borbone (*Charles III of Spain*), built the San Carlo in 1737 with a secret passageway linking the royal box to his apartments in the adjacent palazzo. And his son Ferdinando, went a little native in the city by the bay, playing fishmonger on the waterfront and throwing hot pasta on the heads of people in the pit beneath his box at the San Carlo. Sounds kind of like Hollywood, doesn't it?

The theater, where a two-year renovation has been completed, was the wonder of Europe when it opened about four decades before *Milan's La Scala*. The 2,500 - seat, horseshoe-shaped auditorium rises in six tiers of boxes to a ceiling fresco where gods and poets occupy stalls on banks of pink-tinged clouds.

At the height of the Baroque period, the 75-foot-deep stage accommodated 300 to 400 extras and the occasional horse, on which castrati stars liked to make their entrances.

When the next day dawned sparkling and clear, I remembered there aren't many sights I'd rather wake up to than the Bay of Naples. Leaving the Galleria, I passed between the hulking Castel Nuovo and cantaloupe-colored Palazzo Reale to the waterfront.

Cruise ships that had docked here were emitting shore excursionists who doubtless had been warned to watch their pockets and purses. Again, sound like LA.

At the port I could see the whole glorious crescent of the bay from the Amalfi Coast to *Mt. Vesuvius*. Brooding quietly now, the volcano, perhaps best known for its eruption in 79 AD, erupted eight times in the 1770s when a teen age Mozart gave a concert in Naples.

By that time, the same King Carlos who built the San Carlo had authorized excavation at *Pompeii,* helping to make Naples a required stop of Grand Tour travelers from Northern Europe.

On one of those back streets, Via di San Bartolomeo, I found the small Church of Santa Maria della Graziella, now shuttered and forlorn. It marks the site of the *San Bartolomeo* Theater, which predated the San Carlo and staged some of the first operas to reach the city in the early 1600s.

Around the corner on Via Medina, I stopped at a doorway big enough to admit the Trojan horse. Together with the elaborate, braided staircases of Sanfelice, massive portals are signature of Neapolitan Baroque architecture.

These mark the entrance to the Pieta die Turchini, connected to a church where a painting depicts an angel saving a boy from a demon.

Then it was on to the Naples Conservatory of Music, heir to Baroque period academies such as the Pieta dei Turchini. To get here from the Duomo, I plunged into *Spaccanapoli,* a historic district almost as dense and teeming now as it must have been in the 1700s, when Naples, with a population of about 400,000, was the biggest city in Italy.

Rabbit carcasses drip blood in butcher shops. Baby artichokes and zucchini flowers wait in crates along the pavement for Neapolitan mamas to put them in pasta.

Waiters take espresso on trays to people who don't need to make their own morning coffee because they live above ground-floor cafes. A sanitation worker leans on a broom, contemplating the futility of street sweeping in Naples. Once again, similar to LA.

The conservatory on Via San Sevastiano in Spaccanapoli occupies the former monastery of *San Pietro a Majella.* Visitors aren't permitted inside, but I could hear someone practicing the organ when I peeked into the courtyard.

In the church next door — a gothic structure with Baroque decorations — I saw a 1645 altarpiece made of multicolored stone, fronted by a balustrade supporting polished marble globes that could double as bowling balls.

I had a couple of slices of pizza for lunch and then dessert at the nearby Caffe Scaturchio, where baba au rhum is the house specialty. A 17th Century Polish king is thought to have invented the wicked confection, but bakers here discovered how to keep it light and airy while drenching it in enough rum to make you tipsy, another wonder of the *Neapolitan Baroque*.

I saved the best for last: a ride up the hill on a funicular, leaving me an easy walk to the Charterhouse of San Martino, which overlooks the orchestra pit of downtown Naples.

The complex, dating from around 1325, is now occupied by one of the best city museums in Europe, with galleries dedicated to the great plague of 1656, the peasant revolt of 1647 and works by cityscape, or Vedanta, artists who rendered Naples from nearly every angle in the 18th Century.

I found two gorgeous Baroque sedan chairs, suitable for carrying Farinelli.

# CHAPTER THIRTEEN

HOWARD WALLACE (CIA) AND I got prepared to travel to one of the most famous and *exquisite cities* in the whole world, *Venice*. Our investigation has now led us here and I wanted to learn more about the area prior to our arrival. Particularly, some history the islands and Venetian lagoon, some geography and of course, the "sinking city".

Venice (Venezia) is a city in northern Italy known both for tourism and for industry, and is the capital of the region *Veneto*, with a population of 271,367 (census estimate from 2004). Together with Padua, the city is included in the Padua-Venice Metropolitan Area (pop. 1,600,000).

The name is derived from that ancient tribe of Veneti that inhabited the region in Roman times. The city historically was the capital of an independent city-state.

Venice has been known as the "La Dominante", "Serenissima", "Queen of the Adriatic", "City of Water", "City of Masks", City of Bridges", "The Floating City", and "City of Canals". Luigi Barzini, writing in The New York Times, described it as "undoubtedly the most beautiful city built by man". Venice has also been described by the Times Online as being one of Europe's most romantic cities.

The city stretches across 117 small islands in the marshy *Venetian Lagoon* along the Adriatic Sea in northeast Italy. The saltwater lagoon stretches along the shoreline between the mouths of the Po (south) and the Piave (north) Rivers. The population is estimated at

272,000 inhabitants includes the population of the whole Commune of Venezia; around 60,000 in the historic city of Venice; 176,000 in Terraferma, mostly in the large frazioni of Mestre and Marghera; and 31,000 live on other islands in the lagoon.

The Republic of Venice was a major maritime power during the Middle Ages and Renaissance, and a staging area for the *Crusades* and the Battle of Lepanto, as well as a very important center of commerce (especially silk, grain and spice trade) and art in the 13$^{th}$ Century up to the end of the 17$^{th}$ Century.

This made Venice a wealthy city throughout most of its history. It is also known for its several important artistic movements, especially the Renaissance period. Venice has played an important role in the history of symphonic and operatic music, and it is the birthplace of Antonio Vivaldi.

While there is no historical record that deals directly with the obscure and peripheral origins of Venice, tradition and the available evidence have led several historians to agree that the original population of Venice consisted of refugees from Roman cities such as Padua, Aquileia, Altino and Concordia (*modern Portogruaro*) and from the undefended countryside, who were fleeing successive waves of Germanic invasions and Huns.

Some late Roman records reveal the existence of fishermen on the islands in the original marshy lagoons. They were referred to as "lagoon dwellers". The traditional founding is identified with the dedication of the first church, that of San Jacopo at the islet of Rialto ("High Grove"), given a conventional date of 421.

The Venetians traditionally having offered asylum to the Exach, in flight from the Lombard Liutprand, the Byzantine domination of central and northern Italy was subsequently largely eliminated by the conquest of the *Exarchate of Ravenna* in 751 by Aistulf.

During this period, the seat of the local Byzantine governor (the "duke/dux", later "doge") was situated in Malamocco. Settlement on the islands in the lagoon probably increased in correspondence with the Lombardo conquest of the Byzantine territories. Sometime in the first decades of the eighth Century, the people of the lagoon elected their first leader Ursus, who was confirmed by Byzantium

and given the titles of hypatus and dux. He was the first historical Doge of Venice.

In 810, an agreement between Charlemagne and Nicephorus recognized Venice as Byzantine territory and recognized the city's trading rights along the Adriatic coast, where *Charlemagne* had previously ordered the pope to expel the Venetians from the Pentapolis.

In 828, the new city's prestige was raised by the acquisition of the claimed relics of St. Mark the Evangelist from Alexandria, which were placed in the new basilica. The patriarchal sweat was also moved to Rialto.

As the community continued to develop and as Byzantine power waned, it led to the growth of autonomy and eventual independence.

From the ninth to the twelfth Century Venice developed into a city state. Its strategic position at the head of the Adriatic made Venetian naval and commercial power almost invulnerable.

With the elimination of pirates along the *Dalmatian* coast, the city became a flourishing trade center between Western Europe and the rest of the world. In the 12th Century the foundations of Venice's power were laid: the Venetian Arsenal was under construction in 1104; the last autocratic doge, Vital II Michele, died in 1172.

The Republic of Venice seized a number of locations on the eastern shores of the Adriatic before 1200, mostly for commercial reasons, because pirates based there were a menace to trade.

The Doge already carried the titles of Duke of Dalmatia and Duke of Istria. Later mainland possessions, which extended across Lake Garda as far west as the Adda River, were known as the "Terraferma", and were acquired partly as a buffer against belligerent neighbors, partly to ensure the supply of mainland wheat, on which the city depended.

In building its maritime commercial empire, the Republic dominated the trade in salt, acquired control of most of the islands in the Aegean, including *Cyprus and Crete*, and became a major power-broker in the Near East.

By the standards of the time, Venice's stewardship of its mainland territories was relatively enlightened and the citizens of such towns as Bergamo, Brescia and Verona rallied to the defense of Venetian sovereignty when it was threatened by invaders.

Venice remained closely associated with Constantinople, being twice granted trading privileges in the Eastern Roman Empire, through the so-called Golden Bulls or 'chrysobulls' in return for aiding the Eastern Empire to resist *Norman and Turkish* incursions. In the first chrysobull Venice acknowledged its homage to the Empire but not in the second, reflecting the decline of Byzantium and the rise of Venice's power.

By the late 13$^{th}$ Century, Venice was the most prosperous city in all of Europe. At the peak of its power and wealth, it had 36,000 sailors operating 3,300 ships, dominating Mediterranean commerce. During this time, Venice's leading families vied with each other to build the *grandest places* and support the work of the greatest and most talented artists.

The city was governed by the Great Council, which was made up of members of the noble families of Venice. The Great Council appointed all public officials and elected a Senate of 200 to 300 individuals.

Since this group was too large for efficient administration, a Council of Ten, controlled much of the administration of the city. One member of the great council was elected "Doge", or duke, the ceremonial head of the city, who normally held the title until his death.

The Venetian governmental structure was similar in some ways to the republican system of ancient Rome, with an elected chief executive (the Doge), a senate-like assembly of nobles, and a mass of citizens with limited political power, who originally had the power to grant or withhold their approval of each newly elected Doge.

Church and various private properties were tied to military service, though there was no knight tenure within the city itself. The Cavalieri di San Marco was the only *order of chivalry* ever instituted in Venice, and no citizen could accept or join a foreign order without the government's consent. Venice remained a republic throughout its independent period and politics and military were kept separate, except when on occasion the Doge personally headed the military.

War was regarded as a continuation of commerce by other means (hence, the city's early production of large numbers of mercenaries for service elsewhere, and later its reliance on foreign mercenaries when the ruling class was preoccupied with commerce).

Venice's long decline started in the 15th Century, when it first made an unsuccessful attempt to hold Thessalonica against the Ottomans (1423 - 1430). She also sent ships to help defend Constantinople against the besieging Turks (1453).

After the city fell to Sultan Mehmet II he declared war on Venice. The war lasted thirty years and cost Venice much of her eastern Mediterranean possessions.

Next, Christopher Columbus discovered the New World. Then Portugal found a sea route to India, destroying Venice's land route monopoly. France, England and Holland followed them.

Venice's oared galleys had no advantage when it came to traversing the great oceans. She was left behind in the race for colonies.

THE BLACK DEATH devastated Venice in 1348 and once again between 1575 and 1577. In three years the plague killed some 50,000 people. In 1630, the plague killed a third of Venice's 150,000 citizens.

Venice began to lose its position as a center of international trade during the later part of the Renaissance as Portugal became Europe's principal intermediary in the trade with the East, striking at the very foundation of Venice's great wealth, while France and Spain fought for hegemony over Italy in the Italian Wars, marginalizing its political influence.

However, the Venetian empire was a major exporter of agricultural products and, until the mid-18$^{th}$ Century, a significant manufacturing center.

By 1303, crossbow practice had become compulsory in the city, with citizens training in groups. As weapons became more expensive and complex to operate, professional soldiers were assigned to help work merchant sailing ships and as rowers in galleys.

The company of "noble Bowmen" was recruited in the later 14$^{th}$ Century from among the younger aristocracy and served aboard both galleys and as armed merchantmen, with the privilege of sharing the captain's cabin.

Though Venice was famous for its navy, its army was equally effective. In the 13$^{th}$ Century, most Italian city states already were hiring mercenaries, but Venetian troops were still recruited from the lagoon, plus feudal levies from Calmatia (the very famous Schiavoni or Oltremarini) and Istria.

In times of emergency, *all males* between seventeen and sixty years were registered and their weapons were surveyed, with those called to actually fight being organized into companies of twelve.

The register of 1338 estimated that 30,000 Venetian men were capable of bearing arms; many of these were skilled crossbowmen. As in other Italian cities, aristocrats and other wealthy men were cavalrymen while the city's conscripts fought as infantry.

By 1450, more than 3,000 Venetian merchant ships were in operation. Most of these could be converted when necessary into either warships or transports. The government required each merchant ship to carry a specified number of weapons (mostly crossbows and javelins) and armor; merchant passengers were also expected to be armed and to fight *when necessary*.

A reserve of some 25 (later 100) war-galleys was maintained in the Arsenal. Galley slaves did not exist in medieval Venice, the oarsmen coming from the city itself or from its possessions, especially Dalmatia.

Those from the city were chosen by lot from each parish, their families being supported by the remainder of the parish while the rowers were away. Debtors generally worked off their obligations rowing the galleys. Rowing skills were encouraged through races and regattas.

Early in the 15th Century, as new mainland territories were expanded, the first standing army was organized, consisting of condottieri on contract.

In its alliance with Florence in 1426, Venice agreed to supply 8,000 cavalry and 3,000 infantry in time of war, and 3,000 and 1,000 in peacetime.

Later in that Century, uniforms were adopted that featured *red-and-white* stripes, and system of honors and pensions developed. Throughout the 15th Century, Venetian land forces were almost always on the offensive and were regarded as the most effective in Italy, largely because of the tradition of all classes carrying arms in defense of the city and official encouragement of general military training.

After 1,070 years, the Republic lost independence when *Napoleon Bonaparte* on May 12, 1797, conquered Venice during the First Coalition. The French conqueror brought to an end the most fascinating Century of its history: during the Settecento (18th Century) Venice became perhaps the most *elegant and refined* city in Europe, greatly influencing art, architecture and literature.

Venice became Austrian territory when Napoleon signed a treaty with them on October 12, 1797. The Austrians took control of the city on January 18, 1798. It was taken from Austria by the Treaty of Pressburg in 1805 and became part of *Napoleon's* Kingdom of Italy, but was returned to Austria following Napoleon's defeat in 1814, when it became part of the Austrian-held Kingdom of Lombardy-Venetia.

In 1848-1849 a revolt briefly reestablished the Venetian Republic under Daniele Manin. In 1866, following the Third Italian War of Independence, Venice, along with the rest of the Veneto, became part of the newly created Kingdom of Italy.

During the World War II, the city was largely free from attack, the only aggressive effort of note being a precision strike on the German naval operations there in 1945. Venice was finally liberated by New Zealand troops under Freyberg on April 29, 1945.

The city is divided into six areas or "sestiere". These are Cannaregio, San Polo, Dorsoduro (including the Giudecca and Isola Sacca Fisola), Santa Croce, San Marco (including San Giorgio Maggiore) and Castello (including San pietro di Castello and Sant'Elena).

Each sestiere was administered by a procurator and his staff. These districts consist of parishes — initially seventy in 1033, but reduced under *Napoleon* and now numbering just thirty-eight. These parishes predate the sestieri, which were created in about 1170.

Other islands of the Venetian Lagoon do not form part of any of the sestieri, having historically enjoyed a considerable degree of autonomy. Each sestiere has its own house numbering system. Each house has a unique number in the district, from one to several thousand, generally numbered from one corner of the area to another, but not usually in a readily understandable manner.

At the front of the Gondolas that work in the city there is a large piece of metal intended as a likeness of the *Doge's hat*. On this sit six notches pointing forward and one pointing backwards. Each of these represent one of the Sextieri (the one which points backwards represents the Giudecca)

SINKING OF VENICE — The buildings of Venice are constructed on closely spaced wood piles, which were imported from the mainland. (Under water, in the absence of oxygen, wood does not decay. It is petrified as a result of the constant flow of mineral rich water around and through it, so that it becomes a stone-like structure.)

The piles penetrate a softer layer of sand and mud until they reach the much harder layer of compressed clay. Wood for piles was cut in the most western part of today's *Slovenia*, resulting in the barren land in a region today called Dras, and in two regions of Croatia, Lika and Gorski Kotar (resulting in the barren slopes of Velebit). Most of these piles are still intact after centuries of submersion. The foundations rest on the piles, and buildings of brick or stone sit above these footings.

The buildings are often threatened by flood tides pushing in from the Adriatic between autumn and early spring.

Six hundred years ago, Venetians protected themselves from land-based attacks by diverting all the major rivers flowing into the lagoon and thus preventing sediment from filling the area around the city. This created an ever-deeper lagoon environment. During the 20$^{th}$ Century, when many artesian wells were sunk into the periphery of the lagoon to draw water for local use, Venice began to *subside*. It was realized that extraction of the aquifer was the cause.

This sinking process has slowed markedly since artesian wells were banned in the 1960s. However, the city is still threatened by more frequent low-level floods (called acqua alta, "high water") that crept to a height of several centimeters over its quays, regularly following certain tides. In many old houses the former staircases used by people to unload goods are now flooded, rendering the former ground floor uninhabitable.

Some *recent studies* have suggested that the city is no longer sinking, but this is not yet certain, therefore, a state of alert has not been revoked. In May 2003 the Italian Prime Minister Silvio

Berlusconi inaugurated the MOSE project (Modulo Sperimentale Elettromeccanico), an experimental model for evaluating the performance of inflatable gates; the idea is to lay a series of 79 inflatable pontoons across the sea bed at the three entrances to the lagoon. When tides are predicted to rise above 110 centimeters, the pontoons will be filled with air and block the incoming water from the *Adriatic Sea*. This engineering work is due to be completed by 2011.

Researching the marvelous and historic old city of Venice was fascinating as well as a lot of fun. I was in Venice about 1996, but only for two days. It was so very romantic, and 'love' was in the air!

Unfortunately, I was traveling alone at the time and therefore I could not enjoy the magnificent 'ambiance' of the city to its fullest. There is nothing more romantic or invigorating to a man than to visit a truly enchanting city with a lovely young woman on his arm. Oh, yes, the wonders of male-female chemistry! Something human beings have been trying to figure out for the past eight-thousand years.

# CHAPTER FOURTEEN

A FEW MORE THINGS I wanted to know about beautiful Venice were its famous canals, its transportation system, and its musical history (I love its ancient music). Equipped with the important back ground information on the city of Venice, Howard and I can now proceed with our visit (and investigation into the "Bank of Italy, LLC" case).

Many cities in the world are named after Venice, Italy. One very well known one is Venice, California, which is right by my home town of Hermosa Beach. I also have been in beautiful and very romantic Venice, Italy. It is an absolutely magnificent city, however Venice, California is really not that hot an area.

Venice is world famous for its canals. It is built on an archipelago of 117 islands formed by 177 canals in a shallow lagoon. The islands on which the city is built are connected by 455 bridges. In the old center, the canals serve the function of roads and almost every form of transport is on water or on foot.

In the 19$^{th}$ Century causeway to the mainland brought a railway station to Venice, and an automobile causeway and parking lot was added in the 20$^{th}$ Century. Beyond these land entrances at the northern edge of the city, transportation within the city remains, as it was in centuries past, entirely on water or on foot.

Venice is Europe's *largest* urban car free area, unique in Europe in remaining a sizable functioning city in the 21st Century entirely without motorcars or trucks.

The classical Venetian boat is the gondola, although it is now mostly used for tourists, or for weddings, funerals, or other ceremonies.

Many gondolas are lushly appointed with crushed velvet seats and Persian rugs. Gondoliers typically charge between 80 and 100 Euros for a 35 minute "giro" or excursion around some canals. To be a Gondolier you must be an Italian or EU Citizen.

Most Venetians now travel by motorized waterbuses (vaporetti) which ply regular routes along the major canals and between the city's islands. The city also has many private boats. The only gondolas still in common use by Venetians are the *traghetti,* foot passenger ferries crossing the Grand Canal at certain points without bridges. Visitors can also take the water taxis between areas of the city.

Azienda Consorzio Trasporti Veneziano (ACTV) is the name of the public transport system in Venice. It combines both land transportation, with buses, and canal travel, with water buses (vaporetti).

In total, there are 25 routes which connect the city. A one way pass good for one hour costs 6.50 Euros; longer term passes for 12 to 72 hours are available, costing 14 to 31 Euros. An even better deal is the "Venice Card" for 7 days, starting at 47.50 Euros, which includes unlimited vaporetto travel.

The Venice People Mover (managed by ASM) is a cable operated public transit system connecting Tronchetto Island with Piazzale Roma. Venice also has water taxis, which are fast but quite expensive.

Venice is served by the newly rebuilt *Marco Polo* International Airport, or Aeroporto di Venezia Marco Polo, named in honor of its famous citizen. The airport is on the mainland and was rebuilt away from the coast; however, the water taxis or Alilaguna waterbuses to Venice are only a seven-minute walk from the terminals.

Some airlines market Treviso Airport in Treviso, as a Venice gateway. Some simply advertise flights to "Venice" without naming the actual airport except in the small print.

Venice is serviced by regional and national trains. One of the easiest ways to travel from Rome or other large Italian cities is to use the train. Rome is only slightly over four hours away; Milan is slightly over two and a half hours away. Treviso is thirty-five minutes away.

Florence and Padua are two of the stops between Rome and Venice. The St. Lucia station is a few steps away from a vaporetti stop. The station is the terminus and starting point of the Venice Simplon Orient Express from or to London, Victoria and Paris.

The maritime portion of Venice has no streets as such, being composed almost entirely of narrow footpaths, and laid out across islands connected by staired stone footbridges, making transportation impossible by almost anything with wheels.

Cars can reach the car/bus terminal via the *Ponte della Liberta* bridge. It comes in from the West from Mestre. There are two parking lots which serve the city: Tronchetto and Piazzale Roma. Cars can be parked there any time for around 30 Euros per day.

A ferry to Lido leaves from the parking lot in Tronchetto and it is served by vaporetti and buses of the public transportation.

Venice has been the setting of chosen location of numerous films, novels, poems and other cultural references. The city was a particularly popular setting for novels, essays, and other works of fictional or non-fictional literature.

Examples of these include Shakespeare's Merchant of Venice and Othello, Ben Jonson's Volpone, Votaire's Candide, Casanova's autobiographical History of My Life, Anne Rice's Cry to Heaven, and Philippe Sollers' Watteau in Venice, to name but a few.

The city has also been a setting for numerous films and music videos, such as the *James Bond series* From Russia with Love, Moonraker and Casino Royale, Death in Venice, Fellini's Casanova, Indiana Jones and the Last Crusade, A Little Romance, The Italian Job, and Lara Croft: Tomb Raider, Siouxie and the Banshees "Dear Prudence" and Madonna's Like a Virgin (song).

Venice has a rich and diverse architectural style, the most famous of which is probably the Gothic style. Venetian Gothic architecture is a term given to a Venetian building style combining use of the Gothic lancet arch with Byzantine and Arab influences.

The style originated in $14^{th}$ Century Venice where the confluence of Byzantine style from Constantinople met Arab influence from Moorish Spain. Chief examples of the style are Doge's Palace and the Ca'd'Oro in the city. The city also has several Renaissance and Baroque buildings, including the Ca'Pesaro and the Ca'Rezzonico.

THE CITY OF Venice in Italy has played an important role in the development of the music of Italy. The Venetian state — i.e. the medieval *Maritime Republic* of Venice — was often popularly called the "Republic of Music", and an anonymous Frenchman of the 1600s is said to have remarked that "in every home, someone is playing a musical instrument or singing. There is music everywhere."

During the 16th Century, Venice became one of the most important musical centers of Europe, marked by a characteristic style of composition (the Venetian school) and the development of the Venetian polychoral style under composers such as Adrain Willaert, who worked at *St. Mark's Basilica*.

Venice was the early center of music printing; Ottaviano Petrucci began publishing music almost as soon as this technology was available, and his publishing enterprise helped to attract composers from all over Europe, especially from France and Flanders.

By the end of the Century, Venice was famous for the splendor of its music, as exemplified in the "colossal style" of Andrea and Giovanni Gabrieli, which used multiple choruses and instrumental groups. Venice was the home of many famous composers during the baroque period, such as Antonio Vivaldi, Ippolito Ciera, Giovanni Picchi, and Girolamo dalla Casa, to name a few.

Venice arguably produced the most unique and refined *Rococo designs*. At the time, Venice was in a state of trouble. It had lost most of its maritime power, was lagging behind its rivals in political importance, with nobles wasting their money in gambling and partying. But without a doubt, Venice remained Italy's fashion capital, and was a serious contender to Paris in terms of wealth, architecture, luxury, taste, sophistication, trade, decoration, style and design.

Venetian Rococo was well-known for being rich and luxurious, with usually very extravagant designs. Unique Venetian furniture, such as the divani da portego, or long Rococo couches and pozzetti, objects meant to be placed against the wall.

Venetian bedrooms were usually sumptuous and grand, with rich damask, velvet and silk drapery and curtains, a beautifully carved Rococo beds with statues of putti, flowers and angels.

Venice was especially famous for its beautiful girandole mirrors, which remained amongst, if not the, finest in Europe. Chandeliers were usually very colorful, using Murano glass to make them look more vibrant and stand out from others, and precious stones and materials from abroad were used, since Venice still held a vast trade empire.

Lacquer was very common, and many items of furniture were covered with it, the most famous being lacca povera (poor lacquer), in which allegories and images of social life were painted. Lacquerwork and Chinoiserie were particularly common in bureau cabinets.

In the 16$^{th}$ Century Venetian painting was developed through influences from the Paduan School and Antonello da Messina, who introduced the oil painting technique of the Van Eyck brothers. It is signified by a warm color scale and a picturesque use of color.

Early masters where the Bellini and Vivarini families, followed by Giorgione and Titian, then Tintoretto and Veronese. In the early 1500s, also, there was rivalry between whether Venetian painting should use disegno or colorito.

Canvases (the common painting surface) *originated* in Venice during the early renaissance. These early canvases were generally rough. In the 18$^{th}$ Century Venetian painting had a renaissance because to Tiepolo's decorative painting can Canaletto's and Guardi's panoramic views.

Venice is famous for its ornate glass-work, known as Venetian glass. It is world-renowned for being colorful, elaborate, and skillfully made. Many of the important characteristics of these objects had been developed by the 13$^{th}$ Century. Toward the end of that Century, the center of the Venetian glass industry moved to Murano.

Byzantine craftsmen played an important role in the development of Venetian glass, an art form for which the city is well-known. When Constantinople was sacked by the Fourth Crusade in 1204, some fleeing artisans came to Venice.

This happened again when the ottomans took Constantinople in 1453, supplying Venice with still more glassworkers. By the 16$^{th}$ Century, Venetian artisans had gained even greater control over the color and transparency of their glass, and had mastered a variety of decorative techniques.

Despite efforts to keep Venetian glassmaking techniques within Venice, they became known elsewhere, and Venetain-style glassware was produced in other Italian cities and other countries of Europe.

Some of the most important brands of glass in the world today are still produced in the historical glass factories on Murano. They are Venini, Barovier & Toso, Pauly, Millevetri, and Seguso. Barovier & Toso is considered one of the 100 oldest companies in the world, formed in 1295.

One of the most renowned types of Venetian glasses are made in Murano, known as *Murano glass*, which has a famous product of the Venetian island of Murano for centuries.

Located off the shore of Venice, Italy, Murano was a commercial port as far back as the 7$^{th}$ Century. By the 10$^{th}$ Century it had become a well-known city of trade.

Today Murano remains a destination for tourists and art and jewelry lovers alike. Also, the popular automobile, the Nissan Murano, is named after the lovely little island.

Again, more interesting facts and figures concerning Venice. Nothing that pops-out to me as some information that will help me on my bank investigation. But we will see later on if it does or not. It did not take that long and was fascinating even if not useful to the current case.

Just so you know I plan on returning to Venice (and Roma) one day, *the Lord willing and the creek don't rise.* As John Wayne (the Duke) the famous movie actor use to say when he was not absolutely sure that he would be able to do something that he wanted (or planned) to do later on, in the movies anyway.

# CHAPTER FIFTEEN

MS. FELICIA ALEMANNO THE EVP (Executive Vice President) in charge of "The Bank of Italy, LLC" retail banking division, was just identified as a possible perp in our 'counterfeiting' case. *Giovanni Colonna*, through his families Mafia connections, was told to 'take a look' at Ms. Alemanno, a serious look.

She was a very classy dresser when I saw her. She wore a black necklace to coordinate with the black band of her diamond lady Rolex watch and her soft Italian made red heeled leather shoes.

I spotted the French pedicure on her little toes. It matched the manicured fingers that sported that lovely three carat diamond ring with about one carat of sapphires on each side of the gem stone. She was in my humble opinion very prosperous, very put together, very pampered, and very different from most women I knew. Too bad she was a suspect.

The head of the local Italian Mafia family (Camorra) was named Giuseppe Gotti Fabrizi. He was a local God Father as well as a senior member of the Mafias central council which controlled all organized criminal activity in all of Italy and Sicily. His eyes were mean, looked right through you, and were an imperious hazel shade.

His voice was creepy, very low pitched, obviously angry, laced with derision and snake venom. And, if that were not bad enough, he was a class A certified *psychopath* (psychopaths have no feelings, for themselves or for anyone else. They just go after what they want.

They never feel revenge or regret. Or grief, for that matter. Moral imagination. That's what my philosophy professor had said they lacked. He'd suggested that people who couldn't imagine the feelings of others couldn't feel empathy for them). Nothing can be done with them. Psychopaths are born that way — sociopaths the same thing — and they die that way. Now, he just became our third "person of interest."

Renzo Borghese a CI (confidential informant) had told our Giovanni that Fabrizi had a lot of knowledge concerning "The Bank of Italy, LLC" counterfeit loss. Also, that he was involved in it up to his eyeballs.

And, that he had something to do with the 'supposed' suicide of the bank's central cash vault supervisor (Celio Virabilli). The CI said it was definitely not a suicide nor an accidental death. And, that Celio's wife had not run off with an executive from the *Lamborghini* factory.

The man was from the *Ferrari* factory in Florence, and that Celio already had a new 'love of his life' who also was pretty and younger and also a gorgeous model.

Angel Ortega Bermudez (in our CIA war (control) room) has been monitoring her 'global hawk' unmanned sky drone for several days now.

She has been working ten to twelve hours per day and I am sure that her 'eyes and ears' are sore by now. Her persistence and skill *have paid off* though.

She has picked up 'radio traffic' concerning a possible suspect in our bank fraud case. A Ms. Anna "Gigi" Sordi, the administrative assistant to the president of "The Bank of Italy, LLC" (Vittorio Capitolini).

I thought to myself, no not "Gigi", she is just too lovely to be a criminal — thief. Besides I had planned to date her when the case was solved. What a bummer.

The information that Angel keenly developed, said that "Gigi" was spending thousands of dollars on Italian designer clothes, shoes, and handbags. That did not surprise me as each time I saw her, she

looked like she had just stepped *off the runway* at one of the famous designers shows.

Now, the question was, where is she getting that kind of money? From a wealthy admirer-boyfriend, possibly. From her family, she was said to come from a very old, wealthy and very prestigious Italian family. Again, a possibility. Or, from money she stole from the "bank", via counterfeit fraud. Yet another possibility.

I said to myself: "*Charlie*, you must endure some (or a lot) pain in order to achieve mastery in any area of your personal or professional life. As wonderful as obtaining that mastery is, the path to getting there — becoming even better at something you care very much about — (something you deeply desire to accomplish) is not lined with flowers or spanned by rainbows."

If it were, more of us would make the trip. *Mastery hurts*. Sometimes — many times —it's not much fun. That is one lesson of the work of psychologist Anders Ericsson, whose groundbreaking research on expert performance has provided a new theory of what fosters mastery.

As he puts it, "Many characteristics once believed to reflect innate talent are actually the results of intense practice for a minimum of 10 years."

And, if you wish to become a better Private Eye (Investigator) and proficient at your chosen vocation in life, then you must learn to master all of the necessary skills associated with your line of work.

Namely, surveillance, legal wire taps, various weapons usage and maintenance, fast speed chases, pilotless drone usage, foreign languages (just conversational is enough), foreign banking laws (off shore banking locations), Swiss, Lichtenstein, and Panamanian numbered bank accounts, et cetera.

Since I was already contemplating how to "master" the skills to become a more efficient Private Investigator, I decided to continue my contemplative mood and call my 'life coach', Chuck Booher, back in LA.

He has a beautiful and nicely decorated suite of offices on the corner of Hollywood Boulevard and Cahuenga Street — right in the center of Hollywood.

He is an outstanding, and renowned psychologist, life coach, and MFT (Marriage and Family Therapist). Although not that old of a man, he has exceptional wisdom into peoples' inner wants and needs. His keen insight into an individual's personal trials and tribulations, helps him to help them more effectively.

Chuck has assisted me on many occasions over the years. For example, while I was going through my excruciating and very painful divorce, after my wife of thirty (30) years left me for another man, my decision to take early retirement from the LAPD, some female dating relationships that did not work out the way that I had hoped they would (more shattered dreams), and after being shot (on more than one occasion, unfortunately), just to name a few.

He is a very articulate and well educated man, as well as an extremely gifted story teller. He is a frequently sought after public speaker for Universities, corporate visionary meetings, various police departments, the FBI, the CIA, and psychology conventions around the USA and even overseas.

One of the many important life lessons which he taught me over the years, is to embrace difficulties when they come into our lives. And trust me, they will come and keep coming as long as you are breathing here on old planet earth. I can guarantee you of that.

Chuck has shown me that when big — or even little — problems invade our lives (space), accept them and endure them with spirit. And, do not just complain about them and keep asking why poor little me, et cetera.

On a personal level, Chuck has an absolutely wonderful wife, Pam, two very neat married sons, Tim and Michael, and his three beloved grandkids. He is always bragging about his just fantastic grandchildren (and yes they are very cool kids), but I have to interrupt him and advise him that my two terrific grandkids are better. Then we always laugh because we know that they are all just magnificent young people. Chuck is a great and very knowledgeable teacher (life coach) and a very good friend as well.

# CHAPTER SIXTEEN

THE MONEY CHANGER: UNA DENARO cambio sta uno che occupato een girare uno spicie di denoaro een un altro. Or loosely translated by my broken, very broken, Italian is as follows: A money changer is one who engages in turning one type of currency into another.

And, to continue: een questo investigare qualcuno cambio vero uno conto een falso denaro. Roughly meaning: In this investigation someone changed real $100.00 bills into fake counterfeit money.

Then: Charlie's ottenere sta een travare fuori che fare questo molto cattivo cosa! Definition: Charlie's goal is to find out who did this very bad thing.

Finally: Io promessa voi questo, Charlie fare trovare questo investigare pari se stah ammazzare lui. Ed, stah molto prozzo potere fare giusto quello!

Equals: I guarantee you this, I will solve this case, even if it kills me. And, it very well may do just that!

If you do a little bit of research in your almanac, encyclopedia or better yet, the internet, you will find that there have been money changers around the world for over four thousand plus years. The most common definition of money is that it is a medium of exchange.

The important word in the definition is *medium*. "Money" has really no value in itself at all, unless it is melted down and put to some practical use, such as gold for filling teeth or silver for contact points in a radar set.

Money came into being because someone in authority decided that gold, silver, or other metals should *stand for* the value of goods. Money was at first merely a matter of convenience and it remains a convenience today.

No longer is it necessary to carry around a load of hay on your back to exchange for a dozen bushels of wheat. The value of the hay and the value of the wheat are symbolized by money. Before the invention of money, the custom of *barter*, or "swapping", was about the only way of exchanging goods.

Most workers today specialize in producing just one thing. Barter would be too inconvenient and too cumbersome a way to exchange all these specialized products. That is why in most societies man has found some product that *everyone* will accept. He uses this product for exchange.

Money is not the only medium of *exchange* for goods and services. It also serves as a measure of value. Under a barter system, it would be difficult to compare the value of an automobile with that of an alarm clock. But it is easy to compare their prices in money.

Money, or currency as it is often called, also serves as a means of *storing up value*, and savings accounts usually take the form of money. Finally, it acts as a standard of deferred payments, so that it is possible to know how much is owed on a product purchased by the installment plan.

Shortly after Howard and I arrived in the ancient and *magnificent* city of Venice, and after a too short but absolutely breathtaking sightseeing tour, we met up with two CI's. Mr. Marcello Villaggio and Mr. Angelo Mastroianni. Marcello was a former member of the Italian Mafia (the Camorra family). He was fairly high up in the organization when he had an affair with his Capo's mistress (Ragazza). Luckily for him he had several family members in the mafia who convinced the Capo not to kill (uccidere) Marcello, but to just excommunicate him from the Camorra. Which cost him thousands of dollars a year in money. He went to mass everyday to give thanks for his 'life'. He was a serious man still. Serious as a heart attack. You could still see stark fear in his very dark (scuro) brown eyes. They never stopped moving, left-to-right and then right-to-left.

Next we talked (parlare) to Angelo, he was also a former member of the mafia but a different crime family (the Cosa Nostra). His father (padre) Agostino Mastroianni, was the family patriarch. He wanted Angelo to have a better future so he allowed him to resign "from the life", something that is normally never done in the mafia.

It was a nice gesture by his father which allowed Angelo and his family to live a regular life after many years of very frightful experiences.

Angelo had an old dueling scar on his right cheek. He wore an exquisitely tailored blue silk suit (vestito), hand painted silk tie, and custom made Italian shoes (of course). He looked every bit like the successful businessman that he had become after leaving — the life.

He now owns a fleet of fancy gondola's which service the many beautiful canals of Venice. And, he also owns a chain of pizzerias here and also in Florence and Tuscany. Even though retired, he still had a stare that could scold your face, for real.

I noticed that he was ‘strapped', and asked what kind of gun he carried, he said a 9mm Berretta automatic pistol with a 15 round clip. Also, he volunteered that he carried a lightweight five shot American made *Smith and Wesson* .38 caliber on his left ankle under his suit pants. He favored his Berretta, but said that Smith and Wesson made the finest and most dependable revolvers in the whole world.

We talked to Marcello first, he had heard rumors, he said, there seemed to be a lot of chatter ‘on the streets' about someone making a *score of a lifetime*. He had heard the name of "Giuseppe Gotti Fabrizi (an Italian mafia god father) however, had no further details but added that some people in Paris might have more information that could possibly assist our investigation.

Second we talked to Angelo. The name he had heard 'in the wind' — so to speak was that of a lovely banker who just loved to gamble. Her name, he said was Ms. Dora De Pisis — assistant to the President at "The Bank of Italy, LLC".

It was said that she usually lost big — real big. She kept telling her friends, "I will win next time. I will win it all back and then some." She wished!

He further suggested that we talk to *Interpol* in Paris, as he had heard it through "the grapevine" that they had some knowledge of the bank fraud. He had no further information, but was very kind (possibly due to his guilt over his criminal past) and said he would call us if he heard anything else. Nice man, I thought.

Since all of our current leads, Intel (intelligence) and CI's seem to indicate that the trail to the answer to solving our 'bank' case, would direct our paths to France and to Interpol (just outside of Paris). Before you could say James Bond (or Sean Connery), Howard and I were "on a jet plane" headed for the "City of Light" — Paris, France. And the headquarters of the world renowned Interpol (International Police Organization).

Oh, by the way, I forgot to tell you, that I just finished a "fudo shin tai martial arts" class right before I left my beloved LA for magnificent and picturesque Italy. Fudo is a unique blend of aikido, iaido, karate, and good old fashioned street fighting. It will better enable me to be much more effective in handling any verbal, physical, or emotional attacks.

These techniques work regardless of age, body size, physical abilities, or health. This was a *good thing* because I am not a kid anymore (as you know), I am not that big, I am not as strong as I use to be, and while my health is good for my age, I am clearly not a twenty-five year old any longer!

Fudo teaches you how to take control of armed and unarmed assaults upon your body. I took the class at the famed LAPD Police Academy next to Dodger Stadium, just off of the 5 freeway in downtown LA. It only cost me $140.00 and I thought that was a bargain. The instructor was named Dave Campbell. He was a retired LA County Sherriff/LAPD officer with thirty years on the job. He was 6 foot, about 225 pounds of muscle, and just as tough as a marine DI (Drill Instructor). He loved bikes (motorcycles) and rode a Harley on the "white line" on the very dangerous freeways all over LA County.

I have had a lot of self-defense training during my lifetime while I was working for the LAPD (over 20 years), some special FBI training in Quantico, Virginia and even some detailed and in-depth CIA terrorist training in Langley, Virginia.

In addition, I have taken several karate and kung fu courses over the years in and around LA. In my line of business (a state and federally licensed and fully certified private investigator) you need all of the training that you can get (believe me on that) because you never know when you are going to be 'in the crap' and you will need it to save your life.

# CHAPTER SEVENTEEN

MOVING OUR FAST PACED AND ongoing investigation into the "Bank of Italy, LLC" fraud case, Howard, our CSI team, and I are now headed for fabulous France.

Some research, in advance is required, for example same basic history, of course, the French Revolution, their military and police, its transportation network and airports.

And, most importantly, Interpol (the International Police Network and Organization) located in Lyon, France.

France, officially the French Republic, is a state in Western Europe with several overseas territories and islands located on other continents and in the Indian, Pacific, and Atlantic Oceans.

Metropolitan France extends from the Mediterranean Sea to the English Channel and the North Sea, and from the Rhine to the Atlantic Ocean. It is often referred to as L'Hezagone ("The Hexagon") because of the *geometric shape* of its territory.

It is bordered (clockwise starting from the northeast) by Belgium, Luxembourg, Germany, Switzerland, Italy and Monaco; with Spain and Andorra to the south.

France's overseas departments and collectivities also share land borders with Brazil and Suriname (bordering French Guiana), and the Netherlands Antilles (bordering Saint-Martin).

France is linked to the United Kingdom by the Channel Tunnel, which passes underneath the English Channel.

France is a unitary semi-presidential republic with its main ideals expressed in the Declaration of the Rights of Man and of the Citizen. France is one of the most developed counties and possesses the fifth largest economy by nominal GDP and seventh largest economy by purchasing power parity.

France enjoys a high standard of living as well as a high public education level, and has also one of *the world's highest* life expectancies. It is the most visited country in the world, receiving 82 million foreign tourists annually.

France is a founding member of the United Nations, and a WTO, and the Latin Union. It is one of the five permanent members of the UN Security Council and possesses the third largest nuclear weapons stockpile in the world.

The word "Frank" had been loosely used from the fall of Rome to the Middle Ages, yet from Hugh Capet's coronation as "King of the Franks" (Rex Francorum) it became usual to refer to the Kingdome of Fancia, which would become France.

The Capetian Kings were descended from the Robertines, who had produced two Frankish kings, and previously held the title of "Duke of the Franks" ("dux Francorum"). This Frankish duchy encompassed most of modern northern France but because the royal power was sapped by regional princes the term was then applied to the royal demesne as shorthand. It was finally the name adopted for the entire Kingdom as central power was affirmed over the entire kingdom.

The name "France" itself comes from Latin Francia, which literally means "land of the Franks," or "country of the Franks". There are various theories as to the origin of the name of the Franks.

One is that it is derived from the Proto-Germanic word frankon which translates as javelin or lance, as the throwing axe of the Franks was known as a francisca. Another proposed etymology is that in an ancient *Germanic* language, Frank means free as opposed to servant.

This usage still survives in the name of the national currency prior to the adoption of the Euro, the Franc.

However, it is also possible that the word is derived from the ethnic name of the Franks, because as the conquering class only the Franks had the status of freemen.

In German, France is still called Frankreich, which literally means "Realm of the Franks". In order to distinguish from the

Frankish Empire of *Charlemagne,* Modern France is called Frankreich, while the Frankish Realm is called Frankenreich. In some languages, such as Greek, France is still known as Gaul.

The borders of modern France are approximately the same as those of ancient Gaul, which was inhabited by Celtic Gauls. Gaul was conquered by Rome under *Julius Caesar* in the 1st Century BC, and the Gauls eventually adopted Roman speech and Roman culture. Christianity first appeared in the 2nd and 3rd centuries AD, and became so firmly established by the fourth and fifth centuries that St. Jerome wrote that Gaul was the only region "free from heresy".

In the 4th Century AD, Gaul's eastern frontier along the Rhine was overrun by Germanic tribes, principally the Franks, from whom the ancient name of "Francie" was derived. The modern name "France" derives from the name of the feudal domain of the Capetian Kings of France around Paris.

The Franks were the first tribe among the Germanic conquerors of Europe after the fall of the Roman Empire to convert to Catholic Christianity rather than Arianism (their *King Clovis* did so in 498); thus France obtained the title "Eldest daughter of the Church" (La fille aine'e de l'Eglise), and the French world adopt this as justification for calling themselves "the Most Christian Kingdom of France".

Existence as a separate entity began with the Treaty of Verdun (843), with the division of Charlemagne's Carolingian Empire into East Francia, Middle Francia and West Francia. Western Francia approximated the area occupied by modern France and was the precursor to modern France.

The Carolingian dynasty ruled France until 987, when *Hugh Capet*, Duke of France and Count of Paris, was crowned *King of France*. His descendants, the Direct Capetians, the House of Valois and the House of Bourbon, progressively unified the country through a series of wars and dynastic inheritance into a Kingdom of France.

The Albigensian Crusade was launched in 1209 to eliminate the heretical Cathars of Occitania. In the end, both the Cathars and the independence of southern France were exterminated. In 1066, the Duke of Normandy added King of England to his titles.

Later Kings expanded their territory to cover over half of modern continental France, including most of the North, Center and West of France.

*Charles IV* (The Fair) died without an heir in 1328. Under the rules of the Salic Law adopted in 1316, the crown of France could not pass to a woman, nor could the line of kinship pass through the female line.

Accordingly, the crown passed to the cousin of Charles, Philip of Valois, rather than passing through the female line to Charles' nephew, Edward, who would soon become Edward III of England. In the reign of Philip of Valois, the French monarchy reached the height of its medieval power.

However, Philip's seat on the throne was contested by Edward III of England and in 1337, on the eve of the first wave of the *Black Death*, England and France went to war in what would become known as the Hundred Years' War.

In the most notorious incident during the French Wars of Religion (1562-98), thousands of Huguenots were murdered in the St. Bartholomew's Day massacre or 1572.

The monarchy ruled France until the French Revolution. It did not fall immediately after the storming of the Bastille on July 14, 1789, but endured until the creation of the First Republic in September 1792.

Louis XVI and his wife, *Marie Antoinette*, were executed in 1793, along with thousands of other French citizens during the Reign of

Terror.

A guerrilla war and counterrevolution, known as the Revolt in the Vende'e, cost more than 100,000 lives before it was crushed in 1796. After a series of short-lived governmental schemes, *Napoleon Bonaparte* seized control of the Republic in 1799, making himself First Consul, and later Emperor of what is now known as the First Empire (1804-1814).

In the course of several wars, his armies conquered most of continental Europe, with members of the Bonaparte family being appointed as monarchs of newly established kingdoms. About a million Frenchmen died during the Napoleonic wars.

Following Napoleon's final defeat in 1815 at the *Battle of Waterloo*, the French monarchy was re-established, but with new constitutional limitations. In 1830, a civil uprising established the constitutional July Monarchy, which lasted until 1848.

The short-lived Second Republic ended in 1852 when Louis-Napoleon Bonaparte proclaimed the Second Empire. Louis-Napoleon was unseated following defeat in the Franco-Prussian war of 1870 and his regime was replaced by the Third Republic.

A small part of Northern France was occupied during World War I. The human and material losses in the first war, which left 1.4 million French soldiers dead, exceeded those of the second where 567,600 French died.

The phase was marked by a variety of social reforms introduced by the Popular Front government. Following the German *Blitzkrieg campaign* in World War II metropolitan France was divided in an occupation zone in the north and Vichy France, a newly established authoritarian regime collaborating with Germany, in the south.

The debate over whether or not to keep control of Algeria, then home to over one million European settlers, wracked the country and nearly led to civil war.

In 1958, the weak and unstable Fourth Republic gave way to the Fifth Republic, which contained a strengthened Presidency. In the

latter role, *Charles de Gaulle* managed to keep the country together while taking steps to end the war. The Algerian War was concluded with peace negotiations in 1962 that led t Algerian independence.

WHILE METROPOLITAN FRANCE is located in Western Europe, France also has a number of territories in North America, the Caribbean, South America, the southern Indian Ocean, the Pacific Ocean, and Antarctica. These territories have varying forms of government ranging from overseas department to overseas collectivity.

Metropolitan France covers 211,209 square miles, having the largest area among European Union members. France possesses a wide variety of landscapes, from coastal plains in the north and west to mountain ranges of the Alps in the south-east, the Massif Central in the south-central and Pyrenees n the south-west.

At 15,782 feet above sea level, the highest point in Western Europe, *Mont Blanc*, is situated in the Alps on the border between France and Italy. Metropolitan France also has extensive river systems such as the Seine, the Loire, the Garonne, and the Rhone, which divides the Massif Central from the Alps and flows into the Mediterranean Sea at the Camargue, the lowest point in France. Corsica lies off the Mediterranean coast.

France uses a civil legal system, that is, law arises primarily form written statutes; judges are not to make law, but merely to interpret it (though the amount of judge interpretation in certain areas makes it equivalent to case law).

Basic principles of the rule of law were laid in the Napoleonic Code. In agreement with the principles of the *Declaration of the Rights of Man* and of the Citizen, law should only prohibit actions detrimental to society.

As Guy Canivet, first president of the Court of Cassation, wrote about the management of prisons: Freedom is the rule, and its restriction is the exception; any restriction of Freedom must be provided for by Law and must follow the principles of necessity and proportionality.

That is, Law should lay out prohibitions only if they are needed, and if the inconveniences caused by this restriction do not exceed the inconveniences that the prohibition is supposed to remedy. French law is divided into two principal areas: private law and public law. Private law includes, in particular, civil law and criminal law.

Public law includes, in particular, administrative law and constitutional law. However, in practical terms, French law comprises three principal areas of law: civil law, criminal law and administrative law.

France does not recognize religious law, nor does it recognize religious beliefs or morality as a motivation for the enactment of prohibitions. As a consequence, France has long had neither blasphemy laws nor sodomy laws. However, "offences against public decency" or disturbing public order have been used to repress public expressions or street prostitution.

In 2007, France is the third largest donor of development aid in the world, behind the US and Germany, but ahead of Japan and the UK. This represents 0.5% of its GDP, one of the highest rate of the developed countries. The organism managing the French help is the French Development Agency, which finances primarily humanitarian projects in sub-Saharan Africa.

The main goals of this help are "developing infrastructure, access to health care and education, the implementation of appropriate economic policies and the consolidation of the rule of law and democracy.

Military: The French armed forces are divided into four branches: Arme'e de Terre (*Army)*, Marine Nationale (*Navy*),

Arme'e de l'Air (*Air Force*), and Gendarmerie Nationale (A military force which acts as a National Rural Police and as a Military police for the entire French military).

After the Algerian War, conscription was steadily reduced and was finally suspended in 1997 by President Jacques Chirac.

The total number of military personnel is approximately 347,000. France spends in 2010 2.5% of its GDP on defense, slightly more than the United Kingdom (2.3%) and the highest in the European

Union where defense spending generally accounts to less than 1.5% of GDP. About 10% of France's defense budget goes towards its nuclear deterrence, or nuclear weapons force.

France has major military industries that have produced the Rafale fighter, the Charles de Gaulle aircraft carrier, the Exocet missile and the Leclerc tank amongst others. Some weaponry, like the E-2 Hawkeye or the E-3 Sentry was bought from the *United States*.

Despite withdrawing from the Euro fighter project, France is actively investing in European joint projects such as the Eurocopter Tiger, multipurpose frigates, the UCAV demonstrator nEUROn and the *Airbus A400M*. France has the most powerful *aerospace* industry in Europe.

France is a *major arms seller,* as most of its arsenal's designs are for the export market with the notable exception of nuclear-powered devices. Some of the French designed equipments are specifically designed for exports like the Franco-Spanish Scorpene class submarines.

Some French equipments have been largely modified to fit allied countries' requirements like the Formidable class frigates (based on the La Fayette class) or the Hashmat class submarines (based on the Agosta class submarines).

Although it includes very competent anti-terrorist units such as the GIGN or the EPIGN, the gendarmerie is a military police force which serves for the most part as a rural and general purpose police force. Since its creation the GIGN has taken part in roughly one thousand operations and freed over five-hundred hostages; the Air France Flight 8969's hijacking brought them to the world's attention with a very successful antiterrorist operation.

French intelligence consists of two major units: the DGSE (the external agency) and the DCRI (domestic agency). The latter being part of the police while the former is associated to the army. The DGSE is notorious for the Sinking of the Rainbow Warrior, but it is also known for revealing the most extensive technological spy network uncovered in Europe and the United States to date through the mole Vladimir Vetrov.

The French deterrence, (formerly known as "Force de frappe"), relies on complete independence. The current French nuclear force consists of four submarines equipped with M45 ballistic missiles. The current Triomphant class is currently under deployment to replace the former Redoutable class.

The M51 will replace the M45 in the future and expand the Triomphants firing range. Aside of the submarines the French dissuasion force uses the Mirage 2000N; it is a variant of the Mirage 2000 and thus is designed to deliver nuclear strikes. Other nuclear devices like the Plateau d'Albion's Intermediate-range ballistic missile and the short range Hades missiles have been disarmed.

With 350 nuclear heads stockpiled France is the world's third largest nuclear power. *The Marine Nationale* is regarded as one of the world's most powerful navies. The professional compendium flottes de combats, in its 2006 edition, ranked it world's 6th biggest navy after the American, Russian, Chinese, British and Japanese navies.

It is equipped with the only non-American nuclear powered Aircraft Carrier in the world. Recently Mistral class ships joined the Marine Nationale, the Mistral itself having taken part to operations in Lebanon.

For the 2004 centennial of the Entente cordiale President Chirac announced the Future French aircraft carrier would *be jointly designed* with Great Britain.

The French navy is equipped with the La Fayette class frigates, early examples of stealth ships, and several ships are expected to be retired in the next few years and replaced by more modern ships, examples of future surface ships are the Forbin and the Aquitaine class frigates.

The attack submarines are also part of the Force Oceanique Strategique although they do not carry the nuclear dissuasion, the current class is the Rubis Class and will be replaced in the future by the expected Suffren Class.

The Arme'e de Terre employs as of 2009 123,100 people. It is famous for the Legion Etrange're (French Foreign Legion) though the French special forces are not the Legion but the Dragons Parachutists and the Marines Parachutists.

The French *assault rifle* is the FAMAS and future infantry combat system is the Felin. France uses both tracked and wheeled vehicles to a significant point, examples of older AMX 30 tanks are still operational. It uses the AMX 30 AuF1 for artillery and is equipped with Eurocopter Tiger helicopters.

The Arme'e de l'Air is the oldest and first professional air force worldwide. *It still today* retains a significant capacity. It uses mainly two aircraft fighters: the older Mirage F1 and the more recent Mirage 2000. The later model exists in a ground attack version called the Mirage 2000D. The modern Rafale is in deployment in both the French air force and navy.

Transport: The railway network in France, which as of 2008 stretches 18,314 miles is the second most extensive in Western Europe after the German one. It is operated by the SNCF, and high-speed trains include the Thalys, the Eurostar and TGV, which travels at 199 MPH in commercial use.

The Eurostar, along with the *Eurotunnel Shuttle*, connects with the United Kingdom through the *Channel Tunnel*. Rail connections exist to all other neighboring countries in Europe, except Andorra. Intra-urban connections are also well developed with both underground services and tramway services complementing bus services.

There are 475 airports in France. Paris-*Charles de Gaulle* Airport located in the vicinity of Paris is the largest and busiest airport in the country, handling the vast majority of popular and commercial traffic of the country and connecting Paris with virtually all major cities across the world.

Air France is the national carrier airline, although numerous private airline companies provide domestic and international travel services. There are ten major ports in France, the largest of which is in *Marseille*, which also is the largest bordering the Mediterranean Sea.

Some 7,619 miles of waterways traverse France including the Canal du Midi which connects the Mediterranean Sea to the Atlantic Ocean through the Garonne River.

France is ripe with very rich history. Of course, reading about Napoleon's escapes was interesting. Also, France's legal system, their military and especially the Gendarmerie (National Police), and the DGSE and the DCRI.

France is a major arms seller, I also found out. And I have always been interested in the famous, or infamous, "French Foreign Legion". It is one of the oldest and best fighting forces in the whole wide world.

I was in Paris and the beautiful country side in 1991 on a tour with one of my son's. We took an 'overnight' sleeper car train from the historic and very old, Paris train station. The orient express 'type' train took us to marvelous Madrid, Spain. I just loved Spain, much more than France, if the truth be told. And, I always try to tell the truth as you know.

# CHAPTER EIGHTEEN

I CONTINUED MY RESEARCH INTO France so that upon arrival I would be completely knowledgeable concerning the wonderful country.

Some additional subject matters included the following: its government, their economy (fifth largest in the world), languages (very important to our team), as well as a 'little' more history. It is said to be one of the best countries "to live in" in the whole world.

The administrative divisions of France is divided into *26 administrative* regions. Twenty-two are in metropolitan France and four are overseas regions. The regions are further subdivided into 100 departments which are numbered (mainly alphabetically). This number is used in postal codes and vehicle number plates which are, in turn, subdivided into 4,032 cantons.

These cantons are then inter-communal entities grouping 33,414 of the 36,680 communes (i.e. 91.1% of all the communes). Three communes, Paris, Lyon and Marseille are also subdivided into 45 municipal arrondissements.

The regions, departments and communes are all known as territorial collectivities, meaning they possess local assemblies as well as an executive. *Arrondissements* and cantons are merely administrative divisions. However, this was not always the case.

Until 1940, the arrondissements were also territorial collectivities with an elected assembly, but these were suspended by the Vichy regime and definitely abolished by the Fourth Republic in 1946. Historically, the cantons were also territorial collectivities with their elected assemblies.

Overseas regions/departments, collectivities, and territories: Among the 100 departments of France, four (French Guiana, Guadeloupe, Martinique, and Reunion) are in overseas regions (ROMs) that are also simultaneously overseas departments (DOMs) and are an integral part of France (and the European Union) and thus enjoy a status similar to metropolitan departments.

In addition to the 26 regions and 100 departments, the French Republic also *has six overseas* collectivities (French Polynesia, Mayotte, Saint Barthelme, Saint Martin and Miquelon, Wallis and Futuna), one collectivity (New Caledonia), one overseas territory (French Southern and Antarctic Lands), and one island in the Pacific Ocean (Clipperton Island).

Overseas collectivities and territories form part of the French Republic, but do not form part of the European Union or its fiscal area (with the exception of St. Barthelme, which seceded from Guadeloupe in 2007).

The Pacific Collectivities (COMs) of French Polynesia, Wallis and Fortuna, and New Caledonia continue to use the Pacific Franc whose value is linked to that of the Euro. In contrast, the four overseas regions used the French Franc and now use the Euro.

A member of the "G8" group of leading industrialized countries, it is ranked as the fifth largest economy by nominal GDP. France joined the 11 other EU members to launch the euro on January 1, 1999, with euro coins and banknotes completely replacing the French franc in early 2002. France has a mixed economy which combines extensive private enterprise (nearly 2.5 million companies registered) with substantial (though declining) state enterprise and government intervention. The government retains considerable influence over key segments of infrastructure sectors, with majority

ownership of railway, electricity, aircraft, nuclear power and telecommunications. It has been gradually relaxing its control over these sectors since the early 1990s.

The government is slowly corporatizing the state sector and selling off holding in France Telecom, Air France, as well as the insurance, banking, and defense industries. France has an important aerospace industry led by the *European consortium Airbus*, and has its own national spaceport, the Centre Spatial Guyanais.

According to the WTO, in 2009 France was the world's sixth-largest exporter and the fourth-largest importer of manufactured goods. In 2008, France was the third-largest recipient of foreign direct investment among OECD countries at 4117.9 billion, ranking behind Luxembourg (where foreign direct investment was essentially monetary transfers to banks located in that country) and the United States ($316.1 billion), but above the United Kingdom ($96.9 billion), Germany ($24.9 billion), or Japan ($24.4 billion).

In the same year, *French companies* invested $220. Billion outside of France, ranking France as the second most important outward direct investor in the OECD, behind the United States ($311.8 billion), and ahead of the United Kingdom ($111.4 billion), Japan ($128 billion) and Germany ($156.5 billion).

Within 2010, 39 of the 500 biggest companies of the world, France ranks 4$^{th}$ in the Fortune Global 500, behind the US, Japan and China, but ahead of Germany and the UK.

With an estimated population of 65.4 million people (as of January 2010), France is the 20$^{th}$ most populous country in the world. In 2003, France's natural population growth was responsible for almost all natural population growth in the European Union.

In 2004, population growth was 0.68% and then in 2005 birth and fertility rates continued to increase. The natural increase of births over deaths rose to 299,800 in 2006. The total fertility rate rose to 2.02 in 2008, from 1.88 in 2002.

In 2004, a total of 104,033 people immigrated to France. Of them, 90,250 were from Africa and 13,710 from Europe. In 2008, France granted citizenship to 137,000 persons, mostly to people from *Morocco, Algeria and Turkey.*

According to the French National Institute for Statistics and Economic Studies, it has an estimated 4.9 million foreign-born immigrants, of which 2 million have acquired French citizen-ship.

France is *the leading asylum destination* in Western Europe with an estimated 50,000 applications in 2005. The European Union allows free movement between the member states. While UK and Ireland did not impose restrictions, France put in place controls to curb Eastern European migration.

A perennial political issue concerns rural depopulation. Over the period 1960-1999 fifteen rural departments experienced a decline in population. In the most extreme case, the population of Creuse fell by 24%

According to Article 2 of the Constitution, amended in 1992, French is the sole official language of France. France is the only Western European nation to have only one officially recognized language.

However, 77 regional languages are also spoken, in metropolitan France as well as in the overseas departments and territories. Until recently, the French government and state school system discouraged the use of any of these languages, but they are now taught to varying degrees at some schools.

*Other languages*, such as Portuguese, Italian, Maghrebi Arabic and several Berber languages are spoken by immigrants.

Technically speaking, there is no standard type of "French" architecture, although that has not always been true. Gothic Architecture's old name was French Architecture. The term "Gothic" appeared later as a stylistic insult and was widely adopted.

The Gothic Architecture was the first French style of Architecture to be copied in all Europe. Northern France is the home of some of the most important *Gothic cathedrals and basilicas*, the first of these being the Saint Denis Basilica; other important French Gothic cathedrals are Notre-Dame de Chartres and Notre-Dame d'Amiens.

The kings were crowned in another important Gothic church: Nortre-Dame de Reims. Aside from churches, Gothic Architecture had been used for many religious palaces, the most important one being the Palais des Papes in Avignon.

DURING THE MIDDLE Ages, fortified castles were built by feudal nobles to mark their powers against their rivals. When King

Philip II took over from King John, for example, he demolished the ducal castle to build a bigger one.

Fortified cities were also common, unfortunately most French castles did not survive the passage of time. This is why *Richard the Lionheart's* Chateau Gaillard was demolished, as well as the Chateau de Lusignan. Some important French castles that survived are Chinon, Chateau d'Angers, the massive Chateau de Vincennes and the so called Cathar castles.

Before the appearance of this architecture France had been using Romanesque architecture like most of Western Europe. Some of the greatest examp0les of Romanesque churches in France are the Saint Sernin basilica in Toulouse (*largest Romanesque* church in Europe) and the remains of the Cluniac Abbey (largely destroyed during the revolution and the Napoleonic Wars).

The end of the Hundred Years' War marked an important stage in the evolution of French architecture. It was the time of the French Renaissance and several artists from Italy and Spain were invited to the French court; many presidential palaces, inspired by the Italians, were built, but mainly in the Loire Valley.

Such residential castles were the Chateau de Chambord, the Chateau de Chenonceau, or the chateau d'Amboise. Following the renaissance and the end of the Middle Ages, Baroque Architecture replaced the traditional gothic style.

However, in France, baroque architecture found a greater success in the secular domain than in a religious one. In the secular domain the *Palace of Versailles* has many baroque features.

Jules Hardouin Mansart was said to be the most influential French architect of the baroque era, with his famous dome, Les Invalides.

Some of the most impressive provincial baroque architecture is found in places that were not yet French such as the Place Stanislas in Nancy.

On the military architectural side, Vauban designed some of the most efficient fortresses in Europe and became an influential military architect; as a result, imitations of his works can be found all over Europe, the Americas, Russia and Turkey.

Under Napoleon III a new wave of urbanism and architecture was given birth. If extravagant buildings such as the neo-baroque Palais Garnier were built, the urban planning of the time was very organized and rigorous. For example, Baron Haussmann rebuilt Paris.

The architecture associated to this ear is named Second Empire in English, the term being taken from the Second French Empire. At this time there was strong Gothic resurgence across

Europe and in France the associated architect was Eugene Viollet-le-Duc.

In the late 19$^{th}$ Century Gustave Eiffel designed many bridges, such as Garabit viaduct, and remains one of the most influential bridge designer of his time, although he is best remembered for the iconic Eiffel Tower.

In the 20$^{th}$ Century, Swiss Architect Le Corbusier designed several buildings in France. More recently French architects have combined both modern and old architectural styles.

The *Louvre Pyramid* is an example of modern architecture added to an older building. Certainly the most difficult buildings to integrate within French cities are skyscrapers, as they are visible from afar.

For instance, in Paris, since 1977, new buildings must have been under 121 feet. France's largest financial district is La Defense, where a significant number of skyscrapers are located.

Other massive buildings that are a challenge to integrate into their environment are large bridges; a good example of the way this has been done in the Millau Viaduct. Some famous modern French architects include Jean Nouvel or Paul Andreu.

The earliest French literature dates from the Middle Ages, when what is now known as modern France did not have a single, uniform language. There were several languages and dialects and each writer used his own spelling and grammar.

The authors of French mediaeval texts are unknown, such as Tristan and Iseult and Lancelot and the Holy Grail. Much mediaeval French poetry and literature were inspired by the legends of the Mater of France, such as The Song of Roland and the various Chansons de geste.

The "Roman de Renart", written in 1175 by *Perrout de Saint Cloude* tells the story of the mediaeval character Reynard ('the Fox') and is another example of early French writing. The names of some authors from this period are known, for example Chretien de Troyes and Duke William IX of Aquitaine, who wrote in Occitan.

According to a BBC poll based on 29,977 responses in 28 countries, France is globally seen as a positive influence in the world's affairs: 49% have a positive view of the country's influence, whereas only 19% have a negative view, however, I am one of the 19%.

I visited France in 1991 and noticed that Americans were treated very poorly, unless they could speak French. The Nation Band Index of 2008 suggested that France has the second best international reputation, only behind Germany.

In January 2010, the International Living ranked France as "best country to live in", ahead of 193 other countries surveyed, for the fifth year running, according to a survey taking into account nine criteria of quality of life: Cost of Living, Culture and Leisure, Economy, Environment, Freedom, Health, Infrastructure, Safety and Risk, and Climate.

France has historical strong ties with Human Rights. Since the Declaration of the Rights of Man and of the Citizen of 1789, France is often nicknamed as "the country of Human Rights". Furthermore, in 1948, a Frenchman, *Rene Cassin,* was one of the main redactors of the Universal Declaration of Human Rights which was adopted by the UN members in Paris.

Marianne is a symbol of the French Republic. She is an allegorical figure of liberty and the Republic and first appeared at the time of the French Revolution. The earliest representations of Marianne are of a woman wearing a Phrygian cap.

In 1792, the National convention chose Marianne to incarnate the French Republic. The origins of the name Marianne are unknown, but Marie-Anne was a very common first name in the18th Century.

Anti-revolutionaries of the time derisively called her "La Gueuse" ("the Commoner"). It is believed that revolutionaries from the South of France adopted the Phrygian cap as it symbolized liberty, having been worn by freed indentured servants in both Greece and Rome.

Mediterranean seamen and convicts manning the galleys also wore a similar type of cap. Under the Third Republic, statues, and especially busts, of Marianne began to proliferate, particularly in town halls.

She was represented in several different manners, depending on whether the aim was to emphasize her revolutionary nature or her "wisdom".

Over time, the Phrygian cap was felt to be too seditious, and was replaced by a diadem or a crown. In recent times, *famous French women* have been used as the model for those busts: recent ones include Sophie Marceau, and Laetitia Casta. She also features on everyday articles such as postage stamps and coins.

My continued research into France which I visited in 1991 on a fabulous trip though Europe (including: Belgium, Germany, Switzerland, and also Spain) revealed a lot of information that I was not aware of.

Their six overseas territories (i.e. collectivities), their fifth largest economy in the world, fourth largest importer of goods (mainly oil from the Middle East), and they are the twentieth most populated country.

Something that I found very interesting was they have a large and very violent Albanian population, some of which are heavily involved in organized criminal activities. *Interpol* says that even the Russian Mafia stay clear of the "Albanians".

# CHAPTER NINETEEN

AFTER HOWARD, HIS SEVEN MEMBER CIA team, and I arrived in Paris and as soon as it was humanly possible, we took a night train out of Paris' ancient and absolutely exquisite old railway train station. Our destination was the famous *Interpol* complex in *Lyon, France* (just 30 miles outside of Paris).

Interpol is the world's Largest International Police Organization, with 188 member countries. *Created in 1923*, it facilitates cross-border police co-operation, and supports and assists all organizations, authorities and services whose mission is to prevent or combat international crime.

Working with the world's best police organization (next to the Masad (Israel); the CIA; and British MI-5 of course) should really assist us in finding our evil counterfeit criminals.

Interpol aims to facilitate international police co-operation even where diplomatic relations do not exist between particular countries. Action is taken within the limits of existing laws in different countries and in the spirit of the *Universal Declaration of Human Rights*.

Interpol's constitution prohibits 'any intervention or activities of a political, military, or religious character.' The President of

Interpol and the Secretary General work closely together in providing strong leadership and direction to the organization.

As defined in Article 5 of its Constitution, Interpol (whose correct full name is *'The International Criminal Police Organization* — INTERPOL') is comprised of the following:

General Assembly

Executive Committee

General Secretariat

National Central Bureaus

Advisors

The Commission for the Control of Interpol's files

The General Assembly and the Executive Committee form the organization's Governance.

*General Assembly* — Interpol's supreme governing body, it meets annually and comprises delegates appointed by each member country. The assembly takes all important decisions related to policy, resources, working methods, finances, activities and programs.

*Executive Committee* — this 13-member committee is elected by the General Assembly, and comprises the president, three vice-presidents and nine delegates covering the four regions.

*General Secretariat* — located in Lyon, France, the General Secretariat operates 24 hours a day, 365 days a year and is run by the Secretary General. Officials from more than 80 countries work side-by-side in any of the Organization's four official languages: Arabic, English, French and Spanish. The Secretariat has seven regional offices across the world; in Argentina, Cameroon, Cote d'Ivoire, El Salvador, Kenya, Thailand and Zimbabwe, along with Special Representatives at the United Nations in New York and at the European Union in Brussels.

*National Central Bureaus* (NCB) — Each Interpol member country maintains a National Central Bureau staffed by national law enforcement officers (The US has an NCB located in Washington DC). The NCB is the designated contact point for the General Secretariat, regional offices and other member countries requiring assistance with overseas investigations and the location and apprehension of fugitives.

*Advisors* — these are experts in purely advisory capacity, who may be appointed by the Executive Committee and confirmed by the General Assembly. Note: *Howard Wallace* (CIA) is currently an appointed Interpol advisor and was confirmed by their General Assembly. He was appointed back in 2001. After the heinous and totally unprovoked attack on the World Trade Center Towers (the Pentagon and the Capital Building).

*Commission for the Control of Interpol's Files* (CCF) — this is an independent body whose mandate is threefold: (1) to ensure that the processing of personal information by Interpol complies with the organizations regulations, (2) to advise Interpol on any project, operation, set of rules or other matter involving the processing of personal information and (3) to process requests concerning the information contained in Interpol's files.

I looked up the very old and prestigious, world renowned company (Interpol) and found out some very interesting facts. In addition, I asked Howard to check with the CIA in the USA to see what confidential and non-public background information his agency had on the very clouded in secrecy (i.e. almost a military type) organization.

Interpol has the ability to exchange crucial data quickly and securely and is a cornerstone of effective International Law Enforcement. This is why Interpol developed the I-24/7 global police communications system.

The system connects the Interpol General Secretariat in Lyon, France, National Central Bureaus (NCBs) in member countries and regional offices, creation a global network for the exchange of police information and providing law enforcement authorities in member countries with instant access to the organization's databases and other services.

Member countries can also choose to grant consultative access to authorized law enforcement entities outside NCBs, such as border control units or customs officials.

Interpol continues to develop new services and training programs to ensure that users are able to make full use of the I-24/7 system.

MIND/FIND technical solutions (Mobile and Fixed Interpol Network Databases) help countries access the system, by integrating into their existing computer-assisted verification systems. I-24/7 was created in 2003, with Canada being the first country to connect to the system. The final of Interpol's 188 member countries to join was Somalia, which was connected on July 10, 2007.

Interpol provides operational support to its National Central Bureaus and regional offices with the aim of enabling them to work as efficiently as possible. This support is centered on the Organization's priority crime areas: fugitives, public safety and terrorism, drugs and organized crime, trafficking in human beings, financial and high-tech crime and corruption.

The Command and Coordination Center (CCC) operates 'round the clock in all of Interpol's four official languages (English, French, Spanish, and Arabic) and serves as the first point of contact for any member country faced with a crisis situation.

The CCC staff monitors news channels and Interpol messages exchanged between member countries to ensure the full resources of the organization are ready and available *whenever and wherever* they may be needed.

In the event of a disaster or major crime, Interpol Response Teams or Disaster Victim Identification teams composed of officers from the General Secretariat and member countries can be dispatched to the scene within hours of an event.

Interpol Major Event Support Teams can assist member countries with the implementation of security arrangements for high-profile conferences or sporting events.

An important component of Interpol's operational police support is the notice system, of which the Red notice for wanted persons is the most well known.

In addition to the six color-coded notices (Red, Blue, Green, Yellow, Black and Orange), is the Interpol United Nations Special Notice issued for groups or individuals who are the targets of UN sanctions against *Al Qaeda and the Taliban.*

Criminal intelligence analysis is recognized by the law enforcement community as a valuable tool, helping to provide timely warning of threats and operational police activities.

Interpol contributes to investigations by assisting officers working at the General Secretariat and in member countries with research and analysis on crime trends and with training courses in criminal analysis techniques.

To fight international crime, police need access to information which can assist investigations or help prevent crime. Interpol manages several databases, accessible to the Interpol bureaus in all member countries through its I-24/7 communications system, which contain critical information on criminals and criminality. These include:

I-link project

FASTID

MIND/FIND

Suspected terrorists

Nominal data on criminals (names, photos)

Fingerprints

DNA profiles

Lost or stolen travel documents

Child sexual abuse images

Stolen works of art (recovering priceless oil paintings is one of Charlie's specialties)

Stolen motor vehicles

As one of the four Interpol core functions, Police Training and Development continues to evolve as a priority for Interpol and their member countries. The aim is to help officials in Interpol's 188 member countries to improve their operational effectiveness, enhance their skills and build their capacity to address the increasingly globalized and sophisticated nature of *crime today*. Interpol offers many tools and services — for example, databases — to its member countries. To ensure that member countries can maximize their use, Interpol has launched a number of initiatives to develop expertise and facilitate knowledge-sharing.

The strategic objectives for Interpol's police training activities for 2008-2010 are as follows:

Assist member countries in bridging the gap between national and international policing;

Provide member countries with the knowledge, skills and best practices to meet the policing challenges of the 21st Century;

Ensure that law enforcement agencies are fully aware of and take advantage of the services provided by Interpol.

In 2009, a total of 141 police training programs were delivered in 25 different areas, benefiting 4,583 participants from 165 countries. Interpol has developed *advanced training programs* for police officers from law enforcement agencies and National Central Bureaus.

The Interpol International Police Training Program (IIPTP) is aimed at officers with responsibility for international police co-operation, and of sufficient rank to bring about change and improvement upon return to their respective administrations.

Participants gain knowledge and skills, in particular of Interpol's systems and services. Duration of the program is changing based on evaluations and it is now six weeks. Two or three sessions are conducted each year.

A project to shorten and implement the IIPTP programs in different regions through the Interpol Mobile Teams focusing on the regions' *needs and priorities* is in process, which is called IMPTP (Interpol Mobile Police Training Programs).

NATIONAL CENTRAL BUREAUS are Interpol's link with national police forces and they are increasingly called upon to play a greater operational role as Interpol expands the range of its activities and services.

Core competency guidelines for NCB staff have been developed by a group of NCB volunteers representing each of Interpol's regions, together with representatives from the General Secretariat. The guidelines outline five main areas of competencies required of NCB staff.

In support to the NCBs and in collaboration with regional police chiefs' bodies and other organizations, Interpol's Regional Bureaus (RBs) are being strengthened.

Each Bureau is equipped with modern training facilities, and one Regional training officer per Bureau has been designated and trained facilities, and one Regional training officer per Bureau has been designated and trained with a view to coordinating and enhancing the regional training services.

The Interpol "Training Quality Assurance" (TQA) has been defined. The aims of the TQA are to ensure that General Secretariat training programs apply the standards as recommended in the "Interpol Guide to Effective Training", that the training cycle is fully respected to reach the best quality, and that resources are used efficiently.

A number of initiatives are in place in order to facilitate cooperation and the sharing of learning resources among member countries:

The Interpol *Global Learning Center* (IGLC) is a web-based learning platform, which enables timely and efficient capacity building internationally.

It centralizes available Interpol police training information, a library of e-learning modules, a calendar of training events and a list of online links to law enforcement related websites.

IGLC is aimed at Interpol's National Central Bureaus, the wider police community across the world and staff at the General Secretariat in Lyon.

A knowledge bank allowing member countries to input and share their training resources and feed the repository of research papers and best practices is in development.

Thanks to recent funding from the Canadian Government, IGLC is now available in English, French and Spanish.

Interpol is *exploring opportunities* to develop a network of training institutions and universities that can address priority crime areas and enhance the skills in using hi-tech tools.

Several co-operation agreements have been signed, and efforts to establish partnerships with external entities are continuing. For instance, an Interpol Anti-Heroin Smuggling Training Center has been established in *Moscow, Russia*.

The Interpol Group of Experts of Police Training (IGEPT) was also created in 2009. The purpose of the IGEPT is twofold:

To advise Interpol Police Training & Development Directorate in the execution of its mandate and facilitate the deliberations of the Interpol Senior management.

To inform and encourage and update Interpol stakeholders regarding police training options and developments and encourage participation or adoption.

In order to achieve these objectives, staff developmental needs are identified and managed so that performance gaps are addressed through well-designed familiarization, awareness, and formal training programs. Training is competency-based, meaning that a set of *common capabilities* (knowledge, skills, experience, values, behavior and attitudes) have been identified and are applied as appropriate to individual posts. In addition, continuity and "organizational memory" is being promoted through the sharing of knowledge.

Definitions of what constitutes organized crime vary widely from country to country. Organized groups are typically involved in many different types of *criminal activity* spanning several countries.

These activities may include trafficking in humans, weapons and drugs, armed robbery, *counterfeiting* and money laundering.

Interpol acts as a central repository for professional and technical expertise on transnational organized crime and as a *clearinghouse* for the collection, collation, analysis and dissemination relating to organized crime and criminal organizations.

It also monitors the organized crime situation on a global basis and coordinates international investigations.

Interpol's mission in this regard is to enhance co-operation among member countries and stimulate the exchange of information between all national and international enforcement bodies (including "America's Most Wanted" with John Walsh) concerned with countering organized crime groups and related corruption.

Drawing on the wide investigative and analytical experience of its multinational staff, Interpol helps 188 member countries:

Indentify, establish and maintain contracts with experts in the field.

Monitor and analyze information related to specific areas of activity and criminal organizations.

Indentify major criminal threats with potential global impact.

Pursue strategic partnerships with various organizations and institutions.

Assist in finding solutions to problems encountered by law enforcement agencies (LEAs).

Evaluate and exploit information received at the General Secretariat from National Central Bureaus, LEAs, open sources, international organizations and other institutions.

Monitor open-source information and reports.

Initiate, prepare and participate in programs to improve the international sharing of information.

Promote and carry out joint projects with other international organizations and institutions active in specific crime areas.

Research, develop and publish documents for investigators.

Provide support to member countries in ongoing international investigations on a case-by-case basis.

This enables the possibility of making links between transnational organized crime cases being conducted by national administrations that would otherwise seem unrelated.

*A special project* will be initiated when it has been clearly established that there is real potential for further development.

Interpol currently has projects targeting organized/specialized crime in five areas of high activity:

Project Millennium — Targeting Eurasian criminal organizations

Project AOC — Targeting Asian criminal organizations

Project Scream — Targeting serial murderers and rapists

Project Bada — Targeting maritime piracy (i.e. Somali Pirates)

Project Pink Panther — Armed jewelry robberies committed by nationals or former Yugoslavia. (remember the Pink Panther movies by famous director Blake Edwards — husband of Julie Andrews — Sound of Music movie)

Financial and high-tech crimes — "*currency counterfeiting*", money laundering, intellectual property crime, payment card fraud, computer virus attacks and cyber-terrorism, for example — can affect all levels of society.

"*Currency counterfeiting*" and money laundering have the potential to destabilize national economies and threaten global security, as these activities are sometimes used by terrorists and other dangerous criminals to finance their activities or conceal their profits.

Intellectual property crime is a serious financial concern for car manufactures, luxury goods makers, media firms and drug companies.

Most alarmingly, counterfeiting endangers public health, especially in developing countries, where the World Health Organization estimates more than 60% of pharmaceuticals are fake.

'Spam' is becoming more than just a nuisance for Internet users, as criminals are using it in increasingly sophisticated ways to defraud consumers, cripple computer systems and release viruses.

In 2000, the so-called 'Love Bug' virus, which affected millions of computers around the world within hours, exposed the *vulnerability* of corporate and government networks to such attacks.

New technologies open up many possibilities for criminals to carry out traditional financial crimes in *new ways*. One notable example is 'phishing', whereby a criminal attempts to acquire through e-mail or instant messaging sensitive information such as passwords or credit card details by pretending to be a legitimate business representative.

With this information, the criminal can commit fraud and even money laundering.

Interpol has stepped up its efforts in this area, working with stakeholders such as pharmaceutical makers, Internet service providers, software companies, *central banks* and other relevant bodies to devise solutions to thwart criminals and protect consumers.

Carlo Piacentini, a key member of our very sophisticated CIA TAC team, once worked for Interpol as a Senior Detective. He still had friends in supervision at the police agency, and that should prove to be very helpful in our interaction with them.

We definitely need all of the assistance we can get in solving this "Bank of Italy, LLC" fraud and counterfeiting case. Carlo knows the Interpol "Secretary General" very well. They used to be detectives together 'back in the day'. The President, and Secretary General, provide the leadership and direction for the very prestigious International Law Enforcement Agency.

# CHAPTER TWENTY

WHILE IN PARIS, I STAYED at the "Park Hyatt Vendome Hotel" (originally built in 1850). It is one of the most expensive, luxurious, and exquisite Hotels in Paris — and also in Europe — for that matter.

The first night I stayed in the "*Imperial Suite*", as it was the only room available. There was an art exhibit at the famous "Louvre" Museum in Paris and most of the nicer hotels were filled. The cost was $19,000.00 (US Dollars) per night, -WOW!- but well worth it. And besides, I was not paying, "The Bank of Italy, LLC" was!

I did not want to take advantage of their "good will" and trust, therefore, the next night I moved to a smaller suite (although just as lovely) which only cost $2,000.00 per night.

The second suite I moved to was: 840 square feet, very high ceilings, a spa bathroom (with a massage table, of course) — just in case I need an ala carte rub down — and you just know I will need two or three or more of those, a large living room, dining room, and a private office (I will need this to keep in touch with the CIA in the US and our own war room in Roma).

The suite also had 'round-the-clock room service, an in-room safe for valuables and weapons, and a set of weights for keeping in shape. With the delicious and very rich food here in Paris, and my love of good cuisine, I was going to need the exercise.

The only hotel rooms that I have ever stayed in that were as nice, although not as elaborate nor majestic, were the ones at the Warner suite at the "Four Seasons Hotel" in New York City, USA. At a cost

of $40,000.00 per night, the *Ty Warner Penthouse* gives guests a wide-angle view of Manhattan, on display from the nine-room suite's glass balconies and floor-to-ceiling bay windows.

Inside, guests will enjoy the creativity of Ty Warner, Peter Marino and I.M. Pei, who planned every detail from the 25-foot cathedral ceilings to the cut-glass chandeliers. If all this isn't luxurious enough, penthouse guests are also promised the use of a personal butler, personal trainer/therapist and personal chauffeur.

And, the other was the Royal Plaza Suite at the "Plaza Hotel" also located in New York City. This will run you $30,000.00 per night. The *Royal Plaza Suite* was inspired by Louis XV's royal court. Sumptuous décor complements square footage — 4,400 to be exact — which is at a premium in the city that never sleeps.

But along with all of that, guests will enjoy a state-of-the-art kitchen (for their personal chefs, of course), a dining room that seats 12, a library lined with a thoughtful selection of books, and magnificent views of Central Park South and Fifth Avenue.

To top it all off, there are even 24 - carat gold faucets in the bathrooms — yes bathrooms, there are three.

Oh, I almost forgot, I did stay at the Royal Penthouse Suite at the very prestigious "President Wilson Hotel" in Geneva, Switzerland. One night only, I hasten to add, at the exorbitant price they charged my client (a Saudi Arabian oil Sheikh - prince). Then I moved down stairs in the hotel, way down stairs.

The Royal Penthouse Suite here cost $65,000.00 a night. For that lofty price, guests can enjoy 18,083 square feet of luxurious accommodations overlooking sparkling *Lake Geneva*. Enter the marble bathroom and guests will find their own personal hot tub.

By the way, you'll be scrubbing up with Acqua di Parma bath products. Room service 24 hours, and rumor has it, this suite is quite secure — with the ability to lockdown and watch suspicious hotel guests on closed-circuit TV.

Of course there's also satellite TV and a nearly limitless selection of movies and music. The suite also features a safe because if you can afford this room, you'll be traveling with lots of treasures.

And I just remembered, the hotel that I stayed at while we were in Roma (The Royal Palatine Hill Hotel and Casino) was just absolutely magnificent.

Also, the view was quite breathtaking. The service was above reproach and the women on staff all looked like models and were 'drop dead gorgeous'. I just love Italian women, or have I told you that before?

Most beautiful women make my heart "beat a little bit faster", however, I do believe that lovely *Italian* ladies almost cause me to go into "cardiac arrest". I certainly hope that women from the good old USA, and other great countries that also have a lot of lovely women, and pretty lasses (Ireland), will not be upset with me for my admitted bias toward Italian beauties!

One night while I was laying in my bed after just having a marvelous massage on the special table in the bathroom of my lovely suite in Paris, so I was only half awake, if that much. Therefore, after I dreamed about my massage therapist (Marie Val de Seine Blanc).

No, I will not tell you about my dream, however I will describe Marie for you men out there. She made a man a little bit weak in the knees, if you know what I mean. She reminded me a little bit of Christina Agularia in her new movie (with Cher): "Burlesque". Her smile was so disarming that I almost dropped my towel six times, at least.

Her hands were like angel wings and her fingers were like strings on a violin. They were both magic! Just plain magic. No matter what was wrong with you: arthritis, bad knees or back, severe migraines, whip lash, surgery, and/or a fracture, Marie would make you forget all-of-your troubles, trust me on that my friends.

I am an expert when it comes to massages. I have had them all around the world and next to my regular physical massage therapist in Hollywood, on Sunset Boulevard (*Hope Champion*), Marie was

the next best thing. Hope was just as talented, or better, however she happens to be about 5,700 miles away the time. She is married (unfortunately for me). Hope is a very beautiful red-head.

Just the last few years, I have become attracted to red-heads (and blondes). For some reason, prior to that, for thirty some odd years I always preferred brunettes, go figure. She is married to a great man named John. I have always admired a man who likes a good cigar every now and then. They have four neat kids, Little Loren, Jacob, Sarah and Clint.

Anyway, back to little Marie. She was about five foot three inches. And, about 110 pounds, petite, and absolutely wonderfully put-together. Wow.

She brought tears to my eyes even before she touched me. And, after that school-was-out my dear friends. She had blonde hair, with highlights, and her eyes were so emerald green that you thought that they were little Irish streams and you just fell into them, and to her as well.

Then I started, or should I say attempted to start in a sort of dreamy state-of-mind to contemplate our counterfeit fraud case at "The Bank of Italy, LLC". Oh, Marie what have you done to me?! Alright, get it together Charlie, good lord she is only a beautiful woman with the hands and fingers of a *Greek French goddess*.

I started going over in my *little* mind, the who, what, when, and where of the investigation.

Those are the basic questions for any case. We had some people-of-interest, some of the usual suspects, and some possible perps. Then I passed out from my wonderful massage. When I awoke six hours later, I said to myself out loud again: "suspects: we had one, Vittorio — the bank president, two, Doria — the assistant to the chairman of the board at the bank, three, Felicia — the executive vice president at the bank, four, Giuseppe — the alleged Mafia god father, and five, Gigi — the bank president's administrative assistant".

Did I tell you that she was 'drop dead gorgeous', yes, I guess I did. But you know I repeat myself a lot sometimes.

I probably do not have to tell you that I and my CIA TAC team, believe that there are other possible suspects besides these listed. We are all working very hard to identify them as we speak.

Some of us are here in Paris, France, some in our war (operation) room in Roma, Italy, some of our friends at Interpol, and not to even mention, Howard's information counter-intelligence agent/operatives back at CIA Headquarters in Langley, Virginia.

Soon, very soon, we would have all of our possible culprits (villains) on our list and then we could go about eliminating them or identifying them. Some of our suspects were brilliant, some had the Midas touch, some were breathtakingly beautiful, and at least one was a 'pure psychopath'.

By the way, while I was in France, I have picked up the Parisian style of driving pretty fast, with a lot of nerve, verve and sometimes reckless abandonment. If someone tried to cut me off, I did not give them some of the local gestures though, just thought about it. When I am in my PI, or *hunter mode,* I search very diligently for my prey (i.e. suspects).

Usually my heart starts to pump a little bit faster (probably not a good thing since I have high blood pressure), I sweat a little more than normal, my ulcer (GERD) usually ends up in my throat, and more often than not, my mind works overtime trying to catch the bad guys.

An opportunity like this usually comes only once in a person's lifetime. Staying at a luxurious hotel (for free) in Paris, France. How can you even beat that? And I only have to find a crook and one hundred million dollars (USD).

And, that should be easy, right? By the way, I know that there are some people in this world who are so inherently evil, that they do not deserve to live. However, I do not feel that our 'thief', is one of them.

I could be wrong, of course, but I think possibly, just possibly, *our guilty party*, just got in-over-their heads. That can happen to good people, it has almost happened to me on several occasions over the years.

I am so very honest, I never thought about stealing money from drug dealers, money from the LAPD evidence room, or large sums of money that I recovered for some clients.

However, on one occasion, after my ex-wife left me for another man (after 30 years of marriage), I did think about swallowing my .40 caliber *Glock* automatic pistol. But, just for a second, I hasten to add.

All of us may do things that we would never normally do, when we are confronted with the 'trials and tribulations' of this crazy old life in this crazy old world.

The loss of a job, loss of your home, loss of your spouse, loss of some family members, loss of your life savings, loss of your 401K plan, et cetera, can all drive someone over-the-bend. Also, in this day and age drugs are so very prevalent in our society that when addicted to them, people do things that they would never even *imagine* if they were 'clean'.

That brought a thought to my little brain. I was going to check and see if any of our possible perps were suspected of using illegal drugs.

# CHAPTER TWENTY-ONE

AS HOWARD WALLACE AND I arrived back in Paris after our tour of Interpol, I needed to do some last minute research on the magnificent "City of Lights". We may need some, or at least a *little* bit, of this knowledge, to assist us in our fraud case.

I reviewed the history of the incredible city, of love, its geography, some important landmarks, and its very well known and famous hotels.

Paris is the capital and the largest city of France. It is situated on the river Seine, in northern France, at the heart of the Ile-de-France region (or Paris Region, French: Region Parisienne).

The *city of Paris*, within its administrative limits largely unchanged since 1860, has an estimated population of 2,193,031 (as of January 2007), and is one of the most populated metropolitan areas in Europe. The most populated metropolitan area in the EU is Greater London and Paris/Ile0de-France is the second.

In 2009 and 2010 Paris has been ranked among the first 3 most important and influential cities in the world, among the first 3 "European cities of the future" — according to a research published by Financial Times and among the *first 10 cities* in the world "where to live in" according to the British review Monocle (June 2010).

An Important settlement for more than two millennia, Paris is today one of the world's leading business and cultural centers, and its influences in politics, education, entertainment, media, fashion, science, and the arts all contribute to its status as one of the world's major global cities.

Paris is one of the most popular tourist destinations in the world. The Paris region receives 45 million tourist annually, 60% of whom are foreign visitors. The city and region contain numerous iconic landmarks, world-famous institutions and popular parks.

The earliest archaeological signs of permanent habitation in the Paris area date from around 4200 BC. The paresis, a sub tribe of the Celtic Saneness, inhabited the area near the river Seine from around 250 BC.

The Romans conquered the Paris basin in 52 BC, with a permanent settlement by the end of the same Century on the Left Bank Sainte Genevieve Hill and the ilea de la Cite. The Gallo-Roman town was originally called Lutetium, but later Gallicized to Lutes.

It expanded greatly over the following centuries, becoming a prosperous city with a forum, palaces, baths, temples, theatres, and an amphitheatre.

The collapse of the Roman Empire and the fifth-Century Germanic invasions sent the city into little more than a garrison town entrenched into the hastily fortified central island.

The city reclaimed its original appellation of "Paris" towards the end of the Roman occupation. The Frankish king Clovis I established Paris as his capital in 508.

Paris's population was around 200,000 when the *Black Death* arrived in 1348, killing as many as 800 people a day, and 40,000 died from the plague. According to Biraben, plague was present in Paris for almost one year in three in the $16^{th}$ and $17^{th}$ centuries to 1670.

Paris lost its position as seat of the French realm during occupation of the English-allied Burgundians during the Hundred Years' War, but regained its title when Charles VII of France reclaimed the city from English rule in 1436.

Paris from then became France's capital once again in title, but France's real center of power would remain in the Loire Valley until King Francis I returned France's crown residences to Paris in 1528.

During the French Wars of Religion, Paris was a stronghold of the Catholic party. In August 1572, under the reign of Charles IX, while many noble Protestants were in Paris on the occasion of the marriage of Henry of Navarre, the future Henry IV, to Margaret of Valois, sister of Charles IX, the St. Bartholomew's

Day massacre occurred; begun on August 24th and lasted several days and spread throughout the country.

During the Fronde, Parisians rose in rebellion and the royal family fled the city in 1648. King Louis XIV then moved the royal court permanently to Versailles, a lavish estate on the outskirts of Paris, in 1682. A Century later, Paris was the center stage for the French Revolution, with the Storming of the Bastille on July 14, 1789 and the overthrow of the monarchy in September 1792.

Paris was occupied by Russian Cossack and Kalmyk cavalry units upon Napoleon's defeat on March 31, 1814; this was the first time in 400 years that the city had been conquered by a foreign power. The ensuing Restoration period, or the return of the monarchy under Louis XVIII (1814-1824) and Charles X, ended with the July Revolution Parisian uprising of 1830.

The new 'constitutional monarchy' under Louis-Philippe ended with the 1848 "February Revolution" that led to the creation of the Second Republic. Throughout these events, cholera epidemics in 1832 and 1849 ravaged the population of Paris; the 1832 epidemic alone claimed 20,000 of the population of 650,000.

The greatest envelopment in Paris's history began with the *Industrial Revolution* creation of a network of railways that brought an unprecedented flow of migrants to the capital from the 1840s.

The city's largest transformation came with the 1852 Second Empire under Napoleon III; his prefect Haussmann leveled entire districts of Paris' narrow, winding medieval streets to create the network of wide avenues and neo-classical facades that still make much of modern Paris; the reason for this transformation was twofold, as not only did the creation of wide boulevards beautify and sanitize the capital, it also facilitated the effectiveness of troops and artillery against any further uprisings and barricades that Paris was so famous for.

During World War I, Paris was at the forefront of the war effort, having been spared a German invasion by the French and British victory at the First Battle of the Marne in 1914. In 1918-1919, it was the scene of Allied victory parades and peace negotiations.

In the inter-war period Paris was famed for its cultural and artistic communities and its night life. The city became a gathering place of artists from around the world, from exiled Russian composer Stravinsky and Spanish painters Picasso and Kali to American writer Hemingway.

In the post-war era, Paris experienced its largest development since the end of the Belle Époque in 1914. The suburbs began to expand considerably, with the construction of large social estates known as cites and the beginning of the business district la Defense.

A comprehensive *express subway network*, the RER, was built to complement the Metro and serve the distant suburbs, while a network of freeways was developed in the suburbs, centered on the Peripherique expressway circling around the city.

Paris is considered today to be one of the most beautiful and vibrant cities in Europe. In order to alleviate social tensions in the inner suburbs and revitalize the metropolitan economy of Paris, several plans are currently underway.

The office of Secretary of State for the Development of the Capital Region was created in March 2008 within the French government.

Its office holder, Christian Blanc, is in charge of overseeing president Nicolas Sarkozy's plans for the creation of an integrated Grand Paris ("Greater Paris") metropolitan authority, as well as the extension of the subway network to cope with the renewed growth of population in Paris and its suburbs, and various economic development projects to boost the metropolitan economy such as the creation of a world-class technology and scientific cluster and university campus on the Saclay plateau in the southern suburbs.

Meanwhile, in an effort to boost the global economic image of metropolitan Paris, several *skyscrapers* (984 feet and higher) have been approved since 2006 n the business district of La defense, to the west of the city proper, and are scheduled to be completed the end of 2010.

Paris authorities also made public they are planning to authorize the construction of skyscrapers within the city proper by relaxing the cap on building height for the first time since the construction of the tour Montparnasse in the early 1970s.

The name Paris derives from that of its inhabitants, the Gaulish tribe known as the Parisii. The city was called Lutetia during the Roman era of the 1st to 6th Century, but during the reign of Julian the Apostate (360-363) the city was renamed Paris.

It is considered that the name of the Parisii tribe comes from the Celtic Gallic word parisio meaning "the working people" or "the craftsmen". Since the mid-19th Century, Paris has been known as Paname in the Parisian slang called argot.

The singer Renaud repopularized the term amongst the young generation with his 1976 album Amoureux de Paname ("In love with Paname").

Paris has many nicknames, but its most famous is "La Ville-Lumiere" ("The City of Light"), a name it owes first to its fame as a center of education and ideas during the Age of Enlightenment, and lager to its early adoption of street lighting.

PARIS' INHABITANTS ARE known in English as "Parisians" and in French "Parisians". Parisians are often pejoratively called Parigots, a term first used in 1900 by those living outside the Paris region, but now the term may be considered endearing by Parisians themselves.

Much of contemporary Paris is the result of the vast mid-nineteenth Century urban remodeling. For centuries, the city had been a labyrinth of narrow streets and half-timber houses, but, beginning in 1852, the *Baron Haussmann's* urbanization program involved leveling entire quarters to make way for wide avenues lined with neo-classical stone buildings of bourgeoisie standing.

Most of this ‘new' Paris is the Paris we see today. The building code has seen few changes since, and the Second Empire plans are in many cases still followed. The "alignment" law is still in place, which regulates building facades of new constructions according to a pre-defined street width.

A building's height is limited according to the width of the streets it lines, and under regulation, it is difficult to get an approval to build a taller building.

Some points of interest in Paris are; Place de la Bastille is a district of great historical significance, not only for Paris, but for France, too. Because of its symbolic value, the square has often been a site of political demonstrations; Champs-Elysees is a seventeenth Century garden-promenade-turned-avenue connecting the Concorde and Arc de Triomphe.

It is one of the many tourist attractions and a major shopping street of Paris; Place de la Concorde is at the foot of the Champs-Elysees, built as the "Place Louis XV", site of the infamous guillotine. The Egyptian obelisk is Paris' "oldest monument".

On this place, on either side of the Rue Royale, there are two identical stone buildings: the eastern one houses the French Naval Ministry, the western the luxurious Hotel de Crillon.

Nearby Place Vendome is famous for its fashionable and deluxe hotels (Hotel Ritz and Hotel de Vendome) and its jewelers. Many famous fashion designers have had their salons in the square; Les Halles was formerly Paris' central meat and produce market, and, since the late 1970s, a major shopping center on an important metro connection station. The past Les Halles was destroyed in 1971 and replaced by the Forum des Halles.

The central market of Paris, the biggest wholesale *food market in the world*, was transferred to Rungis, in the southern suburbs; Le Marais is a trendy Right Bank district. It is architecturally very well-preserved, and some of the oldest houses and buildings of Paris can be found there. It is a very culturally open place; Avenue Montaigne, next to the Champs-Elysees, is home to luxury brand labels such as Chanel, Louis Vuitton, Dior and Givenchy.

MONTMARTRE IS an historic area on the Butte, home to the Basilique du Sacre-Coeur. Montmartre has always had a history with artists and has many studios and cafes of many great artists in that area; Montparnasse is a historic Left Bank area famous for artists' studios, music halls, and café life.

The large Montparnasse-Bienvenue metro station and the lone Tour Montparnasse skyscraper are located there; Avenue de l'Opera is the area around the Opera Garnier and the location of the capital's densest concentration of both department stores and offices.

A few examples are the Printemps and Galleries Lafayette grands magasins, and the Paris headquarters of financial giants such as BNP Paribas and American Express; Quartier Latin is a twelfth-Century scholastic center formerly stretching between the Left Bank's Place Maubert and the Sorbonne campus.

It is known for its lively atmosphere and many bistros. Various higher-education establishments, such as the Ecole Normale Superieure, TELECOM ParisTech, and the Jussieu university campus, make it a major educational center in Paris' high-fashion districts, home to labels such as Hermes and Christian Lacroix; La Defenseis a key suburb of Paris and is one of the largest business centers in the world.

Built at the western end of a westward extension of Paris' historical axis from the Champs-Elysees, La Defense consists mainly of business high-rises. Initiated by the French government in 1958, the district hosts 37,673,686 square feet of offices, making it the largest district in Europe specifically developed for business.

The Grand Arch of la Defense, which houses a part of the French Transports Minister's headquarters, ends the central Esplanade, around which the district is organized.

Plaine Saint-Denis is a former derelict manufacturing area that has undergone large scale urban renewal in the last 10 years. It now hosts the Stade de France, around which is being built the new business district of LandyFrance, with two RER stations and possibly some skyscrapers.

In the Plaine Saint-Denis are also located most of France's television studios as well as some major movie studios; Val de Seine is the new media hub of Paris and France, hosting the headquarters of most of France's TV networks, as well as several telecommunication and IT companies such as Neuf Cegetel in Boulogne-Billancourt or Microsoft's Europe, Africa and Middle East regional headquarters in Issy-les-Moulineaux.

Three of the most famous *Parisian landmarks* are the twelfth-Century cathedral Notre Dame de Paris on the Ile de la Cite, the

Napoleonic Arc de Triomphe and the nineteenth-Century Eiffel Tower.

The Eiffel Tower was a "temporary" construction by Gustave Eiffel for the 1889 Universal Exposition, but the tower was never dismantled and is now an enduring symbol of Paris.

The historical axis is a line of monuments, buildings, and thoroughfares that run in a roughly straight line from the city-center westwards: The line of monuments begins with the Louvre and continues through the Tuileries Gardens, the Champs-Ilysees, and the Arc de Triomphe, centered in the Place de L'Etoile circus.

From the 1960s, the line was prolonged even further west to the La Defense business district dominated by square-shaped triumphal Grande Arche of its own; this district hosts most of the tallest skyscrapers in the Paris urban area.

The Invalides museum is the burial place for many great French soldiers, including Napoleon, and the Pantheon church is where many of France's illustrious men and women are buried.

The former Conciergerie prison held some prominent Ancient regime members before their deaths during the French Revolution. Another symbol of the Revolution are the two Statues of Liberty located on the Ile des Cygnes on the Seine and in the Luxembourg Garden. A larger version of the statues was sent as a gift from France to America in 1886.

The Palais Garnier, built in the later Second Empire period, houses the Paris Opera and the Paris Opera Ballet, while the former palace of the Louvre now houses one of the most renowned museums in the world.

The Sorbonne is the most famous part of the University of Paris and is based in the center of the Latin Quarter. Apart from Notre Dame de Paris, there are several other ecclesiastical masterpieces including the Gothic thirteenth-Century Saninte-Chapelle palace chapel *and the* Eglise de la Madeleine.

Paris, France, what one word can one conjure up in one's mind? It is one of the most *romantic* and renowned cities in the entire world. Visiting the "City of Light" in 1991 was a once in a life time experience for Charlie as strange as it may sound; and as absolutely incredible a city as Paris is, I still preferred Rome.

But that is just me, however, I completely understand the adoration of millions of people especially women, to the fabled metropolis. Since 1860, the city limits have not changed.

Archeologists have found evidence of human habitation dating back to 4200 BC. Paris is considered today to be one of the most *'beautiful and vibrant'* cities in Europe as well as the entire globe. I visited the majestic and ecclesiastical "Eiffel Tower" (built in 1889) that was also in 1991.

Almost as magnificent as the tower was the "Palace at Versailles" it is one of the most breathtaking and *spectacular* sights that I have ever seen. I would rank it up there with: the Roman Coliseum; Leaning Tower of Pizza; and Windsor Castle (London).

# CHAPTER TWENTY-TWO

JUST A FEW MORE SUBJECTS about Paris and then Howard, our CSI team, and I will be ready to 'hit the bricks', and continue our investigation into the "Bank of Italy, LLC" fraud case.

Thus far it has led us from Roma (Rome), to lovely Venice and now to the "City of Lights" (Paris, France). These topics include the opera houses (I need more class in my life when I return to the good old USA), its world renown culinary reputation so well deserved (and you know me, I must *'eat my way'* through every city that I visit on my investigations around the globe), its city and local government, its economy, universities/schools, their transportation system (way important to me), and last but not least — Paris' health care system.

At my *mature* age you never know when I could become ill (or even shot in my line of work), and luckily for me their health care is one of the best in the world.

Paris' largest opera houses are the nineteenth-Century Opera Garnier (historical Paris Opera) and modern Opera Bastille; the former tends towards the more classic ballets and operas, and the latter provides a mixed repertoire of classic and modern.

In middle of 19$^{th}$ Century, there were active two other competing opera houses: Opera-Comique and Theatre Lyrique.

Theatre traditionally has occupied a large place in Parisian culture. This still holds true today, and many of its most popular actors today are also stars of French television.

Some of *Paris' major theatres* include Bobino, Theatre Mogador, and the Theatre de la Gaite-Montparnasse. Some Parisian theaters have also doubled as concert halls. Many of France's greatest musical legends, such as Edith Piaf, Maurice Chevalier, Georges Brassens, and Charles Aznavour, found their fame in Parisian concert halls. Legendary yet still-showing examples of these are Le Lido, Bobino, l'Olympia, la Cigale, and le Splendid.

Parisians tend to share the same movie-going trends as many of the world's global cities that is to say with a dominance of Hollywood-generated film entertainment. French cinema comes a close second, with major directors such as Claude Lelouch, Francois Truffaut, Jean-Luc Godard, Claude Chabrol, and Luc Besson, and the more slapstick/popular genre with director Claude Zidi as an example.

European and Asian films are also widely shown and appreciated. A specialty of Paris is its very large network of small movie theaters; in a given week, the movie fan has the choice between around 300 old or new movies from all over the world.

Many of Paris' concere/dance halls were transformed into Movie Theater when the media became popular form the

1930s. Later, most of the largest cinemas were divided into multiple, smaller rooms: Paris' largest cinema today is by far *le Grand Rex Theatre* with 2,800 seats, whereas other cinemas all have fewer than 1,000 seats. There is now a trend toward modern multiplexes that contain more than 10 or 20 screens.

Paris' culinary reputation has its base in the diverse origins of inhabitants. In its beginnings, it owed much to the 19th-Century organization of a railway system that had Paris as a center, making the capital a focal point for immigration from France's many different regions and gastronomical cultures.

This reputation continues through today in a cultural diversity that has since spread to a worldwide level thanks to Paris' continued reputation for culinary finesse and further immigration from increasingly distant climes.

Paris' most popular sport clubs are the association football (soccer) club Paris Saint-Germaine FC, the basketball team Paris-Levalloisian

Basket, and the rugby union club Stade Francais. The 80,000-seat Stade de France, built for the 1998 FIFA World Cup, is located in Saint-Denis.

It is used for football, rugby union and track and field athletics. It hosts annually French national association football team for exhibition games and major tournaments qualifiers, and several important matches of the Stade Francais rugby team.

Although the starting point and the route of the famous Tour de France varies each year, the final stage always finishes in Paris, and since 1975, the race has finished on the Champs-Elysees.

Tennis is another popular sport in Paris and throughout France. The *French Open*, held every year on the red clay of the Roland Garros National Tennis Centre near the Bois de Boulogne, is one of the four Grand Slam events of the world professional tennis tour.

The 2006 UEFA Chanmpions League Final between Arsenal and FC Barcelona was played in the Stade de France. Paris hosted the 2007 Rugby World Cup final at Stade de France on October 20, 2007.

As the capital, Paris is the seat of France's national government. For the executive, the two chief officers each have their own official residences, which also serve as their offices.

The President of France resides at the Elysee Palace in the 8$^{th}$ arrondissement, while the Prime Minister's seat is at the Hotel Matignon in the 7$^{th}$ arrondissement. Government ministries are located in various parts of the city; many are located in the 7$^{th}$ arrondissement, near the Matignon.

The two houses of the *French Parliament* are also located on the Left Bank. The upper house, the Senate, meets in the Palais du Luxembourg in the 6th Nationale, meets in the Palais Bourbon in the 7th.

The President of the Senate, the second-highest public official in France after the President of the Republic, resides in the "Petit Luxembourg", a smaller palace annex to the Palais du Luxembourg.

FRANCE'S HIGHEST COURTS are located in Paris. The Court of Cassation, the highest court in the judicial order, which reviews criminal and civil cases, is located in the Palais de Justice on the Ile de la Cite, while the Conseil d'Etat, which provides legal advice to the executive and acts as the highest court in the administrative order, judging litigation against public bodies, is located in the Palais Royal in the 1st arrondissement.

The Constitutional Council, an advisory body with ultimate authority on the constitutionality of laws and government decrees, also meets in the Palais Royal.

As part of a 1961 nation-wide administrative effort to consolidate regional economies, Paris as a department became the capital of the new region of the District of Paris, renamed the Ile-de-France region in 1976.

It encompasses the Paris department and its seven closest departments. Its regional council members, since 1986, have been chosen by direct elections. The prefect of the Paris department is also prefect of the Ile-de-France region, although the office lost much of its power following the creation of the office of mayor of Paris in 1977.

The cathedral of *Notre-Dame* was the first center of higher-education before the creation of the University of Paris. The universities was chartered by King Philip Augustus in 1200, as a corporation granting teachers (and their students) the right to rule themselves independently from crown law and taxes.

At the time, many classes were held in open air. Non-Parisian students and teachers would stay in hostels, or "colleges", created for the boursiers coming from afar.

Already famous by the $13^{th}$ Century, the University of Paris had students from all of Europe. Paris' Rive Gauche scholastic center, dubbed "Latin Quarter" as classes were taught in Latin then, would eventually regroup around the college created by Robert de Sorbonne from 1257, the College de Sorbonne.

The University of Paris in the $19^{th}$ Century had six faculties: law, science, medicine, pharmaceutical studies, literature, and theology. Following the 1968 student riots, there was an extensive reform of the University of Paris, in an effort to disperse the centralized student body.

The following year, the former unique University of Paris was split between thirteen autonomous universities ("Paris I" to Paris XIII") located throughout the City of Paris and its suburbs. Each of these universities inherited only some of the departments of the old University of Paris, and are not generalist universities.

Paris I, II, V, and X, inherited the Law School, Paris V inherited the School of Medicine as well, Paris VI and VII inherited the scientific departments, etc.

The Paris region hosts France's highest concentration of the prestigious grandes ecoles, which are specialized centers of higher-education outside the public university structure.

The prestigious public universities are usually considered grandes establishments. Most of the grandes ecoles were relocated to the suburbs of Paris in the 1960s and 1970s, in new campuses much larger than the old campuses within the crowded city of Paris, though the Ecole Normale Superieure has remained on rue d'Ulm in the 5$^{th}$ arrondissement.

The Paris area has a high number of engineering schools, led by the prestigious Paris Institute of Technology (Paris Tech), which comprises several colleges such as Ecole Polytechnique, Ecole des Mines, Telecom Paris, Arts et Metiers, and Ecole des Ponts et Chaussees.

There are also many business scholls, including, HEC, ESSEC, INSEAD, and ESCP-EAP European School of Management. Although the elite administrative school ENA has been relocated to Strasbourg, the political science school Sciences-Po is still located in Paris' Left bank 7$^{th}$ arrondissement.

The grandes ecoles system is supported by a number of preparatory schools that offer courses of two to three years' duration called

Classes Preparatoires, also known as classes prepas or simply prepas.

These courses provide entry to the grandes ecoles. Many of the best prepas are located in Paris, including Lycee Louis-le-Grand, Lycee Henri-IV, Lycee Saint-Louis, Lycee Janson de Sailly, and Lycee Stanislas.

Two other top-ranking prepas are located in *Versailles*, near Paris. Student selection is based on school grades and teacher remarks. Prepas attract most of the best students in France and are known to be very demanding in terms of work load and psychological stress.

Paris has been building its transportation system throughout history and continuous improvements are on-going. The Syndicate des transports d'Ile-de-France, formerly Syndicate des transports Parisians oversees the transit network in the region.

The members of this syndicate are the Ile-de-France region and the eight departments of this region. The syndicate coordinates public transport and contracts it out to the RATP (operating 654 bus lines, the Metro, three tramway lines, and sections of the RER), the SNCF (operating suburban rails, a tramway line and the other sections of the RER) and the Optile consortium of private operators managing 1,070 minor bus lines.

The Metro is Paris' most important transportation system. The system, with 300 stations (384 stops) connected by 133 miles of rails, comprises 16lines, indentified by numbers from 1 to 14, with two minor lines, 3bis and 7bis, so numbered because they used to be branches of their respective original lines, and only later became independent.

In October 1998, the new line 14 was inaugurated after 70-year hiatus in inaugurating fully new metro lines. Because of the short distance between stations on the Metro network, lines were too slow to be extended further into the suburbs, as is the case in most other cities. As such, an additional express network, the RER, has been created since the 1960s to connect more-distant parts of the urban area. The RER consists in the integration of modern city-center subway and pre-existing suburban rail. Nowadays, the RER network comprises five lines, 257 stops and 365 miles of rails.

Health care and emergency medical services in the city of Paris and its suburbs are provided by the Assistance publique — *Hopitaux de Paris* (AP - HP), a public hospital system that employs more than 90,000 people (practitioners and administrative) in 44 hospitals. It is the largest hospital system in Europe.

Once again, more interesting information about Paris the "City of Light". Nothing, note worthy to assist with Charlie's case, however, may come in handy in conversations with 'Parisians' (in French: Parisians).

Knowing some historical facts about Paris and speaking a 'little-bit' of the French language; possibly, just may, help me while investigating the case of "the Bank of Italy, LLC" here in the 'Champs-Elysees" in Paris. Reading about "Notre Dame; the Paris transportation system (with 300 stations); and the local health care system was informative.

# CHAPTER TWENTY-THREE

AS A RE-CAP OF SUSPECTS in "The Bank of Italy, LLC" counterfeiting case — suspects thus far anyway — there very well may be more after more investigation, we have identified the following individuals:

*Vittorio Capitolini* - The President and CEO (Chief Executive Officer) of "The Bank of Italy, LLC". Vittorio was identified early on in our investigation because he was suspected by Luca Perugino, the director of internal security for the bank. Vittorio had his romantic escapades with three mistresses almost as many as the Italian Prime Minister (the PM was always in the new about it). Also, he made big money with an equally big expense account, but unfortunately he spent much more money than he earned. As he liked to live large, real large. Supposedly he was very close to possibly having to file for bankruptcy protection.

*Doria De Pisis* — Assistant to the president, the chairman of the board and a member of the office of the president at "The Bank of Italy, LLC". She was reported by a trusted CI to have been traveling all around the world visiting very expensive and top of the line gambling "casinos". From Monte Carlo to Macow (Hong Kong) to the Caribbean Islands. Also, it was said that usually she lost at the tables and seldom won. In addition, she was hanging around with some very dark and nefarious individuals. Some of them were reportedly: ex-senior agents for the KGB, others high ranking members of the Italian Mafia, and, still others, some right wing military dictators from South America.

*Felicia Alemanno* — Executive Vice President in charge of the retail banking division of "The Bank of Italy, LLC". She also was identified as a suspect by a CI. The use of CI's in criminal investigations is common with law enforcement officers all around the world. In LA for example, Charlie uses CI's frequently and so does the LAPD as well as the LA office of the FBI and the DEA. She was a real "looker", a very classy lady and it was a crying shame that she was a suspect. Her smile was sardonic, very charming and she had just perfect beautiful teeth. But, did that angelic and captivating smile hide a compulsive liar and thief? Only a lot closer, and further observation, would tell.

*Giuseppe Gotti Fabrizi* — The alleged Italian Mafia god father. It was said that he was a heinous ethereal villain. He supposedly like to chop off (personally) the hands of any 'made man' who dared to steal from 'his' organization. He absolutely loved to gamble and would bet on anything that moved! Including horses, dogs, prize fighters, wrestlers, sports, and even once on a cockroach race, believe it or not. From all that I had heard, Giuseppe was definitely a very nefarious character, for real. His voice was like a husky whisper, why do all of the bad guys talk like that, do you suppose? Whenever he entered a room, darkness, gloom, and death seemed to follow. If he were not a 'pure' sociopath, he was as close as one could get.

*Anna "Gigi" Sordi* — Administrative Assistant (and secretary) to the President of "The Bank of Italy, LLC". I will tell you right now, unequivocally, that Gigi just cannot be guilty, period. No woman that was that 'drop dead' gorgeous and had legs that long and well shaped could do anything wrong or commit a crime. Then I stopped and paused and thought for a minute, and remembered the worlds ancient history of beautiful women, who had done "all sorts of evil things" (I also recalled my ex-wife) and decided, yes, possibly Gigi, the new love of my life, could possibly be involved in the theft and fraud. I was sorry to have to admit to myself. Lord, if she was involved, why did I have to be so enthralled and absolutely enchanted with lovely Gigi?

*Sulejman Rama Berisha* — An Albanian Mafia king-pin who operates both in Paris, France (and also Rome, Italy as well as his native Albania) with apparent impunity. His expression was as dark as a black night with no moon shinning. When he smiled, which was seldom, his smile was completely empty, devoid of any normal emotions or humanity, and as ice cold as death itself. Also, he had a hair trigger and frayed temper, that was ready to 'snap' at any second. He was a major player in the very deadly game called organized crime. Although, it was anything but organized or a game.

*Nino Proietti* — The chief legal counsel (i.e. attorney) for "The Bank of Italy, LLC". A big surprise to me, a crooked lawyer, yeah right. I told you some time ago, that you often cannot trust an attorney, remember? Please do not quote me on this, however, some lawyers: lie, cheat and steal for a living. Then they become politicians, and I do not have to tell you what politicians do for a living, do I? Nino was in a high enough position at the bank where he could easily cover things up. Interpol told us that they suspected he had very close ties to the Italian Mafia (the Camorra). To give him the benefit of the doubt, since Nino was an attorney, he could not be honest even if he tried.

Our number six and number seven suspects, were kindly provided to our CIA TAC team by our good friends at Interpol. That was because of the connection of our teams Carlo Piacentini and the Secretary General at Interpol.

As you already know, they have vast and far reaching resources. And, they were able to by using those, and also their deep connections in Roma, to develop sufficient relevant information. That said information, indicated that possibly, quite possibly, Berisha or Nino or both of these individuals, were involved in "The Bank of Italy, LLC's" one hundred million dollar (USD) counterfeit bank fraud case.

# CHAPTER TWENTY-FOUR

THERE WAS THAT *FAMILIAR* ACHE in my stomach 'again'. The one that was my constant companion whenever I worried, which meant I had the stomach ache pretty much *all* the time. I wrote it off as one of the occupational hazards of being a private investigator.

I said to myself, out loud again, I wish I would quit doing that: "Sometimes you have to make a deal 'with the devil' in order to solve a crime." Sad as that is to say, it is true.

In order to solve "The Bank of Italy, LLC" counterfeit case, and *also retrieve* the stolen one hundred million dollars (USD), or at least a 'good' portion of it, I just very well might indeed have to make a deal with the devil. And, in this instance, the devil might be, just possibly, the Italian Mafia (Cosa Nostra and Camorra).

Pretty soon I was going to have to get another one of these terrific table (tavola) massages (massaggio in Italian). The stress of this case, all of the traveling, time (tempo) lag, and worry (anxiety) is killing me. It really is!

Luckily for me, I had people traveling with me who 'had my back' *at all* times. And, individuals who could translate (traduzione) both Italian and French for me (mi). In addition, people who like good food (cibo), as much as I do. Well at least almost as much. All you folks out there know by now just how much I *love my* cuisine, right?

"Primo cosa quello io bisogno ad fare steh distruggere alcuno sospettare quello io latta sacco disfare mio descrivere investigare fino een il prendere".

I am still working on my Italian, you see, and a 'rough' translation of this statement would be as follows: "The first thing that I need to do is to eliminate any suspects that I can, based upon my investigation thus far in the case."

Once I have done that, the major primary culprits *will rise* to the surface. Kind of like baking a cake, although I hasten to add if I baked a cake (as if) you clearly would not want to eat any of it. I can do many things in this life, I really can, baking is definitely not one of them.

Anyway, detailed surveillance by the CIA TAC team, as well as the background investigations by both Interpol and the CIA in Langley, Virginia, have indicated that while *Vittorio Capitolini* — the bank's President (Primo Minister) and CEO just "loved to love" beautiful women (and what good red blooded man does not?) and also spent way too much money (denaro) — more than he earned — he probably was not our perp. While I have eliminated him for now, for the sake of time, I may still "take another look" at him in the future if I do not find my money.

Next, I examined the dossier and file information on *Doria De Pisis* — the bank's assistant to the President and also Chairman of the Board. Yes, she just "loved to gamble" in fabulous casinos all around the world and yes, she picked the wrong kind of men to love (kind of like I always pick the wrong kind of women to love) but there was no strong nor conclusive evidence to support her involvement in this crime.

Once again, I must take a fresh look at her at a later date. Anything is possible. On to *Felicia Alemanno* — Executive Vice President of the bank. Upon in depth and further examination, it appeared that Felicia was not involved at all in the theft. If this is true I will be very happy because she is just too, absolutely beautiful to be guilty.

She really is. It would just destroy my belief in pretty women for her to be involved in the bank's fraud case. I realize that is a stupid thing to say, however, it is not the dumbest thing that I have ever said, trust me on that.

And, *there's Anna "Gigi" Sodi* — Administrative Assistant to the President of the bank. Thorough research into her background, past, relationships (boyfriends), financial files, and her long successful career in banking showed no signs of wrong doing of any kind whatsoever.

Once again that made me very ecstatic, since she was so exquisite looking and sweet as well. As my beloved mother used to say: "Charlie, beauty is only skin deep." And, if I would have listened to her, it would have saved me more 'heartache and emotional pain' than you can ever imagine.

It really would have. Sorry for not listening Mom. Now, there is *Sulejman Rama Berisha* — the head of a large Albanian Mafia crime family. Yes, it has been verified that indeed he may very well be the "son of the devil", and he may possibly have some knowledge of the fraud at the bank, it did not appear to Interpol *nor* the CIA that he was directly involved.

But some good news and outcome of our bank fraud case, Interpol, French, and Italian security services as well as the CIA were filing criminal racketeering, money laundering, prostitution of Albanian nationals, and gun and drug smuggling charges against this despicable and vile individual.

After attentively eliminating five of our top seven suspects, now who does that leave for me and Howard to investigate? Well let me see now, it still leaves our vicious Italian mafia God father — Giuseppe Gotti Fabrizi — and it also leaves Nino Proietti — the crooked lawyer — Chief Legal Counsel for "The Bank of Italy, LLC". There are a couple of other potential perps that we may just have to 'look at' if one of these two do not pan out. There were seven of them and their names were:

*Agostino Giancano*, a high ranking mafia lieutenant, who appears to be unrelated to our investigation, but a possibility still.

*Martin Signorelli*, a race car driver for the Ferrari team and big time Bacharach gambler.

*Leo Ghirlandaio*, a high up auto executive at Fiat-Chrysler Motors.

*Marcus Turcato*, an Italian designer and shoe manufacturer which is in big financial trouble.

*Raphael Bramante*, a computer consultant who did work for the bank in the central cash vault area where the theft was discovered.

Marforio Pirandello, a crooked real estate broker — made a lot of bad real estate loans to the 'bank'.

*Antonine Morandi*, the President of "The Bank of Florence" a major competitor and big rival of "The Bank of Italy, LLC".

There could possibly be one or two more "persons of interest" for our CIA TAC team to examine, however, it appears to Howard and me that the two primary suspects Giuseppe or Nino (my favorite attorney, yeah right) were the most likely guilty parties. If we were wrong then we go to our plan "B", and look closely, real closely, at the "magnificent seven" (so to speak) listed above.

Today, I just received the top secret 'dossier' from Interpol, and just last night I got the classified file from the CIA (at Langley) — on Nino Proietti — the 'bank's' Chief legal Counsel. While Nino was definitely a very "smooth operator", he had left behind some clues that make him appear (quite probably) to be involved in the 'bank's' counterfeit embezzlement-fraud case.

Interpol through its inside contacts in Switzerland uncovered a *numbered Swiss bank account* (at "Credit Swiss Commercial Bank, LLC" — Geneva) with over $50,000,000.00 (USD), yes, that's right — fifty million dollars. WOW!

In addition, they also located another hidden and secret bank account at the "Singapore International Securities Bank" - Asia. That account had $25,000,000.00 (USD) in it. Interestingly enough that accounted for almost all of the One hundred million stolen from

"The Bank of Italy, LLC". The only amount missing was $25,000,000.00 million. Where did that money (denaro) go? And who has it now?

Nino, if I may describe him to you, had thick smooth eyebrows that lowered over the two narrowed black slits for his mean dark brown eyes with thick lashes. All of which gave him a very menacing look. Also, his face was devoid of any expression (like most lawyers, if I must add).

He had a reputation at the 'bank', of not playing well with others. It was his way or the Roma highway, period. Although it was said that Nino could be very charming with beautiful Italian women (or models), and also the key members of the 'bank's' board of directors (his bread and butter for his job — you could say).

When he lost his temper he could 'take it to a whole new level", way up there. He was definitely a certified 'psychopath', although he had never been officially *diagnosed* (because he was an attorney and almost all of them are mean), but Howard and I are quite sure that is exactly what he is!

He had that dark, intimidating and brooding look (stare) down cold. We were never going to get a man like Nino to confess to this crime that was for sure.

We would have to come up with another way to get the rest of the evidence necessary to arrest him. Just after the huge revelation concerning Nino, I got two more files on Giuseppe, the Godfather.

The most important 'material fact' the CIA discovered, was that they found a numbered bank account at the "Bank of the Sudan" located in Dubai in the UAE (United Arab Emirates). It had a balance of about $25,000,000.00 (USD).

I found it more that a *coincidence* that the balance in Nino's Swiss bank account plus the balance in Giuseppe's Dubai bank account almost totaled the exact amount of money (one hundred million dollars) stolen from "The Bank of Italy, LLC".

I was very excited about both of these recent investigative developments. It is nice to have friends in *'high places*' such as the famous CIA and the world renowned Interpol.

Giuseppe had been previously described by several mafia capo's and underlings as someone when they entered a room that everyone, and they meant *everyone'* would be 'terrified' of, and they would be trembling in their custom made Italian designer boots!

A few new members immediately turned pale green when they became 'made men' (i.e. accepted into the mafia family). When I interviewed him later, I was taken aback by the venom in his voice. He is the kind of man who only believes in what he can see, smell, touch, hear, and taste. Nothing else, nothing at all.

The fact that he was a psychopath made him even more dangerous than he would have been if he were just one ordinary street criminal. His personality was described by many as toxic, very volatile and highly radioactive.

He once used an ancient 'cat-of-nine-tails' on a low level thug (member) who had stolen a hundred dollars from him (only a $100.00). He cursed constantly, mostly in Italian, of course, but also he swore in English some of the time. English is spoken in most major cities in Italy. It is only out in the lovely country side and wine country that they only speak Italian, or possibly a little bit of French. We now had our two indentified prime suspects:

1) Nino (*Proietti*) and 2) Giuseppe (*Gotti Fabrizi*). All that we needed now was to figure out how they pulled off the "crime of the Century" at "The Bank of Italy, LLC" and then turn them over to the Italian Carabinieri (police) for prosecution.

And to get paid by the 'bank' of course. Money, money, money.

Just as I have felt on several other previous investigations I have been on (namely in Siberia — Mother *Russia*, my beloved *Vera Cruz*, Mexico, and the fabulous ancient and majestic city of *Roma*, Italy).

And now the very romantic fashion center of the world, "the City of Light", Paris, France.

I can hardly wait to 'jump on a jet plane' and head back home to my beloved sunny Southern California, in the good old US of A.

Ooh, to be "born, live, and then die" in LA, that has always been what I believed would happen to me!

I looked around and said to myself out loud, again? "Arrived-erci" (good-bye) to Italy and France, thank God, and in a **heart-beat** I was gone!

www.ingramcontent.com/pod-product-compliance
Lightning Source LLC
Chambersburg PA
CBHW030624310726
48979CB00003B/866

* 9 7 8 1 7 3 2 6 2 8 3 8 0 *